The Wake

of the

Hound Dogs

A.D. Matson

QUILLKEEPERS PRESS

"In the midst of chaos,

there is also opportunity."

—Sun Tzu

Chapter 1

That's All Right

A one-armed mortician and her Elvis-impersonating nephew aren't your average duo, but this isn't your average story. In truth, there wasn't a psychiatrist seen by Randall who could diagnose or classify his behavior. While the 1998 edition of the *Diagnostic and Statistical Manual of Mental Disorders* lays out the criteria for numerous mental illnesses, they couldn't pinpoint one that encapsulates a 16-year-old needing to adopt the persona of the King of Rock 'n' Roll. One psychiatrist hypothesized it was some form of atypical autism; another thought it could have been triggered by some sort of traumatic brain injury. The last psychiatrist he saw theorized Randall had multiple personality disorder, but all of the personalities were just different variations of Elvis. He came to this conclusion after noting the quick change it took for Randall to go from pretending to be Christmas Elvis to jumping onto the therapy couch and doing a swivel hip dance move while singing 'Viva Las Vegas.' But no matter what his ailment was, it didn't seem to bother him at all. It was like he was the star of his own never-ending improv show, and the rest of the little town of Rockdale, Minnesota, was his captive audience. And boy, was he eager to perform.

"The body of Christ is shed for you. Thank you, thank you very much," Randall repeated as he passed out the wafer crackers to the attendees of the 9:00 am service at First Lutheran Church.

His aunt and legal guardian, Jill Grinager, her assistant funeral director of Grinager Funeral Home, Patrick Loveland, and Randall were all church communion volunteers for Pastor Anna Wilson, given the proximity of their places of work. Randall usually behaved himself, but on more than one occasion, Jill had to reprimand him for fixing his pompadour with the waters of the baptismal font. She gave up trying to get him to take off his yellow-tinted sunglasses during the service. Jill thought they made him look like a young Jim Jones, and because of that, she was thankful he was always on wafer duty instead of the wine.

Jill walked around the pews passing around the offering plate, catching glimpses from the congregation as they stared at her missing arm. She shook off the stares knowing that the service was mostly made up of the near-senile senior citizens of Willow Fields Retirement Community across the street. Like any small-town retirement community, Willow Fields was understaffed, the building was falling apart, and the scent was a mixture of floor cleaner and Raisin Bran. Jill privately referred to the retirement home as "the fridge" because it was only a matter of time before the contents of what went inside would expire. She also knew that she was the one tasked with taking them out of the fridge when their time had come.

As a young girl, it was never Jill's dream to join the ranks of the mortuary services. She never saw herself preparing people for their final rest while balancing the unique and unpredictable emotional baggage each family brought to services. And she certainly could have never predicted that her sister, Jessica, and brother-in-law, Mark, would end up in a fatal car accident, making her the only person her nephew could rely on for a job and a place to live. She and Jessica had fallen out-of-touch after Randall was born. There wasn't any drama or bad blood between the two, which almost made it worse, Jill thought. Their daily phone calls became weekly, and then monthly, and then just around the holidays. Maybe she was just too preoccupied being a mom in Chicago, Jill thought. Maybe she finally had an excuse to get away from the mundane, unchanging life and times of a sister living in a nowhere place like Rockdale. She couldn't blame her for that, she thought. Why waste more time than you need on someone who isn't going anywhere?

But then, the crash happened. Suddenly, there would be no more phone calls ever again. She thought that if there was a Heaven, the resident souls were too preoccupied with the eternal bliss of paradise to concern themselves with the troubles of those they left back on Earth. It was more likely, in her mind, that the residents of Hell were more willing to pay attention to the concerns of the living in order to momentarily escape what she imagined was an eternity of non-stop polka music and wearing wet socks they could never take off.

But even if there was no afterlife, the dead still didn't have to concern themselves with the heavy feelings of loss, unlike those who buried them. But for Jill, she suffered through long nights of staring at her ceiling, flipping through every memory she had of Jessica like a photo album that never ran out of pages. With her parents gone, mournful regret took hold of her in knowing that she failed to stay connected with the only remaining member of her immediate family. Even though her sister was living out in Chicago, Jill knew she didn't do enough to maintain the relationship outside of an occasional phone call during holidays and birthdays. And now, it was too late. In some ways, she felt like she owed it to the memory of her sister to take watch over Randall and become his main source of support. She just never conceived all that would entail.

He spent forty-five minutes in the morning fashioning his hair into a perfectly quaffed pompadour, connecting to his long sideburns. His sparkling cross medallion protruded out the top of his black dress shirt, with his collar popping out of his loose-fitting, flamingo-pink checkered blazer jacket. The outfit was complete with tight black dress pants and burnished black loafers.

"I just love your little suits," said Gloria Ellis, a resident of Willow Fields and the last person in line for communion.

"Why thank you, pretty mama," he replied as he sharply shifted his body to a new pose, "thank you very much."

She smiled widely, making the wrinkles in her face look like stretched-out silly putty.

"I remember back when Elvis was quite the dreamy fella," she recalled with a slight tremor in her voice. "I remember watching him on the television, moving the way he did. There was just something so unique about it back then."

Randall pulled out a comb that was fashioned to look like a switchblade and styled back his hair. He pursed his lips and turned his neck on a swivel to face the elderly woman.

"The King still has it, sweet cheeks," he pressed on, pointing his finger guns her way. "Someone call Cassius Clay. Let him know he ain't the only one out here floatin' like a butterfly. Uh huh, uh huh, uh huh!"

While Randall passed out the wafers, Patrick handled the wine duties of Communion. His usual church attire was the same too-tight short-sleeved orange dress shirt with a yellow tie that stopped two inches short of his belly button.

"The blood of Christ shed for you," Patrick said with a nod as he carefully placed the plastic communion cup into the old woman's grasp.

"Oh, thank you, dear," Gloria said before tipping her chin back, the swallow of wine rattling her goiter. "I hope you enjoy the potluck on Friday."

"I'm sure I will, Ms. Ellis!" Patrick said graciously with a forced grin, "I hope to see you there!"

The heavyset Patrick wiped his brow with the sleeve of his tucked-in yellow buttoned up shirt. His hatred of meaningless small talk made volunteering for each church service an exercise in futility. There were only so many stories and comments he could hear from the old-timers as they made their way up to the front of the altar at the pace of sedated sloths. Nonetheless, he put on a welcoming face for the elderly congregation while periodically looking down at the ticking of his watch. The only person he made an exception for was Ms. Melstad, who lived in his apartment building.

As she walked up to him, he studied the face of his old crone nemesis. Her one hundred and three pounds of pure hatred stared into him like a demon who spawned up from the depths of Hell. Her ashen hair fashioned into an alternative bob with short white bangs that hung an inch below her hairline. She wore a mauve turtleneck sweater and a silver necklace with a single heart dangling above her chest. Her fingernails were always painted red, which Patrick imagined was the collateral blood of the souls she stole before returning to her masters in the underworld.

"Mr. Loveland," she sneered in her raspy tone as the corners of her thin lips curled into a maniacal smile, "I see you managed to make it on time for the service today. I figured the snooze button would have gotten the better of you again."

Patrick's eyes sharpened like two swords before a medieval duel, eager to strike his rival at the ready.

"You know me, Ms. Melstad. I do enjoy my rest. But I guess there's no rest for the wicked, is there? Ya know, given your body of work."

Her smile quickly turned into a jagged scowl. With her bony fingers, she grabbed one of the wine shots out of his container and aggressively threw it back into her mouth without breaking eye-contact. She returned the glass to its slot with forceful authority.

"Now you listen to me, dough boy," she whispered, extending her pointer finger in front of his face, "I want my parking space back, and you're going to give it to me. The property managers had no right to give it to you!"

Right before Patrick moved into the Crosby Estates apartment buildings, Ms. Melstad had her license suspended for refusing to pay a ticket for running a stop sign. Insisting on her innocence, she tore up the ticket right in front of the officer who pulled her over after berating him for what she claimed was a complete inability to comprehend basic traffic law. After being summoned to court and having her citation upheld, she told the judge that he was a stain on the judicial branch. This, of course, would lead to the temporary suspension of her license. As a result, she was unable to renew her premier parking spot near the front entrance of the apartment complex. When Patrick moved in, he claimed the spot and a bitter rivalry was born. He leaned in close enough for her to feel his hot breath on her face.

"I would sooner attend a picnic with the goddamn Donner Party than ever give that parking space to an evil raisin like you," he retorted in a cutting whisper.

"I'm surprised a fridge fiend like you even knows what a raisin is," she snapped back, matching his tone, "I heard you tell Gloria that you'll be at the potluck. I'll have to double my recipe for my tater tot hotdish this year to keep up with a hearty eater like you. Looks like I'm going to have to find a big oven to get the job done!" she snickered with a condescending wink.

"I'll put you in a big oven, wrinkles!" Patrick shot back in an intensified whisper.

The two adversaries realized that the banter had gone on long enough and that eyes were starting to focus on them.

Ms. Melstad shot him another sharp glare before turning around and making her way back to her pew.

"Keep it cool, wrinkles," Randall barked, just out of earshot, with Patrick immediately nudging him in the ribs.

After the organist wrapped up the final song, Pastor Wilson gave the last 'go in peace' blessing. One of Willow Fields' staff members ushered the old folks out of the building. At the same time, their seventy-year-old manager and lead caretaker, Julio Lozano, stayed behind and waved Jill over by putting two fingers to his mouth to indicate smoking a cigarette.

The skinny man had thick silver hair and sharp eyebrows. He was shy but always great company. Jill started joining him for post-church smoke breaks years ago when they realized that the other person was also waiting for church pleasantries and conversations to end. And although she was a Newport girl, Jill would always buy a pack of Marlboro Lights just for him. She looked at him as a nicotine father figure of sorts. The two of them stepped outside through the back exit of the church, standing by the dumpster with 'F.L.C.' painted on it.

"I heard we're going to get some snow on Wednesday. A lot of it, too," Julio said before cupping the end of the cigarette to block the wind from the flame of his black Bic lighter.

Jill signaled him over with a single head movement with the cigarette already in her mouth. In routine fashion, Julio cupped his hands around the end of the cigarette for her as she lit it with her own Zippo lighter. After it lit up, she took a long, vigorous drag, exhaling a small stratus cloud into the winter sky.

"Don't become one of those weather schmucks, Julio," she taunted haughtily before taking another drag.

"Weather schmucks?" he asked, with a bewildered eyebrow raised.

"Yeah, you know, people who get to that point in their lives where they're no longer capable of carrying on an interesting conversation, so their default becomes talking about the weather."

Julio exhaled an exuberant chuckle and tipped the end of his Marlboro, the ashes falling to the salted concrete steps below.

"You know many of these people, do you?" he asked, half-smiling.

"Too many," she said with a wink as she took another puff, "I'm never going to point it out–unless I know you, that is–but too many people get to the point where they eat the same stuff every day, they watch the same old reruns of their favorite shows, and tell the same stories they've told for twenty years. Eventually, all they can muster to talk about is the weather. And why not? It's low-hanging fruit. All you gotta do is pop your head out the window, and there it is. What's easier than that shit?"

"And you think that's boring, huh? You think I'm becoming boring?" he asked, pushing out a cloud of smoke.

"No, I'm not calling you boring at all. I'm simply bringing this geriatric phenomenon to your attention in hopes that you avoid a future of monotony and Wheel of Fortune," she explained, pointing her thumb behind her toward Willow Fields. "I think once you reach that point, you might as well take up a drinking problem. At least, it'll keep things interesting for ya."

Julio let out a hearty laugh that sounded like a man three times his size. He flicked his cigarette on the ground and relit another, gesturing for Jill to do the same. She met him with an unspoken shake of the head as she continued to nurse the remainder of her dart.

"I've got Peruvian blood in my veins, so the weather in this deep freezer of a state tortures my family and me. To this day, my wife curses the day we moved up here from Texas," he said with a laugh, "but you have my word: no boring weather talk," he promised, patting her on the shoulder.

"Good," she said with another smile.

"Speaking of never boring, I think Randall's Elvis mannerisms get better each time I see them. I gotta say, I'm impressed."

"I never took you for an aficionado of famous music men," Jill joked with a wink, peering above the top wire of her glasses.

"I can't say that I am," he confessed, gently tapping her shoulder with his fist, "but I admire the commitment. You know, the sparkly suits, the hair, and all that stuff."

"The kid is something else, Julio," she admitted, looking out toward the insulated landscaping shed thirty yards to their left. "I've never seen anything like it."

"Have you ever figured out...you know?" he asked with cautious curiosity.

"What's wrong with him?" Jill inquired, her smile now completely reset to a resting frown.

"Oh, sorry, not like that," he said, apologetically putting his hands up. "I just mean, like, have you ever figured out why he dresses up all the time?"

Jill took another long drag, bowing her head down and exhaling onto the front of her coat.

"No, I haven't. And trust me, I've addressed it multiple times. He just ends up answering me in character and ends up going on a tangent about Graceland or how Colonel Tom Parker screwed him over."

Sensing potential discomfort on the horizon, Julio took a step back in hesitation before asking his next question. This was the first time he'd ever addressed the subject of her nephew. Of course, in a small town, people gossiped and made assumptions. The leading theories were that Randall had some sort of autism, suffered from multiple personality disorder, or suffered from some kind of brain injury. The brain injury hypothesis was theorized by the leader of the Willow Fields bridge club, Margaret Tomlinson, whose cousin Bill was institutionalized in the 1950s after he pretended to be a bullfighter and was mauled by his father's bovine, sustaining significant brain damage. Aside from other developmental issues, one notable symptom of the brain trauma had poor Bill shouting "Here, bull!" at random pedestrians. The town quickly nicknamed him 'Bully Bill' and added their own variations to the story. Bully Bill's misfortune became a warning to misbehaving children.

"You better be careful, or you'll hit your head and end up screaming at the color red the rest of your life like Bully Bill!" Jill's mother told her several times.

Julio took another drag as the two stood with the winter breeze creeping in. He coughed a couple of times, feeling a smokey tickle in the back of his throat.

"In all seriousness though, Jill, I didn't mean any offense with the Randall question. I was just curious because he's a different cat, you know?" Julio explained, leaning his shoulder against the dumpster.

"Oh, I know. You aren't the first and won't be the last to be curious about Randall," Jill said, looking up at the overcast sky above her head. "It may come as a shock that he is pretty brilliant-at least when he wants to be."

Julio took another inhale as he stewed on her comment.

"Randall? I don't doubt it, I guess. He certainly stores a lot up in his head," he said, his sharp black eyebrow raised like an L-end wrench moving up his forehead.

"I've never seen someone who had the ability to comfort a grieving person with such ease," Jill said as she took another drag of smoke and slowly returned it to the air, her breath opaque and white from the cold winter day. "I can't tell you how many times he was able to calm down someone crying hysterically during a wake. That's not an easy thing to know how to do either. But to be honest, I don't know if it's an act of altruism or if he just says whatever he wants, and it somehow all works out for him."

Jill flicked the ashes of the tip of her cigarette near her black matte boots.

"Maybe it's both," Julio guessed as a cold shiver of wind touched the back of his neck. "Who knows, though? He might be the one who's got it all figured out. Maybe we all ought to pretend to be other people now and then to liven things up. It sure beats talking about the weather, huh?"

"That it does, Julio. That it does," Jill agreed as she inhaled the last bit of her roach.

At that moment, Pastor Anna opened the back door and walked out between them. Her blonde, shoulder-length hair shook from side to side like a straw bell that sat on top of her head.

"Oof! This weather is something else, huh guys?" She asked with a shiver, while Jill sent a sly smirk and a nod Julio's way, "I hear we're gonna get plenty of the white stuff this week, and all before Ash Wednesday! The Lord is good to us, but gosh darn it, I wish he'd cut us a break in the old flurry department!"

"It sure is something," Julio said, giving Jill a wink as he ashed the rest of his cigarette. "I'm gonna head back to the facility. It was good seeing you, Pastor Anna. I hope you both have a Happy Ash Wednesday."

"A blessed Ash Wednesday to you, too, Mr. Lozano!" Pastor Anna said as she extended her neck out like she was trying to get taller.

Julio gave them a head nod before walking around the side of the church.

"What a nice fella, huh?" Pastor Anna said before feeling a subtle shiver in her robe.

"That he is, Anna," Jill replied.

"So...have you given much thought to my date idea?" she asked eagerly.

For the past two weeks, Anna persistently pestered Jill over setting her up on a blind date with her friend's brother. Even as a lonely 38-year-old woman whose dating past was as exciting as a late-night infomercial, Jill was apprehensive about being set up with someone. With her deformity, she had almost gotten used to the lack of romantic pursuit men gave her. Besides, she enjoyed her independence. And with Randall in the picture, it wasn't like there was a shortage of excitement in her life.

"Thanks for the offer, Anna, but I think I'm going to pass this time," she rebutted, taking a drag. "I just have a lot going on, you know, with Randall and work and all that."

"Oh, come on now, Jill. We girls have to look out for each other," Anna insisted, nudging her, "it will be good for you! I personally swore off men when I took up the cloth-that's not ELCA policy, it's just my own-but trust me when I tell you that the best mindset for Jill Grinager is the Cyndi Lauper approach. Come on. Say it with me: girls just wanna have fun!"

"I'm not saying that, Anna," Jill replied, shaking her head.

"They just want, they just wanna!" Anna started chanting.

"Anna, please. I said no," Jill snipped, creating a tense silence between them.

Pastor Anna furrowed her brows as her lips formed the signature grimace of a church lady, which made its last appearance when she was asked about Noah's Ark's logistical plot holes by an eleven-year-old girl. In Anna's defense, the girl came prepared with extensive research on marsupials, explicitly citing the antisocial tendencies of koalas.

"Well, I'm just trying to look out for you, Jill. I'd be darn happy to see you with someone special," she said, folding her arms and shivering. "I also wish you were nicer to your lungs! Yikes, those cigarettes are as bad for you as sticking your head inside an old school bus muffler," she quipped with timid scorn.

"They sure are," Jill agreed, pulling another Newport out of the pack in her shirt pocket and sticking it in her mouth.

She took out the lighter and flicked it, but the wind immediately blew out the flame.

"You mind giving me a hand?" she asked, peering over her glasses at Anna.

Anna's church lady grimace returned to her face. She was full of hope and excitement that her closest friend would quit such a dangerous habit, but it was beginning to sour at Jill's request for lighting assistance. Anna then took a breath and remembered to do what Jesus would do. She closed her eyes momentarily and thought of the story of Jesus forgiving Peter, even after he denied Jesus three times. However, this recollection became clouded after she wondered if Jesus would have helped Peter light up a cigarette as the two of them made small talk.

As she inhaled the maiden voyage puff of smoke, Jill reluctantly pulled up the sleeves of her robe to avoid contact with the flame. She inhaled deeply and slowly puffed it out into the air above them, with Anna's disappointed look going unnoticed.

"Jill, date stuff aside, the reason I came back here is because, well, we've got a death-call situation on our hands that needs your attention," she admitted with another shiver.

"What kind of situation?" Jill asked, rubbing her temples.

"Bud Veitch just passed. The family is pushing for arrangements."

Jill stood still as if someone had just held up a blade to her neck. Her eyes widened as a chill ran down her spine, causing goosebumps to form up her arm. She looked down at the ground and then turned to face Anna directly.

"They want to do the service in Rockdale? Like *all* of them?" She asked with a shaky tone.

"Well, I think they wanted to keep it small and with immediate family only, ya know, given his history and such. I was hoping to speak to his son, Grant, but Grant's wife—"

"—Vicky," Jill interrupted, holding the cigarette just an inch away from her mouth.

"Yes, Vicky," Anna confirmed, "Ya know, he is just the nicest guy, that Grant. I was over at Elmer's Hardware the other day and saw him helping this old Carl Peterson lift these tractor parts in the back of his pickup. I says to Carl, "well, it's a good thing ya ran into Mr. Muscles, huh?" and ya know, Grant just had a good chuckle over that. Of course, these days, old Carl is just about as deaf as a boulder with earmuffs on, so I had to repeat myself about three times."

Jill remained still. A paleness had overcome her face as her mind wandered elsewhere.

"Are you doing okay, hon? You're looking like a Wiseman who just got spooked by one of the angels."

Jill sighed and took a 7-second drag from her cigarette before prematurely ashing it on the railing once more. Old memories started to shuffle through her head.

"It's nothing," she said, flicking her cigarette butt.

"Oh, absolutely. But it's a part of life, I 'spose," Anna said as she opened the door behind her.

Jill followed Pastor Anna down the corridor to her office. The church bulletin, overflowing with papers and volunteer opportunities, was on the right side of the narrow hallway adjacent to the bathrooms. On the opposite side was a portrait of a Caucasian Jesus holding a baby lamb. The exterior of her office door was decorated with an assortment of welcome signs, a bumper sticker of Martin Luther that read, "Nailed it." and her favorite Far Side comic strip, where the top panel showed people going to Heaven with an angel saying, "Welcome to Heaven...here's your harp." and the bottom panel depicted people going to Hell with the devil saying, "Welcome to Hell...here's your accordion."

Randall and Patrick were already in the office, sitting on her orange velour couch that looked fresh out of the early 1970s. Anna's desk was covered with an unorganized pile of sermon notes, prayer requests, and an old TV Guide magazine that featured George Costanza on the cover titled 'Seinfeld's Loveable Loser.' Next to that was a half-eaten container of scotcheroo bars.

Many of the papers contained mug-shaped coffee stains on them. The mug had an indolent clipart image of praying hands surrounded by coffee beans and read, "Inspired by God. Fueled by coffee." Behind each end of the desk were cedar bookshelves filled with religious publications, seminary journals, and three Martha Stewart cookbooks. Directly behind the desk were pictures from her travels around the world in front of famous landmarks, like Machu Picchu, the Eiffel Tower, and one where she's pretending to hold up the Leaning Tower of Pisa. Jill could tell in all the pictures that she had asked a random stranger to snap the photo based on the crookedness of each shot and the fact that she was alone in each one.

Anna sat down in her swivel desk chair and adjusted the height to her liking.

"Oh, for Pete's sake," she grumbled as she accidentally lowered the chair too far.

While she adjusted it back up, Jill noticed that Randall had pulled out his switchblade comb to adjust his hair while looking in the mirror on the opposite side of the room. Jill glared at him, prompting him to put the comb back into his jacket pocket.

"Before we begin, would anyone like a bar?" She asked, holding out the container of scotcheroos, "Connie Paulson swung by here yesterday and brought me a whole pan of 'em! My waistline is going to hate me come spring, but, gosh darn it, they are just to die for."

Everyone met her with a no thank you, but for any person of the Upper Midwest, an initial no thanks often meant you were still open to the proposal.

"Oh, ya gotta try 'em. Pat. This bar's got your name on it," she insisted, holding up the treat in her hand.

"Oh, I really shouldn't, Pastor Anna. I gotta save some room for the potluck coming up," he replied.

"Oh, a little extra treat shouldn't do too much harm," she retorted, pulling a small paper plate out of her desk drawer and putting the scotcheroo on top.

"Oh, I know. I just don't want you to have to go through all the trouble, is all," Patrick replied.

"Oh, they'd just be going to waste anyhow," she insisted, handing him the plate.

"Well, I wouldn't want them to be going to waste," he said, taking the plate and digging into the bar with a big bite.

"Pretty good, huh?" she asked with an eager smile.

"Not too bad at all," he replied.

The same routine of offering three times went on with Jill and Randall, who found themselves with bars that neither wanted. Anna wiped her mouth and rubbed her hands together to remove the chocolate and caramel residue between her fingers.

"Well, I'll get right into it," she began as she put the saran wrap back over the bars, "Bud Veitch passed late last night. As you may or may not know, he had a longstanding series of health issues. His son called me this morning and said he was just having a rough go of it. The poor guy couldn't sneeze without a screw coming loose somewhere, by the sounds of it. Cripes... it's just a sad, sad deal."

"How old was he?" Jill asked.

"Seventy-seven. He was getting up there, but still, just a real bummer," Anna added.

"That's too bad," Patrick chimed in.

"Cryin' shame right there, mama," Randall muttered as he shook his head.

"Well, I'm willing to do whatever I can for Grace. I know she's a little more frail these days. Did she mention anything about the arrangements or pick up?" Jill asked before taking a tiny nibble off of the bar.

Anna paused and scrunched her lips like she had tasted something incredibly bitter. She looked down at a notepad on her desk and then peered back up at Jill.

"Well, that's sort of what I wanted to bring everyone in for," she continued. "I got a very...shall we say catty message left on the machine by some...fella...who said he works for Bud's daughter-in-law. Apparently, he tried getting ahold of you first and was a little perturbed by the fact that you didn't pick up. Now, I know losing a loved one can be stressful, but the way I see it, there's just no sense in getting your undies in a bunch when someone doesn't pick up during church hours on a Sunday."

"There ain't no fighting on the Lord's Day," Randall said, motioning his hands into karate chops.

"Thank you, Randall. My thoughts exactly," Anna agreed.

Jill took off her glasses and began rubbing her temples. She put her glasses back on and took a deep breath.

"So what did he say, exactly?" she asked.

Anna sighed as she leaned back in her chair, slowly shaking her head from side to side. Jill could tell that even Anna, a pinnacle of politeness, was put off by whatever was said.

"I'll just play the message and let ya hear it for yourself," she said, pressing the button below the red light on her desk phone. The message machine started up with Pastor Anna's greeting:

Hello! You've reached Pastor Anna Wilson at First Lutheran Church. Unlike the good Lord, I am unable to be everywhere at once and am away from the phone right now. But if you leave me a brief message with your name and number, I will get back to you as soon as I can. Rain, shine, and yes, even snow, our worship hours are Saturday at 6:00 p.m. and Sunday at 9:00 a.m. and 11:00 a.m.. Thank you so much, and have a blessed day!

BEEP

This is Colton Lorenzo. I am the Chief of Staff for United States Representative Veitch. I need to make funeral arrangements for Bud Veitch, the former United States

Secretary of Transportation and father-in-law of the representative. I called the funeral home at 8:38 and again at 8:41, and no one picked up. What kind of clown show of a funeral home doesn't have an answering machine set up, by the way? In this day and age, that is absolutely ludicrous. At least you were able to check that box, even though you also neglected to answer your phone. Real professional. It's insulting that I have to play phone tag with you people to lay a prominent figure to rest, but that's fine. We expect a swift pickup of the body and transport to the funeral home, so when you've located the funeral staff, call me back immediately. Representative Veitch's preferred scheduling for the proceedings would be on a Wednesday, open casket, midday service. We don't have all day, so figure this out and get back to me.

CLICK

"Well, ain't he a peach?" Randall said before biting into the Scotcheroo bar.

Images of her childhood bully ran through Jill's mind. The thoughts alone put her stomach in knots. But the idea of her childhood bully having a capricious hot head doing her bidding made those knots feel like industrial strength clamps. Judging by the tone of the phone call, she anticipated her worst fears about putting Bud Veitch to rest were about to unfold. She badly wanted a cigarette.

"I love it when people don't make arrangements in person and just shout them over the phone," Jill muttered sarcastically. "What an unbelievable prick."

"He certainly has all the charm of one of those Washington folks, doesn't he?" Anna said.

"All except for my fellow 'Federal Agents at Large'-HOO WAH!" Randall shouted out sound effects as he stood up and performed karate moves in the air.

"Elvis was a federal agent?" Patrick asked with an eyebrow raised as he watched the teenager continue to practice his movements in place.

"Unfortunately..." Jill sighed.

"Appointed to the-HIYAH-Bureau of Narcotics and Dangerous Drugs-COBRA TWIST!" He shouted in a crouching stance as he twisted his forearm 180 degrees.

"Well, we just learn something new every day with you, don't we, Randall?" Anna said with a faint smile.

Randall bowed to her as he placed his hands together in front of him.

"Thank you very much," he said before taking his seat.

"You are welcome very much," she smiled. "Anywho, I called him back right away and got even more of an earful about our professionalism-or lack thereof, according to this grumpy Gus-and we made the arrangements for a wake Wednesday at noon with the full ceremony at 1:30," she announced reluctantly.

"But Anna, that's Ash Wednesday. How can they expect you to officiate?" Jill asked.

Anna sighed deeply and leaned back in her chair far enough to make it creak. As she leaned back, Rice Crispy crumbs from the bars ran down the front of her shawl.

"Well, I completely agree with you. Not to mention that it's supposed to snow something fierce midday Wednesday," she said, raising her eyebrows as she took a sip of her lukewarm coffee. "But I learned from Grant Veitch that his mom is starting to show signs of dementia. And to tell ya the truth, Jill, I just feel so gosh darn bad for the lady. The whole town knew that her husband was shackin' up on her. Cripes, the man, had more harlots than a Babylonian harem. But she's so kind, Jill. Really, she is. She helps out with the Christmas pageant every year, and she's in the bell choir; I just don't have the good heart to turn them away now that she's starting to lose her marbles."

Jill also found herself taking pity on Grace Veitch. She shuddered, imagining what it would be like to be married to such a pig of a man while having a daughter-in-law like Vicky. Dealing with mistresses and constant snide remarks would take a toll on anyone. It was remarkable Grace made it this long without her mind starting to wither away, she thought.

"The body is ready for pickup at hospice. Grant asked if you could come by tomorrow at 3:00 to go over logistics and pick up some of the sentimental items." Anna stated, "Send my best to Nathan at the hospice center, by the way."

"Tomorrow at 3:00? Yeah, that should be fine," Jill said. "Patrick, is it alright that we go get the body after this? I know you probably didn't want to spend your Sunday doing more work."

"It's fine, really," Patrick said, eager to please. "I've got nothing going on today, so I don't mind."

"Oh, bless your heart, Pat," Anna purred, putting her hand to her chest.

"Heartbreak Hotel," Randall interjected.

"I appreciate it, Pat. I think the three of us can do the final setup on Tuesday night before Wednesday's wake," Jill added.

Patrick wiggled in his chair like a daydreaming high school student who had just gotten called on. He adjusted his glasses as he positioned himself to face Jill.

"Tuesday?" he asked.

"Yes," Jill replied, "Tuesday night, preferably."

"I can't make Tuesday night work, actually," he said. "I, uh, have plans with a couple of friends," he announced in an almost apprehensive tone that caught Jill off guard.

It would surprise her that Patrick would have plans on the weekend, let alone a random Tuesday night. He was a good worker, but she felt he came off as a little standoffish and odd in the few years he worked for her. On several occasions, she witnessed him dip a finger into a cooling pool of candle wax at the end of a wake when he thought the room was empty and put it up to his nose, sniff it, and then eat it. While she had trouble imagining what the friends of a serial wax eater would look like, she knew the smell of their hangout spot would be far from a bed of roses.

"That's alright. We'll have to get it done early Wednesday morning, then. Sorry, Anna, I don't think we'll be able to make the Ash Wednesday service."

"Oh, no biggie, Jill! God still loves ya, last time I checked," Anna assured her before popping up in her desk chair like a groundhog. "That said, he and I need a favor if it isn't too much trouble."

She turned her chair around and lifted a large cardboard box of dried-out palms from last year's Palm Sunday service. She dropped it on her desk in front of the three of them with a thud.

"Since my week is going to be pretty jam-packed, could one of you do me a solid and burn these for the ashes on Wednesday? It takes me forever with my little lighter, and it would be a big help if one of you could roast them down for me."

"I can help you out," Patrick said as he looked at the box with palm leaves sticking out of the openings like a porcupine's back.

"Oh, you are just a rock star, Pat!" Anna said, clamping her hands with joy, "Here, take a couple of scotcharoos for the road," after pulling a plastic sandwich baggie from her desk drawer and filling it with two bars.

"Oh, no, Anna. It's fine, really," Patrick refuted, holding the cumbersome box in his arms.

"Oh, I insist. You've earned them!" she protested, zipping up the bag.

"Oh, I've already had two, though," he said.

"Oh, it's alright! Leave the caloric worry for the warmer months," she insisted, placing the bag on the box.

"Well, if you say so," he obliged.

Chapter 2

Don't Be Cruel

William "Bud" Veitch was an infamous figure in Minnesota politics and the most famous person ever to call Rockdale home. After a close failed bid for Governor in 1964, Bud was later appointed by Richard Nixon in 1969 as his Secretary of Transportation. While attending his D.C. cocktail party, Bud was overheard by Tricky Dick saying, "If I were that bus driver, I would have picked up that Rosa Parks and thrown her to the back faster than a rat gets fucked," which immediately propelled him into his good graces. Nixon's original preferred pick for his Secretary of Transportation was also at that party. He got so drunk that he vomited all over Nixon's beloved French Poodle, Vicky, and consequently, fell out of favor with the soon-to-be President.

Bud coasted through most of his duties. His most difficult weekly tasks were juggling his mistresses at social gatherings and keeping them hidden from his wife, Grace. That all changed with Watergate. During one of the most prolific scandals in American history, the White House Tapes incriminated Nixon when he and H.R. Haldeman discussed a plan to cover up the break-in at DNC headquarters at the Watergate Hotel. Bud Veitch, however, was also heard on later tapes apologizing to Nixon for an incident days prior. In what would be dubbed 'Motorgate,' Bud admitted to the President that he and two secret service agents used the Presidential Motorcade to pick up prostitutes for an orgy in the vehicle and engage in illicit drug use. The tape transcripts also revealed that Nixon forgave Bud for his actions, but he later laughed as

Veitch joked about an obscene birthmark on one of the secret service agent's left buttcheek. This was followed by homophobic ramblings from the negativistic 37th President:

Veitch: "Dick, you wouldn't believe it. Agent Roscoe has a birthmark on his ass that looks like the goddamn Mona Lisa."

Nixon: "(laughs) The Mona Lisa, you say?"

Veitch: "Swear to God! I couldn't even focus on the broad I was with; I was mesmerized by it. It looked like she was staring straight at me. I never knew the Louvre was located on his big pimply ass."

Nixon: "(laughter) You see, this is why I can't stay mad at you. I (laughter and incoherent mumbling) and I can just picture Roscoe's big white tuckus with her face right on it."

Veitch: "It was a sight for sore eyes, that's for sure (laughter). Hell, I bet even Da Vinci would have been impressed by it."

Nixon: "Oh, most certainly. Da Vinci was a well-known pervert back in his day."

Veitch: "You're shittin' me."

Nixon: "No, not at all! He and all the other Italian sexual deviants of the day were sought out and commissioned by the Medici Family for most Renaissance artwork."

Veitch: "All of them?"

Nixon: "Oh, yes. Michelangelo, too–huge pervert. His sculptures were ostensibly anatomical inspirations derived from the lovers he'd take at Florentine orgies. That's the Italians for you, though–a bunch of wine-guzzling debaucherers. When you think about it, the Romans were the original hippies."

The release of the tapes prompted Bud's resignation, effectively ending his political career. His marriage almost ended soon after, until he convinced his wife to stay for the sake of their two boys, Dale and Grant. Dale would end up indulging in more risky behavior than even his father, landing him some jail time (which he is currently serving). As the more mild-mannered of the two, Grant would go on to start his own crop insurance business and marry his high school sweetheart, Vicky Turner.

Jill, Randall, and Patrick exited the hearse and walked into the lobby of Rockdale Hospice Center, Bud's residence, during his final days. Patrick and Randall pulled in the largest of the three stretchers owned by the funeral home in preparation for hauling the corpse of the rotund man. Despite being associated with doom and gloom, the hospice facility looked like a pristine ski lodge with the best natural view in the area. It sat on top of a scenic hill overlooking the town, with a perfect view of the old Mainstreet buildings, residential homes, and an array of warm leaf-colored trees in the fall. It was like a weekend spa getaway without a checkout policy. There were worse places to be if you knew your days were numbered, Jill thought.

The director, Nathan Peterson, marched in with his purple dress shirt and a blue bowtie. The slim man had slicked-back brown hair and a goatee with a pointed end wrapped around his sharp chin. While she was always polite to him, she considered him the Grim Reaper, if the Grim Reaper had a stamp collection and used monotonous conversation to collect souls instead of a scythe. The feeling of listening to this man's dull voice was the embodiment of being trapped in a discussion at the grocery store with someone you wanted to avoid. Though she would never be able to prove it, she believed that his mere presence as the facility director moved people closer to their ultimate demise. To make matters worse, he hailed from a place most Minnesotans knew as the evil empire: Wisconsin.

As a proud transplant from Chippewa Falls, Wisconsin, Nathan's presence was usually filled with condescension when discussing his grievances with Minnesota. Jill knew that behind the phony pleasantries, his bobblehead nod and raised eyebrows while he pressed his lips together was an unearned superiority complex from a place known for cheese, drinking, and the occasional serial killer. Something was exasperating about hearing the words come from someone with the charisma of stale bread.

"I guess they'll just let anyone in here these days," Nathan noted with a robotic laugh. "How are we doing today, gang?"

"Just rockin' and rollin', brother," Randall blurted before meeting a slight glare from Jill.

"Good to see you, Nathan," Jill greeted him, hiding her contempt. "Pastor Anna sends her best."

"Oh, that's too kind," he said, placing the tops of his fingers into his front pants pockets. "Speaking of Anna, she told me that you might be going on a date pretty soon. That is quite exciting."

"Looks like you can't help fallin' in love, auntie," Randall added as he ran his fingers through his pompadour.

Jill put her fingers to the base of her forehead as if to thwart a migraine.

"I haven't agreed to anything, Nathan," she said, exasperated. "I think Anna is just trying to speak it into existence. You know how she gets."

Nathan smiled as he shook his head. He pulled on the sides of his bowtie as if trying to straighten it into a perfect line.

"Well, if you do end up going on the date, nothing wins a guy over more like some home cooking," he started in as Jill stared at the grossly discolored front tooth in his smile. "When Judy busted out her world-famous cheesy scalloped potatoes, she had me hook, line, and sinker...you gotta cross the border for the good stuff, though. Nothing beats some Wisconsin-aged cheddar."

An intrusive depiction of Nathan and his wife, Judy, shoved its way into Jill's mind. She imagined the couple gazing seductively at each other across the table, not breaking sustained eye contact with each bite of sliced Yukon golds covered in cheese. Nathan would say something about how her eyes reminded him of the Wisconsin skies from his youth at Camp Waupaca. She imagined the two would throw themselves at each other, looking like two ostriches wrestling in a pen, and go on to have the most vanilla three-minute sexual experience imaginable. She shuddered and shook her head at her own mind's betrayal of her.

"That sounds delicious," Patrick chimed in.

"I'll certainly keep it in mind," Jill said. "How is Judy?"

"Oh, the old ball-and-chain is keeping me busy these days," Nathan said out of the side of his mouth with a joking nudge. "Only kidding, of course. No, but she's good, she's good. We've got the kiddos signed up for some traveling hockey tournaments, so she's off doing mom duty while I'm at work."

"Hockey parents. I bet that's an experience, huh?" Jill replied.

"It ain't nothin' compared to good old-fashioned Mississippi mud wrestling," Randall chimed in.

"Zip it, Randall," she commanded while shooting him a look.

"Oh, I bet," Nathan said, sidestepping the interjection, "and yeah, it's been interesting, that's for sure. I just wish we didn't have to travel so far from town to town, ya know? Back in Wisconsin, our hockey leagues were pretty centralized. Well, also much more organized in general, to tell you the truth. But that's just the hand we're dealt, I suppose."

Jill hardened the muscles of her eyelids to avoid a massive eye roll in the face of a Wisconsinite. Politeness was a tenet that she had to adhere to. *Don't be cruel,* she thought to herself.

"Well, I'm sure it's exciting for the kids nonetheless," she noted, desperately hoping to move on from the conversation entirely.

"Yeah...you'd think so, but it's unfortunately been kind of a mixed bag," he said, denying her the relief altogether. "My Dylan has an allergy to modified corn starch, and Judy made that pretty darn clear to the other hockey parents and coaches... Well, you'd never guess what kind of corny chip

Kevin Wooster's mom paired with the Capris Suns for the after-game snack."

His eyes widened as if he were gossiping about an extramarital affair, waiting for Jill to respond with interest. She reacted with an exhausted sigh.

"Was it Fritos?" she asked with complete indifference.

"Bingo. Like a little red bag of health hazards just staring my Dylan in the face," he said with his hands on his hips. "Now, I don't want to sound like I'm being a negative Ned, but I tell ya what, back in Chippewa Falls, the parents just put a little bit more thought and care into the needs of each kid. Dylan just got some playing time, and his reward? No snack."

"I guess it's hard to get playing time when you can't even swallow a corn chip, huh?" Jill smirked , laughing at her own joke.

She soon realized she was the only one among them laughing. Randall, typically lost in his world, gave her a concerned look. Nathan raised his chin, looking confused and offended by the blatant remarks.

"I'm only kidding, of course. That's, uh, pretty sad for Dylan," she added.

"Ah," Nathan replied with an insulted expression still on his face, "must be that famous mortician's sense of humor. The body is in room 132. I'll need to review some of the next of kin details before you leave."

"Go on, guys," she signaled to Randall and Patrick.

As they made their way down the white and gray hallway with the stretcher, Nathan retrieved a manilla envelope from the front desk beside them with the label "Veitch" on the front. Every set of documents had a designated color-coded label on it. Despite his monotony, Jill found his organizational skills incredibly helpful. He licked the tip of his finger and thumb before flipping through the small stack of paper inside.

"Let's see, the official time of death was 2:20 a.m. We ended up putting diabetic complications as the cause of death after examining the body. His son, Grant, has power of attorney.

He came by when it was clear things weren't going too well and gave express written consent to embalm," he said, extending the two documents to Jill. "I'll have you sign off on the provisional."

She stared at him blankly as if there was something he was neglecting to remember. He realized she needed support to sign off on the papers, given she only had one free hand. Embarrassed, he ushered her over to the front desk counter.

"Sorry about that," he said, with guilt in his voice.

"No need to apologize, Nathan. It happens more than you'd think," Jill assured him as she silently signed through the documents.

The stretcher with a navy blue body bag covering the figure of a heavy corpse made its way down the hall, with Patrick pushing it from behind and Randall strutting in front of it. Like a malfunctioning shopping cart, the back left wheel on the stretcher didn't function properly, forcing Patrick to correct course after continually veering to the side. Judging by the sweat on Patrick's forehead, Jill doubted Randall was much help getting the body transferred onto the cart.

As they said their goodbyes to Nathan, the three made their way out of the facility and to the back of the hearse. Jill opened the back, and Patrick positioned the end of the stretcher above the lip of the truck. The three awkwardly lifted the heavy stretcher with Jill's side tilting, nearly causing the body to fall onto her. Seeing this, Randall quickly shifted his body and picked up the drooping side with impressive strength. The stretcher finally clicked into place on the platform. Jill shut the back door and started the vehicle.

Chapter 3

It's Now or Never

The dreary Monday morning sky started to open as Jill and Randall approached Grace Veitch's ranch-style home in the black hearse. Jill's eyelids still felt heavy from Bud's late night embalming. It had taken longer than usual due to Patrick's complaining of his sciatic back pain while they lifted the body onto the table. Randall also proved to be little help, given that he was pretending to sing into the chemical hose that pumps formaldehyde into the body.

The passenger side of the hearse contained a decal of the "Grinager Funeral Home" logo, incorporating the name in white lettering with a burnt-orange sunset behind it. "No Rain" by Blind Melon played on the stereo, causing Randall to sway his head. Hearses usually aren't recreational vehicles and are primarily used for services. However, her sedan was currently at Rigg's Auto Body for a constant rattling noise that sounded as if someone had filled the muffler with quarters.

They stopped at the only McDonald's within thirty miles. Jill found eating McNuggets while driving doable with one-armed, but she still managed to spill some ketchup on her collar. In hindsight, she thought about how strange of an experience it must have been for that young drive-thru worker to watch a hearse pull through with someone dressed as Elvis in the front seat. What was one person's unbelievable story was her everyday reality, she thought.

As they pulled into the driveway, Jill realized that her childhood tormenter was likely inside. She thought back to every horrible name yelled at her, every push to the ground, and, of course, the Barbie incident.

During the Barbie incident, Jill, a 5th grader, kept as much to herself as a girl with one arm could by burying herself in her books. Although she had few friends, she never felt alone because of her Barbie. Everywhere Jill went, her Sunset Malibu Barbie with a teal romper, long blonde hair, and a tan complexion for fun in the sun would be by her side or in her backpack. Jill would spend hours taking Barbie on Malibu adventures, confiding in her when she was scared, having sleepovers where she would tell her about boys she had crushes on, and chastising Ken for being lazy (a routine that typically involved Barbie telling Ken that "the damn furnace isn't working again" inspired by multiple exchanges at home).

Barbie didn't care that Jill was different. She didn't care if everyone else didn't like her. She was there to listen and to be the tiny shoulder Jill could cry on when life felt so unfair. During the incident, life felt as unjust as ever.

Jill was reading on a bench in Coval Park one afternoon, Barbie at her side when Vicky Turner slapped the book out of her hand.

"Hey Jill, how's my favorite little loner?" she teased, looking down at her with her gaggle of mean girls by her side.

"Go away, Vicky," Jill responded, avoiding eye contact and picking up her book.

"Are you reading to your dolly, Stumpy Jill?" With a smirk forming on her face, Vicky said as the friends giggled, "It must be awfully lonely to be such a loser that your only friend is a doll, huh? Can't grow out of playing pretend if you have to pretend to have friends in the first place."

"Leave me alone, Vicky," Jill huffed as she sat back down on the bench.

"What do you think, Nancy? Do you think this walking water pump will have to take her Ken doll to prom someday because she's so pathetic?" She asked while pacing around Jill.

Jill's eyes made contact with Nancy's, letting out an unspoken plea. Jill knew that plea would be vivaciously denied the moment she pursed her lips.

"Definitely!" Nancy replied.

"So sorry, Stumpy Jill," Vicky mocked, flipping her hair. "Looks like the Ken doll is your only option. Unless you can coerce some guy with no legs to take you. You'd really complete each other then!"

Jill looked at Vicky as if she were the devil incarnate. The unabashed cruelty was all too familiar and not the least bit surprising. She continued to laugh as she folded her arms and stood before Jill as if she were a helpless bug about to be squished.

"Poor Jill. Do you want me to stake out the Special Olympics to see if I can find you a catch?"

Jill adjusted her glasses and fought back her tears. She took a deep breath and calmly glared up at the brazen face with mascaraed eyes. A well-read person who listened more than she talked wasn't the type who typically went nuclear but could if needed. That moment was now.

"Hey Vicky, is your creepy uncle still behind bars?" she asked pointedly.

"What did you just say, bitch?" Vicky barked back, her smirk shifting into a fiery scowl.

Jill leaned back and gave a calm shrug like a Teflon mobster.

"Oh, I'm simply adding to your point! I might end up taking a doll to the prom, sure, but I'd rather be the girl going out with a doll than the one whose uncle can't be within 200 yards of the school because he flashed his weiner at the diner."

As the anger festered on Vicky's face, Jill leaned forward as if she had made contact with a dagger and was ready to twist. Jill leaned back again with a smile as it was readily apparent that Vicky was about to combust into flames of rage.

"Poor Vicky... Her uncle exposed himself to a 14-year-old hostess while on one of his benders. Does he do that often? Family reunions must be pretty awkward, huh? I can't imagine how scary that might be. I feel so bad for you."

Vicky closed her eyes and took a deep breath before immediately sucker-punching Jill in the face. Both girls grabbed each other's hair as the friends gathered around to hold down Jill. With tears in her eyes, she struck Jill a couple more times.

"Get me the Barbie!" she shouted to a friend as she sat on Jill's stomach.

"Leave her alone! Let me go!" Jill shouted back, struggling and squirming.

One of the friends handed the doll over to Vicky, who held it in her hands over Jill, as a girl held her only arm to the ground. Barbie looked like a sacrificial hostage, used to taunt Jill at her very soul.

"It's not fair that one of you gets to have two arms!" Vicky shouted as she began pulling Barbie's left arm out of the socket, "Let's make it a little more even!"

Vicky ripped the arm clean off, dangling in front of Jill's glasses. As she threw the plastic arm to the ground, she took the doll and walked over to the street, 20 meters away. The other girls remained to hold Jill down on the ground. Vicky stood in the road by the curb, holding the doll up like some prized kill.

"Looks like Barbie is going for a swim!" she yelled before throwing the doll into the storm drain.

The girls let Jill go, and she immediately ran over to the drain, reaching with all her might to retrieve her Barbie. Vicky laughed and taunted as she watched. No matter how far she stuck her arm in the drain, the doll was out of reach.

She came back from the memory as the song ended. Collecting herself, she took a deep breath and grabbed her binder. Whether she liked it or not, she had a job to do.

"Shall we?" Jill asked as she turned off the ignition.

"Lead the way, auntie," he replied while running his fingers through his pompadour and looking in the rearview mirror.

The border of the walkway leading up to the front door had an inviting assortment of tulips, daisies, and little knick-knacks like a wooden robin on a stick placed between them. Hanging down on the porch were blue and silver chimes that rattled with the wind. The welcome mat read "Home Sweet Home" with a connecting floral border. Jill pressed the doorbell, setting off a dinging in the melody resembling a grandfather clock reaching a new hour. Randall swiveled his hips with each ding.

The door latched open as Grant Veitch approached the threshold to greet them. Grant would still conduct business in Rockdale and the surrounding towns while his wife spent most of her time in D.C. during and after active congressional sessions. Though they didn't converse regularly, they had a baseline familiarity. Jill found him to be polite and affable but questioned whether or not that was all a facade, considering his choice of spouse.

"My condolences, Grant," Jill said, holding her binder tightly to her chest. "How are you holding up?"

He responded with a warm yet reserved facial expression. Briefly, his eyes averted to the ground before them and then came back with the faint glow of tears he held back.

"I'm hanging in there," he spoke softly. "Thank you for asking."

"Well, rest assured, we plan on making this process as seamless and comforting as possible for you and your family," she replied.

"That's right," Randall said, running his hand through his hair while Jill grimaced in anticipation of his words. "I'll tell ya what, Jack, when my mama's ticker gave out, boy, it felt like mine gave out too. Oh, it broke my heart. She was always my best girl... I hopped on a bird and went straight down to Memphis to console my daddy. Told him how his baby boy was gonna make everything alright."

"Be serious, Randall. Stop it," Jill murmured with a heavy sigh and an eye-roll. "I'm so sorry, he—"

"—that was pretty good!" Grant exclaimed with a laugh and surprisingly joyful expression, "Big Bud loved him some Elvis. He would've gotten a real kick out of that."

"Thank you. Thank you very much," Randall beamed, putting up a finger gun.

As frustrating as he could be for her, Jill was always genuinely amazed at Randall's ability to charm others. Whatever behavioral ailment plagued his mind also acted as his superpower.

"Mom might enjoy it too," Grant remarked, "but just a warning to both of you: she's got dementia. She's hanging in there, but we're having some difficulties with memory lately. We will be moving her into the nursing home soon, and I think Dad's passing has been both hard and confusing for her."

"No worries at all, Grant," Jill added before Randall could say anything. "As I said, we're here to make it as seamless as possible."

She turned to Randall and shot him a sharp, heated look.

"Behave yourself," she firlmy whispered.

As they followed him inside, they walked to the right into an open living room filled with old shag carpet. Hanging over a dusty piano against the wall was a portrait of a younger Grace and the late Bud posing on the White House South Lawn, the backdrop of the President's House behind them. On the opposite side was a burgundy couch, snuggly tucked by the front window, and a fluffy beige chair in the corner where Grace sat. The frail old woman was maybe 95 pounds, dripping wet, and wore bifocals so thick that they magnified the size of her eyes. It was evident by the way she stared out into the ether that the lights were on for Grace, but no one was home.

"Mom, these two are from the funeral home to see you," Grant announced, bending down and gently touching his mother's hand.

The woman looked at him and stared up at Jill and Randall with space cadet eyes.

"Funeral home? Oh... I must be dying then," she said matter-of-factly. "Well, it was a good life. Could have done with less shoveling, but what can you do?"

"No, Mom, you're not dying. Dad passed away, remember?" Grant replied with a patient tone.

"Well, no shit, Buster. Dad's been dead for 30 years," she said confidently, "If you asked me, it was probably that big toe infection he refused to go in for. Mom was always shouting at him, "Harold! You better get that little piggy checked before it gets the whole pork plant shut down!" But dad was always a stubborn one."

Grant took a deep breath as Jill and Randall watched the conversation unfold.

"No, Mom... Not your dad. Your husband, Bud, passed away. These two are here to help us plan the funeral," he said, holding onto the top of her bony hand as he saw the information process in her head.

Finally, it clicked in her brain.

"Ah... Bud... I remember," she stated, folding her arms with a gloomy expression, "what happened again?"

"Diabetes caught up with him, Mom," he replied.

"Oh, that poor fat bastard," she began, shaking her head with a grimace. "My Bud always had a sweet tooth—it was one of his vices. He loved putting away cookies almost as much as he liked...he liked...something or another."

Jill watched in real-time as the woman's brain rejected the inconvenient memories of her philandering husband, which would have completed the thought. Grace looked up again at Jill and gave her a squinted once-over.

"Oh, you poor woman..." Grace said, slowly shaking her head back and forth.

An embarrassed Grant immediately tried to hush his mother from being insulting about Jill's appearance with a missing arm.

"Mom! Don't be rude, please," he pleaded, wanting to cover her mouth with his hand.

"It's quite alright, Grant. Really," Jill said, reassuring him.

"I just feel horrible for anyone with the same glasses as me," the old woman said, continuing to shake her head.

"Cripes, you must be blind as a bat. And at your age? Oh, you poor thing."

The glasses were not even remotely the same. Jill imagined that if you hovered her glasses above an ant on a hot sunny day, it might kill the ant. But if you held up Grace's spectacles on a hot sunny day, it would burn a hole through the center of the Earth. Nevertheless, she rolled along with it.

"Oh, how observant of you, Mrs. Veitch," Jill observed. "I guess we're both just working with the eyes we were given."

"I suppose so," the old woman replied.

"But you know what I love about our glasses? They're great for reading," she explained, pulling out her binder and flipping to the catalog of casket choices. "Can you make out these pages well?"

"Oh, these are lovely," she said, squinting at the book in her lap.

"I like that one, Mom. What do you think?" Grant chimed in, pointing at a standard white economy casket.

"No, that looks like a big bar of soap," she said with an unvarnished tone. "You can't be squeaky clean if you're going in the dirt. I like this one."

She pointed to the solid mahogany casket with an almond velvet interior, known in the mortuary community as the Cadillac of caskets. It was the premier model in Jill's inventory, and the price reflected it. Contrastingly, Grant's suggestion was one of her cheapest options and the most popular amongst Willow Fields Retirement Home residents, making it the Oldsmobile of caskets.

"I don't know, Mom," Grant chimed in, his voice giving off a slight groan as his eyes read the price tag, "that one looks awfully expensive."

"I know you're not farting silk, but you don't need to be a cheap bastard," she blurted out, crossing her arms in response to his input.

"Mom!" Grant replied before turning to Jill in a soft voice. "I'm so sorry. She was never like this before."

"Grant, it's honestly okay," Jill said, putting her hand on his shoulder.

"Fartin' silk," Randall repeated

"Now that's a funny-sounding phrase right there, little lady."

Grace popped her head back up and squinted intensely to make out Randall, whom she noticed for the first time. She studied him with great concentration, flummoxed as she tried deciphering who or what he was. Jill couldn't blame her for that.

"I know you from somewhere," she said, with suspicion in her voice as she extended a bony finger at him. "Who are you?"

"People know me far and wide around these parts," Randall explained, jolting his head to the side, "most recognize me as the one and only King of Rock 'n' Roll."

"Grace, this is Randall," Jill said with a sigh as she nudged him with her arm.

"King Randall..." she said, as everything clicked in her brain.

"No, just Randall," Jill said, defeated.

"It is an honor to meet you, Your Majesty," Grace said earnestly.

"The pleasure's all mine, granny," Randall replied with a bow.

Before Jill could correct her again, Grant looked at her with a shrug, signaling that they should just let it go.

"Mrs. Veitch, are there any items that Bud was fond of? Anything that we could put on display to celebrate him?" Jill asked, trying to get them back on track.

Grace paused to think as she stared at the portrait of Bud on the opposite wall, studying it as if it were a painting in the Louvre. She looked at her late husband's round face, wide smile, and incandescent lightbulb nose as she thought about who he was. Below the portrait sat an antique cedar cabinet that showcased an all-glass case displaying a WWI Luger 9mm pistol. In the portrait, Bud was holding his antique pistol, gifted to him by President Nixon himself.

"Oh, he loved that gun," she replied, pointing at the portrait. "The President gave it to him for his 60th birthday. It was said to be the personal pistol of the Red Baron himself. Oh, how he could talk forever to anyone who would listen about that gun and the legend of the Baron. Poor Grant and Vicky have probably heard it a hundred times over," she recalled, as her eyes glistened with the memory returning to her.

"I think receiving that gun was the only time I ever saw Bud tear up... Well, now that I think about it, he teared up when they made him resign... And also when they closed down his favorite gentlemen's club," she said, adding a sour note to an otherwise joyful memory.

Based on his reputation, Jill imagined that the most significant emotional response came from the closing of the strip joint.

"That's great," Jill added, hunching over. "That sounds like the perfect treasure to display alongside him. I'd also love to have some photos of Bud when he was in office and some photos of him, you, and your children. Anything that can help tell the story of his life. How does that sound?"

"The gun is pretty fragile, so I should bring that to the service, but I'll happily send you some photos with you for the displays," Grant said before turning to his mother. "That sounds like a great plan, doesn't it, Mom?"

"Oh, I suppose," she said blankly, having forgotten the conversation already.

"Well, that's one item off the agenda," Grant sighed with relief.

He looked at Randall and asked, "His Secretary portrait is hanging on the wall in the basement office, first door on your left. Would you run and grab that for me, King?"

"You got it, chief," Randall replied as he hurried toward the staircase.

"Be careful, Randall!" Jill shouted as his footsteps clattered down the stairs.

Grant sighed in anticipation of the impending argument over the casket.

"Mom, can we get back to talking about the casket?" he asked, pointing at the catalog in her lap.

She stared down at it with wonder, as if it were the first time she had laid eyes on it.

"Now, I think this one would be the best for Bud's funeral," he pressed on, pointing to the cherry wine version of his previous casket choice. "I think if he were still here, he'd pick this one for sure."

She looked over the picture, furrowing her brow.

"Hmm..." she muttered, "...I think it looks like a big cough drop."

She pointed back to her original option with her bony finger.

"I like this one. Cough drops make my tongue go numb."

"Mom, it's not a..."

As Jill watched him struggle to argue with his ailing mother, Grant stopped himself and said, "Mom, I think once we get it, you'll like it. Can you trust me on that?"

"No!" she shrilled, her voice raised like a peeved cat.

Grant let out a heavy exhale. Just as Jill was about to intervene, an eerily familiar voice snuck up behind her.

"Grant, we can afford it."

The young woman Jill once knew was nearly unrecognizable. Since her first election in '92, she routinely flew to Orange County, CA, for face fillers and lip injections. Her Chief of Staff, Colton Lorenzo, also hooked her up a year ago with an LA plastic surgeon who he insisted was the "Michael Jordan of cheek lifts and jawline rejuvenation." Unfortunately, Dr. Ortman would later lose his license to a medical malpractice suit after future x-rays indicated that he carved his initials into the breast tissue of a patient whose breast augmentation he considered some of his finest work.

Vicky's lips looked like two inflated red leather couches that sat in the dorm room of a bachelor in the disco era. She had trouble moving her eyebrows as her forehead now served as a roadblock for any movement that was brought upon by sudden surprise. Her cheeks look perpetually raised and stuck in a position that looks like she was smuggling two robin eggs underneath the space below her eyelids. Her eyes themselves were like two hazel solar eclipses, with nothing but darkness behind them. She was sporting designer jeans with semi bell-bottoms to make room for her boots. The black leather jacket she wore shined like a black diamond.

"Honey, I just think-" he started before being cut off.

"Grant," she interupted in a stern tone, "a patriot to this country-who also happens to be your father and her husband-just passed. Money's no object here.

We're getting the casket she wants. Isn't that right, Grace?"

"Yes?" Grace said, having lost track of the conversation.

"Alright," a defeated Grant replied, as his eyes diverted to the shag carpet floors.

Her cold eyes shifted from him to Jill, meeting for the first time in over twenty years.

"As I live and breathe," she boasted, her hands in her jacket pockets, "Jill Grinager! Bring it in!" she said, wrapping her arms around her shoulders, forcing a hug onto a completely shocked Jill.

"My goodness, it's been what? 20 years? How have you been?" She asked as if she were reconnecting with a long-lost sibling.

"I've been good," Jill answered, bewildered. "I've just been running the funeral home in town. How have you been, Vicky?"

"No, no, no—it's Representative Veitch now!" a voice behind her chimed.

"Oh, cram it, Ethan," Vicky shot back with an eye roll.

"Yes, ma'am..."

Standing next to her was her communications assistant, Ethan Bile. As the youngest son of a mega-donor from Marietta, Georgia, Ethan had strict expectations of upholding the family name placed on him. With stunted height and a brunette bowl cut that cut off an inch above his asymmetric eyes, his appearance was unorthodox. His slight overbite protruded his two front teeth over his bottom lip, which sat below a patchy mustache that looked like it belonged in a high school prom picture. Yet despite looking like a hunched-over, scheming henchman who rubbed his hands like a housefly, Ethan was taught that a Bile should be feared and respected.

Ethan remembered his father hitting the roof when he found out he had been hiding a collection of New Kids On The Block CDs, cassette tapes, and memorabilia in his closet. Ethan would quietly bust out the jams with his Walkman at night when his parents fell asleep. The boy band tunes played in his ears while he performed his closet concert with four G.I. Joes and one Cabbage Patch Kid. His father interrupted one such show and stood over him with his arms folded and a face of disappointment that only a Southern Baptist could provide. After a two-hour family prayer session in the living room, his father looked at him and said, "Son, the devil is not welcome in this home. This incident makes me think he has a hold on you. It's high time we assure you're getting the necessary influences to succeed."

After his father called up a televangelist friend, Ethan spent the following summer at a sleepaway camp in Lubbock, TX. The other campers grew frustrated with Ethan, who would frequently report to the counselors if he suspected any nefarious activity. He once noticed a couple of his cabin mates sneaking out at night to go skinny-dipping in the nearby lake. After confirming their tomfoolery with his own eyes, he ran and reported to the counselors that his "fellow campers were disobeying the authority of the camp and should be punished."

And punished they were. While the two skinny dippers had to spend the rest of the summer with the camp clergy, Ethan gained joy from being a tattling teacher's pet. Talking during bedtime hours? Ethan told on you. Using inappropriate language during the nature hike? Ethan told on you. Failing to sing the Johnny Appleseed song before starting lunch? Ethan told on you.

Although ratting out his bunkmates was a behavior they all resented him for, it became an attribute that some of the authoritarian camp leaders admired. This same bunch were the well-connected sons of politicians themselves. Instead of spending the following summers at a camp reciting verses in Leviticus as he glided down the zipline, he would spend them as a page in the US Congress, forever fusing his love of bootlicking with a newfound knowledge of political theater. He attended Hillsdale College in Michigan, where he would major in politics, join their internship program, and become a communications aide for Representative Bob Barr, whose sponsorship and House passage of the Defense of Marriage Act helped Ethan gain the credibility he needed to move up the ladder. He knew of Vicky Veitch and saw her rising star potential. After lunch with Colton and a recommendation from Bob Barr, Ethan was set to become her full-time Director of Communications come the fall. In his mind, he was finally starting to make the Bile name proud.

"Sorry about that," Jill said with a shrug. "I guess it's why I'm not cut out for politics!"

Vicky's fake laugh sounded like a combination of Beavis from "Beavis and Butthead" and the Wicked Witch of the West. It startled everyone in the room, as everyone (Grace included) popped up when she let it out.

"Oh, trust me, not many are," she started. "You'd be amazed if you saw some of the wackjobs I deal with in Washington on a regular basis."

Based on her understanding of Vicky's politics, Jill assumed the "wackjobs" she was referring to were anyone who called for equal rights, equity, or policies that didn't revert everything to the 1950s.

"That sounds rough for sure," Jill replied. "Do you still find yourself enjoying it?"

Vicky paused for a moment, looking annoyed at the audacity of the question. Though her lips were stationary and filled with cosmetic plasma, Jill could see the emotions shifting as the woman tilted her head. There was something so calculated about her, even in the face of something that felt so benign. The internalized processing made Jill feel like she had just asked a robot what it means to feel alive, causing it to short-circuit.

"Well, Jill, that's a great question," she said, placing her hands back into the pockets of her jacket. "I pray and pray for this country all the time, asking the good Lord to restore the values our great founding fathers set forth for our country. I say, 'Oh Lord, we have strayed so far away from you. Give me the strength to help restore this great nation–this shining city on a hill–to the pinnacle of all your creation. Amen.'"

She walked over to Grant and placed her arm around his waist. "After that, I like to think back on what the late great Bud Veitch always said: The great ones don't need to enjoy the job. They just need to be the right person for it."

Bud Veitch actually never said those words in that context. The closest actual quote from Bud was, "I don't like having to do it, but I think I'm pretty damn good at it!" to justify driving drunk through the streets of D.C.

"Well said, Representative Veitch," Ethan added.

"Whatever, Ethan," she grumbled dismissively as he slumped his head.

Vicky pursed her lips together as the heaviness of her surgically modified cheeks stood perfectly in place.

"But enough about me and politics! You're a mortician? I can totally see detailed, curious Jill Grinager being a perfect fit for that role. Good for you!" Vicky said, smiling with her fists on her hips.

Jill didn't know whether or not that was a backhanded compliment. With Vicky and her petulant past, it was safe to assume she was making a dig at you.

"Yep," Jill reacted with a fake chuckle, "it's been a great fit for sure."

"I also eavesdropped a little and can tell you have a knack for sales, too," she said as she picked up the binder out of Grace's lap. "I mean, look at this thing! It's so cute and organized. I mean, no offense, you'd have to be selling someone a casket for their loved ones. That does not sound like a cakewalk of a sales pitch."

"Well, the 'buy one, get one free' promotion hasn't been too popular," Jill said as she broke out in laughter at her own joke.

Her laughter died as the faces in the room stared at her blankly, without any reaction to the statement. Jill swallowed nervously with a dry throat and proceeded to clear it. She felt as if she had just told an Irishman joke in front of an audience of IRA members.

"All joking aside, though, it's a completely manageable part of the job," she pointed out, desperately trying to move on from the conversation.

"Oh," Vicky said, realizing the joke had gone over her head and immediately faking laughter again, "that's a good one, Jill!"

She nudged her assistant Ethan in the rib cage, who nervously joined in with the laughter, too.

"You always were so witty," she admitted, this time sounding more pointed than the possible backhanded compliment. "I'm sure you've settled down by now with someone just as quick as you in the humor department."

"No, actually," Jill replied, the dread ringing in her voice, "I've just been focused on my career so far."

Vicky's eyes sharpened as the corner of her mouth tilted upward to reveal the evil grin Jill remembered growing up. This was the moment she craved. In Vicky's world, there were only two types of people: winners and losers. An admission of loneliness from Jill reassured her that she was still the winner. On the other hand, Jill felt like a dog whose owner zapped her through the shock collar just to see if it was still working.

"That's a shame," Vicky prodded, her subtle grin still on her face. "I guess it just takes a little longer for some of us, huh? I have all the confidence in the world that you will find that special someone, though."

The condescending tone in her voice was insufferable. She walked over to Grace, who was looking like a lost space cadet, and placed her hand on her shoulder.

"Sweet Miss Grace and I found love with these Veitch boys, didn't we?"

"Oh, I suppose," Grace muttered back, her mind worn out and in need of a nap.

"And Grant, honey, I'm taking Bud's pistol for the interview," Vicky said after kissing Grant on the cheek.

"What? But we were going to display it at the wake and—"

"—that sounds great, honey," she said, cutting him off. "I'll be sure to have it back by then."

"Oh," Grant groaned, in an almost fearful tone, "it's just that we've talked about this already, and I told you that I just don't think it's entirely appropriate to bring a gun to an interview."

Her eyes glazed over at him like a snake who noticed a moving rodent in her presence. She prattled a soft, maniacal chuckle as she took a step toward him.

"Do you really want to do this right now, Grant?" she asked in a cutting tone with her head slightly at a tilt. "Because I think it would be a real shame if we did this right now, in front of God and everyone, during your father's passing. Don't you agree, Grant?"

Grant's head slumped like a WWII Polish soldier staring a Blitzkrieg straight in the face. Jill couldn't imagine the harshness of the verbal batterings he must endure behind closed doors.

"Yes, honey," he concluded in an exasperated mutter.

"Good," Vicky said, giving him a pat on his right arm.

She marched toward the front door, Ethan following her like a puppy dog.

"Ethan and I have some constituent meetings we have to attend, honey, so we better take off here. Unfortunately, you have to talk to the people if you want to earn their votes!" she stated, following it with the same witchy cackle.

The two made their way toward the front door before Vicky turned around again to face Jill.

"It really was wonderful to reconnect with you, Jill. Good gosh, let's do it again sometime," she said with that same grin on her face.

"Yeah," Jill replied, swallowing again in her dry throat, "sounds like a plan."

Moments after the door shut, Randall came running back up the stairs, holding in his left hand a medium-sized portrait of Bud standing proudly behind a chair. In Randall's right hand, however, was a scimitar. The sword had a pyrite-colored metal hilt with the inscription "Brother of the Elk" on the handle and a curved Arabian blade that looked decently sharp. He must have been digging through their possessions this whole time, Jill thought. Randall handed the portrait over to Grant.

"Randall!" she raised her voice. "Mr. Veitch asked you to grab the portrait–nothing else. Put that sword back where you found it!"

Randall ignored her and practiced a couple of short jabs with the blade in the open space leading into the kitchen.

"HOO HA!" he yelled, causing the dozed-off Grace to wake up. "I'm the king of the jungle-they call me the Tiger Man! If ya cross my path, you'll take your own life into your hands!"

"Randall! I mean it!" She hollered, "Put the sword back!"

"Oh, let the King have the damn sword!" Grace chirped, to Jill's surprise.

"Mom! That wasn't polite!" Grant replied.

"Oh, pipe it! Bud got that ugly thing from his days at that dirty old lodge a long time ago. It's not like he's got any ceremonies where he can use it anymore. We might as well get rid of it," she said, her eyebrows furrowing at her son.

Grant looked over to Jill and gave a defeated shrug.

"I guess it's yours if you want it. Lord knows we're going to have to clean this place out anyway," he muttered in a soft voice.

After persistent begging from Randall, Jill relented and let him keep the sword, making him swear it wouldn't be brought out in public ever again. The last thing she needed was to plan a funeral and end up in trouble with the law because her minor nephew stabbed someone, she thought. They spent the remainder of the time flipping through old scrapbooks to find the photos they wanted and made floral arrangements using the options in her binder. She collected the photos and the portrait and placed them in the back of the hearse, stowing them neatly in the side compartment.

As they drove home, Jill looked over at Randall, who had his headphones on as he hummed along to a song on his Sony Walkman. He was smiling as he stared at the scimitar on his lap. Her thoughts then shifted back to Vicky—her maniacal grin felt branded into her mind. The jaded comments about not having anyone felt like an unseen sting, but the grin was the buzzing wasp she loathed. It was a not-so-subtle reminder of her own loneliness, the same loneliness that had her crying as she reached for a doll trapped in a storm drain. Jill exhaled a deep sigh and pulled into a Cenex station near the overpass.

Near the entrance doors was a payphone. Jill grabbed a few quarters sitting in her cup holder, got out of the hearse, and put them in the machine. She pulled out the Yellow Pages from the shelf below, flipped to Rockdale, and scrolled down to the W section. The numbers felt sticky to the touch as she dialed, making her want to go inside the convenience store immediately after to wash her hands.

"Yeah, Anna? It's Jill..." she started, "...so about that date with your friend's brother...tell her, I'm in."

Chapter 4

You're the Devil in Disguise

The remote in the Willow Fields Retirement Community lounge was missing, and the TV was stuck on the Weather Channel, giving today's Tuesday morning forecast. Roy Turner sat with his arms crossed in the only recliner chair, glaring at the screen before him. He sat with a perfectly upright posture that made the flat white top of his crew cut perpendicular to the wall behind him. Roy's wife, Rose, sat on the couch, on the furthest seat cushion from him, with needle and thread in hand. She was thankful that the remote went missing, given that he would spend this time watching cable news and shouting about how the country was going to hell, all while being a few non-sequiturs away from triggering a myocardial infarction. However, her relief quickly evaporated after she remembered his inexplicable hatred for weather forecasters.

"Why the hell are they called meteorologists anyway? We haven't had a meteor problem since the goddamn dinosaurs!" he exclaimed in a callous tone, furrowing his brow.

"How lucky for us," Rose agreed without looking up.

"Meteorologists...Give me a break. I bet the same bozos who came up with that came up with 'post-traumatic stress disorder.' Back in Korea, we called it what it was: shell shock!"

"Again with Korea," Rose said, this time rolling her eyes.

"Bill Sanderson doesn't make that turkey noise whenever he hears fireworks because he's *stressed out.*' He's a veteran who had a mortar shell blow up 80 feet behind him in Korea! That's shell shock, dammit!"

Rose pushed her glasses toward the end of her nose as she focused on the final stitchings of the embroidered face of a black cat she was working on for her niece's daughter. The cat's head had bright pink insides to its ears, deep saffron eyes with a stitched black center, and a strand of dark gray for the whiskers to pair with the pitch-black face. Above the cat's head was the name 'Midnight', written with the saffron thread, which was the name of the little girl's first pet cat. Secretly, she hated cats, but only because growing up, one of her family farm cats routinely vomited in the shoes she left outside the entrance to the house.

"The way people are getting soft these days just makes me sick," he said, shaking his head. "Even when you get on a damn airplane, they insist you call them 'flight attendants' now. You can't say stewardess anymore. I mean, for crying out loud! Can you believe it? 'Attending' the flight should be the bare minimum, and they make it their job title. It makes you not even want to get on a plane these days!"

Rose let out the same heavy sigh she'd let out for forty years. She dropped her embroidery in her lap, pushed her glasses back up her nose, and looked him in the eye.

"Roy, you haven't been on a plane in 11 years. What the hell do you care what they call them?"

The scowl he gave her was reminiscent of one a cat might give if you invaded their personal space.

"Well, Rose, if I do, you can sure as hell guarantee that I won't be calling them a 'flight attendant' or any other facade that society wants me to accept!"

He was now tightly gripping the arms of the recliner as if he were receiving a painful dental exam. Roy played out an imaginary scenario in his mind as his brow furrowed further against his glasses, like two caterpillars sitting on a metal railing. He imagined sitting in coach on a flight to Dallas-Fort Worth, where he would hit the button above his seat and request a pillow.

"Stewardess, can I trouble you for a pillow?" he'd asked. When she'd correct him with, "I am a flight attendant, sir, and I refuse to bring you a pillow until you acknowledge me as such!" He would stand up and boldly exclaim, "Ma'am, I've been calling you people *stewardesses* all my life, and I'm not going to change now!"

A smile formed on his face as he imagined his fellow passengers would erupt with applause for him for having the courage to tell it like it was. Charlton Heston, who overheard the exchange from first class, would walk back, shake his hand, and then invite him to go trap shooting together at his private ranch, where Hank Williams Jr. and Ronald Reagan would join them. The Gipper would compliment him on his shooting, the sun starting to set in the distance. The two of them would share a laugh and cheers a glass of fine scotch as they looked at the scenic landscape beyond. It was morning in America once more.

"You were never awake long enough on flights to talk to them. I always had to get your drink order from them while you were asleep," Rose teased, her words bringing down his place of zen faster than the fragments of clay pigeons in his daydream.

"What's that got to do with the price of rice?" He shouted, now hunching forward in the chair. "You always have to contradict me, don't you? If I said, 'It's 5 o'clock,' you'd say, *'Not in Spain.'* I bet you're ecstatic they changed the name from 'stewardess,' aren't you? I bet you just love how much I hate it!" he said, pointing his wrinkled finger at her as his gold watch jiggled on his wrist.

"I promise you, I don't care," she sighed, still staring down at her needle and thread. "You're the only one here who obsesses over trivial things like names, not me."

"There you go again with your slanderous attacks on my character," he said, his finger still extended toward her. "Name one other time I've vehemently objected to a name! Come on."

Rose set her objects in her lap and zeroed in on him with her eyes as if she were a fighter pilot tailing an inferior aircraft.

"Roy, you got a P.O. Box for our mailing address because you were too embarrassed that we lived on Quamclit Avenue. You kept saying that people would think we were 'perverted sex fiends.'"

"Well, Rose, it's not my fault that those four commie British bastards came over to corrupt the youth of this country!" Roy took another irritated swing of his coffee and continued, "Everything became about sex this, and sex that, and 'all you need is sex.' For Christ's sake, you can't even call a good old-fashioned hot dog a 'weiner' anymore without someone giggling! And I'll tell you this much, *Ms. My-Husband-Is-To-Blame:* if people like me didn't take a stand, you would all be speaking Russian by now!"

"Wouldn't it be Mrs.?" Rose quipped without looking up from her project.

"Wouldn't what be Mrs.?" he asked, with dry spit crackling on the corners of his mouth.

"If I have a husband, which I do, it would be Mrs. My-Husband-Is-To-Blame. Not Miss."

Silence fell on them. Roy sat in his chair, seething as Rose continued to pull her thread and smile out of the corner of her mouth. It was a smile that only came about when she watched his silent acknowledgment of defeat. The bulging blue veins in his hands stood atop his leathery skin as he furiously gripped the arms of the recliner chair. He turned his attention back to the TV screen and scowled as he watched the weatherman predict a blizzard this Wednesday with upwards of 13 inches of snow.

"A blizzard already? Give me a damn break," he huffed, taking another sip of his coffee.

One of the lead staff members of Willow Fields, Emily, walked in just as the local weather segment ended. Both Roy and Rose let out a quiet groan. If there was one thing that the two of them could agree on in a marriage that saw less affection than a heavyweight boxing match, it was their disdain for Emily's exaggerated positivity and unnecessary enthusiasm.

She always had an exaggerated smile and talked in a baby-voice tone that felt condescending and patronizing. Emily sported a polo shirt that was the color of an ammonia-heavy floor cleaner with "Willow Fields Staff" embroidered on the chest and khaki pants fastened just above her belly button. On one of her front belt loops, she hung her ID badge with a headshot photo that looked like it was taken inside a racquetball court and a pin that read "I ♡ MY JOB" in the top right corner. But perhaps the aspect the Turners found most off-putting was her machine-gun laughter. The rattling sound of an AK-47 echoed through the halls any time she saw something slightly humorous, and on more than one occasion, it triggered a nervous reaction from veterans like Roy.

"Hello, you two lovebirds!" Emily chirped, holding a clipboard tightly against her chest.

"Hello, Emily," Roy and Rose said simultaneously in monotone voices.

"How is this absolutely gorgeous Tuesday morning treating the both of you?" she asked, radiating the notorious smile that made Rose shudder each time she saw it.

"Every morning is the same when you've got nowhere to be," Roy replied.

Emily put one hand on her hip and tilted her head like a middle school teacher trying to get her students to participate in class.

"Roy, did someone come down with a case of the post-weekend grumpy grumps?" she wisecracked in the baby voice that he despised.

"Jesus Christ," he muttered under his breath before taking another drink of coffee.

"You must be upset about the snow we're going to get Wednesday!" she said, pointing at the TV. "I can't say I blame you there. It's too soon for snow, huh?"

Roy didn't acknowledge her and continued to stare straight ahead.

"Well, lucky for you, I've got the perfect cure! You've got some surprise visitors today!"

Emily opened the door wider to reveal their daughter, Vicky, and two of her political staff members. In the world of American politics in 1998, many elected officials approached civil service with honor and a sense of duty to their constituents. Others, like Vicky Veitch, began to see democracy as an opportunity to use political theater to elevate their personal brand.

On this day, she was wearing her trademark woven cowgirl hat with a leather band and a golden cross at the front to convey that she was a cowgirl at heart who prayed to the Lord at the end of her day wrangling cattle. She often talked about the lessons she learned on her family ranch in western Minnesota during speeches and rallies. Little did the public know that those speeches were nothing but fake platitudes, as her father had sold their family ranch when she was 8 years old and moved onto a rural acreage where the only animals kept were their thoroughbred horse and enough chickens for a backyard coop. Her brown and sandy blonde hair extensions draped over her denim jacket, which paired with her designer jeans and tall ivory rodeo boots.

The two staffers were her Chief of Staff, Colton Lorenzo, and her Director of Communications, Ethan Bile. Colton's buzz cut, pointed chin, and clean-shaven face gave him the appearance of a vulture. The combination of his slender frame, undersized mouth, jaded eyebrows, and beady gray eyes gave him the appearance of an angry mink who was ready to pounce on any rodent he could find and drag it to his burrow. Even starting out as a young intern for Strom Thurmond, he had a vision for his perfect America. A chicken in every pot, two cars in every garage, and two white hoods kept in the storage closet.

It wasn't hard to imagine that Thurmond, a senator who once stood over 24 hours filibustering the Civil Rights Act, immediately took a liking to a staffer who took pleasure in finding new and creative ways to provoke marginalized groups. He was instrumental to Thurmond's strategy in getting the Anti-Drug Abuse Act of 1986 passed through Congress to strengthen the War on Drugs, earning Lorenzo a promotion. Colton suggested that using buzzwords and phrases that could stoke fear in suburban households everywhere was the best approach when speaking of the legislation publicly. Thurmond's favorites of Lorenzo's suggestions were *inner cities*, *crackheads*, and *users are losers*-all of which he passed along to his colleagues.

Unfortunately for Lorenzo, he experienced a fall from grace when he was fired in '89 after D.C. police busted him during a coke orgy he was having with a couple of Ted Kennedy's interns. The incident caused disownment from his father, who couldn't believe his son would stoop so low as to sleep with anyone who "worked for those communist Kennedys."

He was down on his luck until one day, during a routine bender, he ponied up at one of Washington's loneliest dive bars next to a man all too familiar with a political fall from grace: Bud Veitch.

When Vicky announced she was running for Congress in a winnable district back in Minnesota, Bud saw an opportunity. That opportunity was a sunken Colton Lorenzo licking his wounds in a lonely D.C. dive bar. For all of his faults, there was no denying that Bud knew how to play the political game. He also knew that there was no one better to help you win than someone who would crawl on his hands and knees just to get back into the game. And through the manufactured persona of a cowgirl who would buck anyone to keep her god-fearing district free from crime, immigrants, and gay people, he did just that.

"Mom, Dad, it's good to see you again," Vicky said, her hands in her pocket as if posing against a fencepost. "How's this place been treating you?"

Emily perked up as if she had stepped on a thumb tack that pierced the bottom of her all-white Fila Disruptors.

"They are doing just great, Mrs. Veitch! A care facility worker doesn't like to play favorites," she said with a giggle, "but let me tell ya, they are, without a doubt, some of my most cherished two here at Willow Fields. They are truly putting the 'active' in active generations, for sure!"

Without even looking back at her, Vicky put the back of her hand up in acknowledgment of Emily.

"I'm sorry, Emily, was it?" Vicky replied softly.

"Yes, ma'am! Emily Auch. I'm one of the activity leads who—

"—Emily Auch...tell me, Emily, are you a voter in District 3?" she asked as she turned sharply to look at the woman in her smiling pink face.

"Oh, well, I am in District 4. I commute here from just outside of St. Paul—"

"—I see, I see," Vicky interrupted, and to Emily's frightened confusion, she began eerily stroking the right side of the Willow Fields staff member's hair.

She leaned close to Emily's right ear as if she were going to press her inflated lips onto her lobe.

"Listen, Emily Auch from District 4," she whispered with a sharp, menacing tone as the woman began to sweat nervously. "Have you ever seen a toad up close?"

"Y-yes, Mrs. Vei—"

"—No, no, no... Representative Veitch," she corrected her as Emily felt the uncomfortable coolness of her breath against her ear.

"Y-yes, I have Representative Veitch," she responded before swallowing nervously.

"Good, good. So you know all toads are slimy, bloated, and all-around repulsive?"

Like a hawk toying with her prey, who stared up at her with innocent eyes, Vicky said, "You see, Emily, when I look at you, I see a toad. And to be honest, I don't like toads. But I especially don't like toads who croak at me when I don't ask for their toad input. So why don't you and your frumpy self either pipe down or hop on out of here? Can you do that for me?"

Quivering, Emily quickly nodded while Colton and Ethan gave two serpentine half-smiles as they looked at their candidate. Vicky's formidable nature had her voice shattering like a window hit by a gust of wind and stones.

"I... I'll just leave you, folks, to it then," she said before scurrying out the door and making her way down the hallway.

Vicky paced slowly across the room, clicking her boots as she stood in front of the television. She pressed the power button and shut it off completely. She turned around and faced her parents, who remained still, holding back any and all pleasantries.

"I'll make this quick," she said, gazing between them. "Bud's dead."

"Took him long enough," Rose retorted coldly.

"You'd think a lard ass like him would've gone sooner with everything he snorted back in his day," Roy added as his wife gave him a faint nod of approval.

"It's amazing Grant turned out so well, given that the man was a walking advertisement for venereal disease," Rose replied.

Vicky did a slow eye roll and folded her arms like a teenager who had just been cited for skipping class. She bit as much of her bottom lip as her teeth would allow as she slowly shook her head.

"Do you remember that Christmas when he came over after clearly tying one on the night before, and he brought us that lamp?" Roy asked as he perked up in his chair.

"Oh, good lord, the one he clearly stole from whatever hotel he was staying that night? He tried passing that ugly thing off like it was some classy import he got through one of his connections. The buffoon," she recalled.

"Yes!" Roy said with a hearty laugh, "What about that time he took a bite out of one of your pieces of plastic fruit because he thought you put a bowl of grapes on the living room table as a party hors d'oeuvres?"

"I think the moron chipped a tooth!" Rose replied, nearly doubling with laughter, "It took him multiple bites before he even realized it was plastic!"

"That's enough, Mom and Dad," Vicky commanded firmly. "Bud wasn't perfect; we get it."

Colton and Ethan stood awkwardly by a card table near the doors, looking on as the family drama unfolded before them. Ethan pretended to stare at one of the landscape portraits of a church steeple hanging up on the wall opposite the Turners.

"Well, we don't normally speak ill of the dead, but sometimes you have to make exceptions," Rose said, setting her project on the coffee table next to her. "I suppose you want us to attend. Though, I'm unsure what to expect with all this thrown together so quickly."

"I called the local pastor on Sunday and arranged everything for the wake and procession, Mrs. Turner. Rest assured, it will be an expedient wake followed by a quick cremation ceremony," Colton interjected as she stepped toward the old woman, "and may I say, you two look like you're in the best shape of your lives? I don't know if I'm in a retirement home or the Olympic Village! Colton Lorenzo, Vicky's Chief of Staff."

He extended his hand for her to shake, a gesture she blatantly refused as she looked at the hand and then stared him in the eyes. Colton stood there with the grin of a used car salesman, trying to initiate a conversation. The woman continued to stare up at him without any intention of meeting his hand with her own. His extended palm stood hanging for another ten seconds before he slowly dropped his arm.

"I hate to agree with your mother," Roy added, "but are you too important to give us a heads up on things yourself? This will only get worse the longer you stay in politics, you know? Christ, back in my day, your local representative didn't act like he was too good to talk to his own family. Not you, though. You gotta have mop-head and dingleberry over here to do your bidding for you."

"Mop-head?" Ethan asked aloud as he felt the back of his hair.

Colton nervously looked over at Vicky, who now had her hands in her pockets. She looked over at her two staffers and back at her father. The heels of her boots clacked against the porcelain floors as she took a few steps toward him. She bent down, hands on her knees, and met his eyes as their faces sat just a few inches apart.

"You want to talk one-on-one, Dad?" she asked as the two stared down like a couple of old west bandits in a duel. "We can talk one-on-one...why don't you say whatever it is you gotta say to me? No middlemen. Just you and me."

He gripped the arms of the chair even more tightly, to the point where they would produce apparent wrinkles. The corner of his lip curled while his large, elderly ears started getting warmer with his anger. A standoff like this became a weekly ritual during Vicky's upbringing, especially in her teenage years. Be it an older boy she wanted to go out with to disobey him or Roy trying to force her to do farm chores, the relationship between the two was akin to a nuclear arms race between two world superpowers. It was a constant game of chicken, which neither wanted to lose. He turned his head and drank the last sip of his coffee, pretending to ignore her.

"That's what I thought," Vicky said, standing up and walking back in front of the TV. "I didn't drop by just to tell you about Bud. I have a favor to ask."

"Of course," Roy replied, "there's always got to be some strings attached for you to come visit us."

"We've already committed to going to the funeral of that Neanderthal you call a father-in-law. What else could you possibly want from us?" Rose chimed in.

"I need to borrow Frosty for Wednesday," Vicky said, bracing for their reply.

"Out of the question!" Roy screamed, springing up from his chair and standing face-to-face with Vicky again. "He's one of the only living things that brings me any joy in this world!"

"Isn't your only daughter included in that group?" Vicky asked, folding her arms.

"Pfft," Rose replied with a scoff, "don't push your luck."

The prized Camarillo horse, Frosty, was a beautiful steed with a glowing white coat who had been the family's horse for ten years. And despite his curmudgeon tendencies, Roy's attachment to the horse ran deep. So deep, that visitation rights were included in the contract sale of their family farm before downsizing to an apartment and then the retirement home. According to the contract, the Frosty Clause meant the new farm owners were to provide a sanctuary for Frosty to roam free while providing him every day at noon with Granny Smith apples–his favorite treat. The clause explicitly forbade substituting different apples and other fruits instead of the Granny Smiths. Strangely enough, the apple section of the Frosty Clause was not the most bizarre. The new owners were also required to sing a bedtime song Roy made up to Frosty every evening (citing that it was essential to the horse's emotional well-being). The song was a direct rip-off of "Frosty the Snowman" and went like this:

Frosty the snow horse

was a very happy steed,

with some big horseshoes and a long mane, too

on green apples, he will feed.

Frosty the snow horse

the best stallion around,

with a coat so white and his steps so light

he must barely touch the ground.

Buh-ba-dum-dum-dum, buh-ba-dum-dum

look at Frosty run!

buh-ba-dum-dum-dum, buh-ba-dum-dum

I love him like a son!

Although a second and third verse to the song exists (which goes on to mention how Frosty is anointed by God as the greatest of all the horses whose wisdom transcends all human understanding), his attorney advised him to stick to including only the first verse to avoid a legal dispute.

"What the hell do you need Frosty for anyway? This guy just said Bud's wake is Wednesday!" he yelled, pointing his finger at Colton, whose spine twitched like a nervous Puritan who had just been accused of witchcraft by the angry town reverend.

Vicky calmly grabbed a metal folding chair from the card table, flipped it around, and sat in it backward, facing her parents. She sat there silently for a moment, collecting her thoughts, taking off her hat and holding it in front of her while admiring the design along the brim. Her eyes moved to her mother's and then back to her dad's, as if she were intently studying them. The pause made everyone in the room anxious as they awaited her words.

"Dad, I've got an opportunity I simply can't pass up. An opportunity that could take my career to new heights," she pleaded, gripping the edges of the hat tightly between her fingers. "There's a popular reporter from *Time Magazine* who is coming out here to do a big, massive piece on me as a rising star in American politics. It could launch me into the governorship, the Senate, and, God-willing, maybe even somewhere in the White House. He's gonna title the thing 'The Snow Queen' and have my picture right on the front page for all to see. It's simply perfect," she said, standing back up and holding her hat tightly to her chest. "Imagine it, Daddy, your daughter, pictured on the front of *Time Magazine* riding your beautiful white horse across the snowy Minnesota prairies."

Roy stood quiet, with his arms folded and his scowl unchanged. Colton stepped forward nervously beside Vicky and interjected. The ornery owl eyes of the old man shifted toward him.

"Mr. Turner, if I may, our research and data suggest that suburban women will eat this up. Young moms, in particular, will gravitate toward Vicky after seeing their daughters look up to a role model who looks like them. Swing voters in the Rust Belt states will fawn over an outdoorsy candidate who proudly embraces the snow and cold of a long winter. They love a tough champion who fights against handouts and welfare queens. They adore a woman who can go to a gun range and show she's an elite shot," Colton paused, turning to Vicky to look her in the face while biting his lower lip ever so softly like a horny teenager barely holding onto his self-control, "and the men...well, let's just say that white-collar men find your daughter to be very, very, very aesthetically pleasing. Men these days love a confident female candidate who...looks every bit the part." He quickly collected himself after nearly taking a chunk out of his bottom lip and looked back at Roy. "At the end of the day, aesthetics are everything in this business. It is essential, Mr. Turner, that we have your daughter on this horse if we truly want to capture the public's imagination. If you allow us to borrow this horse for just a few hours before the wake Wednesday, there will be no limit to the heights your daughter will climb."

Roy cleared his throat and silently passed his empty coffee cup to his wife. She slowly got up, walked over to the dispenser in the corner near Ethan (still thinking about whether or not his hair resembled a mop), and filled the styrofoam cup halfway with dark, sludgy coffee. The silence continued as she walked back over to her husband, who gave her a nod of gratitude. Without breaking eye contact with them, he took a drink. The sludge worked its way down his throat with a loud gulp.

"No," he bellowed, with a domineering tone in his voice.

"No?" she asked in a shaky, rage-filled voice. "What do you mean by 'no'? I'm your daughter, and this is my big chance, you geriatric tyrant! I bet you can't even ride that damn horse anymore!"

"Doesn't matter," he affirmed with a cold smile. "I said no. I am not letting that wonderful animal become some prop for you to pretend you're something you're not. If you want to become the Ice Cold Queen who lies through her teeth, that's on you. But you leave my sweet Frosty out of it! He is too pure to participate in your political chicanery!"

She turned her head sharply to face her mother in a plea of desperation. Rose had just started back up on her embroidery project.

"Mom, can you please back me up on this? Your husband seems to have lost his mind," Vicky confuted.

"He seems pretty reasonable to me," she said flatly, without looking up.

"Reasonable?!" she yelled, slamming her fist on the television as Colton and Ethan jolted in unison. "How is this reasonable?! Was it reasonable when he threatened a hotel employee for 'conspiring against him' by only providing a bottle of shampoo and not conditioner? Was it reasonable for him to sit on hold with the cable company for hours to berate them for programming MTV? Was it reasonable when he made you drive the two of you home after your gallbladder surgery because he claimed his foot was asleep and thought he would get in an accident?"

Vicky leaned forward toward her mom, placing her hands on her knees and staring at her with laser-focused eyes.

"You know what, Mom? I think you like covering for his antics. I think you're completely fine with Dad ruining my big opportunity because, deep down, you resent me and my success...that's just so typical...your resentment makes you look so weathered these days, Rose. I hope you're happy!"

Rose remained silent, threading her project without moving her head or neck a single inch in response to the verbal insult. Vicky turned back to face her father, who looked more like her adversary. Ethan and Colton looked on as if they were witnessing an execution in real-time.

"And as for you," she scoffed, shifting the plastic, nearly unmovable parts of her face downward with rage, "you've always had it out for me, haven't you, Dad? You just can't take it that people cheer my name when I enter a room but groan at the sight of you. That's probably why you like that stupid horse so much; it can't tell you to your face how unpleasant you are to be around."

After dusting off her hat, she placed it back on her head and adjusted her jacket.

"It never crossed your mind that your daughter was protecting your freedoms, because, at the end of the day, you hate to see me succeed! You'd rather see the godless, the gays, and the guntakers succeed than me!" she yelled at him.

"How dare you call Frosty stupid!" He shouted back at her, "You've got some nerve coming here and hurling these insults at your mother and me! Well, I'll tell you something, Queen Tundra Tantrum: I may not be perfect, but at least I'm not living a lie! You always were an ornery girl, but now you're an ornery girl who will do and say just about anything to get herself noticed so you can be just like all the other cronies running this country into the ground. And now you sit there and expect me to allow you to bring my Frosty into that mess? Well, I say, hell no, Blizzard Queen! Hell no!"

She took the folding chair and threw it across the room as if she were Bobby Knight. It crashed into a display case of Hummel figurines, shattering most of the bottom row made up of porcelain singing German children. Her own rage took her back for a moment as she put her hand to her mouth. The room stood in shock as they looked over at the shattered pieces. Vicky's heels clacked as she stormed out of the room; Colton and Ethan followed closely behind her. As they made their way down the gray hallway, with even more landscape artwork hanging up around them, the thunderous clacking of her cowgirl boots echoed throughout the building. Emily heard it at the other end of the wing and promptly unlocked a door so she could go and hide. They passed the front desk, where a young female worker chimed in with a meek and meager voice.

"Ma'am, if I could just get you to sign out on this form, it would—"

"Oh, kiss my ass," Vicky mocked without turning her head; the girl's jaw dropped and her complexion turned white.

Exiting the building, Vicky leaned up against one of the pillars with one hand as she rubbed her forehead with the other. Colton and Ethan looked at each other and then back at the distressed Vicky.

"What are we going to do?" Colton asked.

She took a deep breath as she looked out into the parking lot and then up at the sky. It was supposed to all come together, but now it was crumbling before her very eyes. She thought momentarily, contemplating every move she could take from here on out.

"Ethan, go start your car. You're taking me to the house," she explained with authority as she stared deeply into Colton's eyes.

"Ok, but Colton rode up here with me. What about his lu—"

"—now Ethan!" she shouted back at him.

Like a cockroach running from under an upturned table, he scuttled along to the parking lot. With his back turned to them, Vicky aggressively gripped Colton's jacket and started making out with him behind the entrance pillar with animalistic passion. He pinned her against the stone before she violently pushed him away moments later. She gripped his coat again, her hands like vice grips. With her nearly paralyzed, overfilled lips, she began kissing him again before stopping abruptly.

"I have a place for us to stay tonight," she said, still gripping underneath the shoulders of his coat, "and I've got your little suit in the back of the truck... I want it bad, and I want it rough."

"I love it when it's a rough one," he said, his serpent-like tongue nearly dangling out of his mouth.

"Oh, I know you do," she replied like a succubus with her prey in her grasp, "but you're going to do something for Mama, alright?"

"Anything for you," he hissed back.

"I need you to steal that goddamn horse," she said, gripping him tighter.

His eyebrows raised, and his eyes widened while his Adam's apple bounced like a pinball in his throat.

"S-steal the horse... But how?" he stammered.

She let go of him and turned her back to him as she maniacally paced away.

"You're going to take my truck and follow me and Ethan back to the house. From there, we'll attach a trailer to the hitch for the horse. I'm then going to write down the directions

to the farm for you and map out the stables. It's about a half-

hour away, and you're going to drive there when it gets dark.

You'll quietly get the horse, put him in the trailer, and drive

back to the Crosby Estates apartment building. My parents still

have another month on the lease after moving out, so we might

as well have some fun. The trailer is insulated, so he'll be fine

to stay in there overnight."

"What about... You know...your husband?" he whispered

with a quiver.

"Grant won't do shit. I'll make something up to tell him,

like that I have to leave to go over talking points with Ethan

or something like that." She turned to face him again and

approached him like a seductive call girl by putting her mouth

up to his ear to whisper, "Then, when the job is done, you're

going to drive back to the apartments, you're going to park the

truck, and then you're going to walk up to 306...and then... I'm

going to rock your world."

He gulped again and gave a shaky exhale. Vicky's voice tingled in his ear, causing goosebumps to run down his arms. Ethan's car pulled around the corner, blocking the entrance to the sidewalk.

"Alright... I'll do it," Colton replied, breathing heavily with his back still pressed against the pillar.

"Good boy," Vicky said as she dropped the keys in his hand.

Colton followed behind her as she made her way to the parking lot, her boots clanking with every step.

Chapter 5

Jailhouse Rock

Jill stood in front of her bedroom mirror, holding a red cocktail dress against her body. Self-conscious thoughts swirled in her head at the sight of the sleeves, which cut off at the shoulder. The idea of going down to the cities to shop for new clothes was never something she looked forward to, like other women. It felt like browsing a car dealership where every car was missing its front left wheel; no matter how sporty the exterior may be, the absence was the only aspect that would attract attention. She threw it on the ground in disgust, next to a pile of unfolded laundry.

She rifled through her closet more, passing on each blouse and dress in an assembly-line fashion. It was the first time in a long while that she spent her time outside of work wearing anything but a flannel shirt and jeans. No to the black dress shirt. No to the peach skirt. No to the blue blouse with white polka dots. Walking into her bathroom in her underwear, she stared into the mirror, examining her freshly curled hair. It had been so long since she accessorized in order to feel pretty. With her foundation applied and her mascara carefully placed on her eyes, she stood there looking down at her lipstick choices. Red felt too aggressive and bold, while pink felt like she was about to attend someone's sweet sixteen birthday party. The only option left was the MAC matte nude color, which served as a convenient neutral option. As she applied it, she stared deeply into her reflection. The vulnerability of the woman staring across from her gave her heart a fearful, sinking feeling that moved like electricity through her body. She put on her glasses and took a deep breath.

"It's just a date, Jill," she assured herself aloud, "it's okay to want to feel pretty."

She walked back to her closet and found a dress hiding in the corner. An all-white polyester minidress with a tiered skirt and single bow back rested in her hands. It feels a little adventurous for a first date, she thought. Nevertheless, she tried it on. The dress fit like a glove as she put it over her body. Glancing it over in the mirror, she noticed that the seam of the shoulder tucked perfectly around her residual limb. The loose twirl of the skirt felt freeing, as though she were Marilyn Monroe standing over an air vent. Sure, this was too summery for February, but for the first time in the process of getting ready, she smiled back at her reflection.

Confidently, she made her way to the living room, a bottle of nude nail polish in her hand. Her feet felt residual crumbs in the gray wool carpet that she hadn't vacuumed in over two weeks. She plopped down on the loveseat and opened it up, setting the wet brush on top of a tissue that she placed on the glass coffee table. She gave her nails a quick once-over and laid her hand out in front of her. With the exception of her ring finger looking a tiny bit shorter than the others, everything looked perfect.

She put the handle end of the brush in her mouth, holding it between her teeth. Holding the bottle with her pointer finger and thumb, she made a '3' with her other fingers. Delicately, she dipped the brush into the bottle while hovering over the coffee table. With gentle strokes, she started with her pinky, filling it in with surgical precision. One down, four to go, she thought. She got halfway through her ring finger before needing to replenish the brush with more polish. Carefully, she dipped the wand back into the bottle, scraping the excess residue along the rim of the opening. Slowly, as if she were threading a needle, she approached the remaining bare nail of her finger.

"On guard! Hoo wah!" Randall shouted as he jumped from the kitchen, pointing his sword at Jill.

Startled, Jill jolted backward, spilling the nail polish all over the midsection of the white dress. The beautiful garment went from the perfect outfit to a flesh-colored Jackson Pollock piece. Randall, still positioned with his sword extended, stood still as his eyes widened over his own mistake. Jill looked down at the stain, her blood pressure rising with every second that went by.

"Goddammit, Randall!" she shouted as she slammed the bottle of nail polish on the coffee table. "My dress is ruined! What the hell were you thinking?"

Sheathing his sword, he approached Jill apologetically.

"I'm so sorry, Auntie. You know how the King gets when he's practicing his karate," he apologized, trying to hand her the box of tissues.

She hit the box out of his hand, sending it flying onto the carpet. He could see in her eyes the severity of his mistake. She stood up and got in his face, resisting the urge to shove him.

"Enough with the Elvis crap! You aren't Elvis, and you never will be, Randall! Newsflash: he died a fat slob on the toilet long before you came around," she yelled as he looked at her with frightened eyes.

"Auntie, I'm sor—"

"—Now I have to change, and I will end up late and looking horrible for my date. I should have never let you have that sword—of course, it was going to come back to bite me somehow because you have zero self-control!" she said, poking him in the chest with her finger. "Why can't you just be normal? Why must you insist on acting like some sort of uncontrollable head case?"

Jill instantly regretted her words as she saw the spirit drain from Randall's face. His head drooped, and the two of them stood in a moment of silence. He exhaled deeply as he lifted his head back up to face her.

"Randall, I'm so sorry," Jill said, trying to put her hand on his shoulder and being met with instant rejection. "Listen,

I didn't mean what I said, okay? That was wrong, and I took it too far."

Randall looked away from her and made his way to the front door, swiftly putting on his boots.

"Where are you going?" she asked as she walked over to him. "Randall, I'm sor-"

"—Sometimes sorry isn't good enough... I need some fresh air to clear my mind," Randall mumbled, still speaking in his southern twang, a single tear rolling down his cheek. "Sometimes you ain't nothin' but a hound dog, Auntie Jill...you got me crying all the time."

He slammed the door behind him, and she followed to see him get on his bike and ride off toward town. Jill ran out and yelled for him to come back. Ignoring her, he pedaled faster, his white cape flapping in the wind. She realized there was no point chasing him down; she just had to let him forgive her on his own. Jill cursed at herself as she stomped back up the concrete steps into her house.

Jill made it to the date after going another round with her closet and a car ride filled with self-deprecating thoughts. Nerves set in during her drive into the city as she fixated on Randall and whether or not he'd ever speak to her again. The watch on her wrist read 5:23 p.m. as she sat at her table alone in DeGidio's Italian restaurant in St. Paul.

Before leaving, she settled on a red blouse that covered most of her severed limb, paired with black dress pants and boots. The bottom of the deformed limb was poking out like a prairie dog, which made her feel extra self-conscious. Surely, Anna would have mentioned to this Todd guy that she was missing a limb, but what if she didn't? It could turn into one of those awkward situations where the guy powers through the date just to get it over with, only to never call her again, given the turn-off. Or, even worse, he could outright leave.

The few dates Jill did have in her life followed that sort of pattern —one she didn't anticipate would get any better at 38. Even the best dates, at some point, prompted the other person to ask how she lost the arm in the first place. She felt it rude at first, but realized that it was only human nature to be curious about anything that stood out. Hell, she barely remembered the accident at all. She was just a six-year-old girl playing in her grandparents' barn, and her arm was trapped under some heavy farming equipment. Her father was able to pull her out, and the arm appeared to be just a little bruised. Little did they know that her arm would continue to swell the following day until it went completely numb. When they took her to the hospital, the doctor told them that Jill had acute compartment syndrome, or swelling inside the fascia, which separates the muscles. When the swelling goes on for too long, blood vessels and nerves get cut off from the muscle, rendering it dead. After that, the only option is to amputate.

Hopefully, it won't cause any issues this time. Hopefully, there would be some sort of baseline humanity shown her way. After all, it's not like she could just grow a new one, she thought.

A tall, slender man with olive skin and slicked-back dark hair entered the restaurant wearing a gray Armani suit with a black tie with white stripes. He approached the hostess and started talking briefly until she turned around and pointed in Jill's direction.

"Shit," Jill said softly to herself. "Okay. Be relaxed...be nice."

The hostess was holding a menu in her arms as she and the man approached the table. The man's chiseled jawline had faint black stubble that looked prickly to the touch. Jill stood up instinctively and took a deep breath.

"Are you Jill?" he asked with a smile, revealing two white rows of perfectly aligned teeth.

"Hi Jill," her mouth spat out as she stood entranced by his smile, confusing both of them. "I mean, yes! Sorry, I am Jill. You must be, Todd."

A feeling of embarrassment swept over her as she fixated on her harebrained response. Hi Jill. What the hell was that, she thought.

"Hi Todd," he introduced himself with a wink and a laugh, causing an embarrassed feeling to balloon inside her. "I'm only giving you a hard time. I slip up like that all the time. Bring it in here!"

Todd walked towards her and embraced her with a hug, wrapping his long arms around her body. She met him in return with a slight pat on the back. For his slender frame, he felt oddly muscular to the touch. They sat down and opened up the menu in front of them. Jill buried her eyes in the cursive font in front of her, nervous to face the eyes from across the table. A server wearing all black with a tie tucked into his vest approached them.

"Hello, you two, and welcome to DeGidio's. My name is Michael, and I'll be your server this evening. Our special tonight is a tagliatelle bolognese tossed in a creamy Roma tomato sauce. Can I start us off with any drinks or appetizers?" he asked.

Before she could even look up, Todd started to rattle off an order as he stuffed his napkin in his collar, forming a bib over his tie.

"Hey Mike, we'll start with an order of Formaggio di Capra, I'll take an old fashioned, and the lady and I are going to also split a bottle of your finest Chianti," Todd replied, radiating more confidence than an Olympic swimmer at a YMCA competition.

"Very good, sir," Michael said, quickly scribbling in his pad. "I'll put that in right away."

An impressed Jill slowly put down her menu like a scared cat around a new person. Usually, she would be annoyed at someone ordering for her; she also didn't care for wine. But for some reason, how he looked in doing so made her temporarily suspend her self-reliant principles. He looked at her with full lips and olive skin that looked mesmerizing in the dim candlelight.

"That's quite an order," she noted with a forced smile, holding her silver necklace between her fingers.

"What can I say?" he said, laying his palms flat outward on the table. "I like to keep things interesting."

Michael came by with the refreshments and began to pour Jill a glass of wine as she and Todd looked at each other quietly from across the table. She averted her eyes and went straight back to the entree section of the menu.

"Were we ready to order, or do we still need a few minutes to look over those menus?" the server asked.

"Umm," Jill said with indecisiveness radiating throughout her voice.

"I'm going to do the rigatoni and porchetta meatballs," Todd decided, handing the menu to Michael and looking back at Jill.

Her eyes combed through the menu as if she were one minute from the time limit on an ACT exam.

"Chicken fettuccine alfredo!" she threw out there, "please and thank you."

Michael finished scribbling down the orders in his notepad.

"Alright, I will put those orders in, and your Formaggio di capra should be on its way out!" he said, taking Jill's menu and walking back to the kitchen area. She looked back over at Todd, who was sipping on his cocktail.

"So," she said, trying to find her center, "Anna tells me you live here in St. Paul?"

"I do. I'm from Southern California originally, though. I moved up here for college and never looked back, I suppose," he said, leaning back in his chair.

"Oh, California sounds nice! I'd much rather be there than here at this time of year," Jill replied with a forced, polite laugh.

"Yeah, can I be real with you for a second?" he asked.

Oh no, she thought. Here it comes. Here comes the brutal rejection from a guy who finds it imprudent to leave out the fact that the woman he is going out on a date with is missing an arm. She felt a gasp of air enter her nostrils and squeezed her diaphragm as she braced for the inevitable.

"Uh...yeah, sure...go ahead," she replied.

He wiped the moisture off his mouth from the drink with the napkin hanging from his collar.

"Well, how do I put this..." he said, looking down at the table. "Everyone around here is so obsessed with talking about the weather, and I just don't get it."

Jill felt like a release valve had just been opened to put her at ease.

"And trust me, this isn't a dig at you or anything. You know, it's just that I get it. It's cold here and everything, but it seems like every day somebody is talking about the weather, and I'm just thinking, 'Yeah, buddy. It's clouds, wind, and shit. They do this all the time. You know what I'm saying?" he asked earnestly.

"Oh, totally," Jill agreed, eager to find common ground. "I can't stand it. I think that everyone who runs out of stuff to talk about just goes to the lowest hanging fruit there is—"

"—and what could be lower hanging than what's happening outside?" he said, finishing her sentence.

"Exactly!" she said with genuine excitement and connection. "I work with dead people and feel like they know how to carry a conversation better than Roger at the hardware store. They're more friendly, too."

Todd threw his head back with laughter.

"Hey, cut Roger some slack now. I hear his friend group is a bunch of tools," he joked. "It's got to be tough dealing with upset customers when you're confiding in a bunch of tools."

Jill nearly spat out her wine as she laughed. She covered her mouth as she checked her surroundings to see if anyone was staring.

"Not that you know too much about angry customers, being a mortician and all," he quipped.

"I can't deny that," she admitted with a smile. "I can confidently say that they've never complained about the comfort of our caskets."

"Oh, that's great," he said with another chuckle.

"It's not for everybody, but it's for a living," Jill replied, giggling.

"Do you just have a booklet of these one-liners somewhere?" Todd asked.

"You pick up a thing or two in mortuary school," she said with a sly grin before taking a sip of her wine.

As the night went on, Jill found herself at ease for the first time in nearly twenty years. Her last romantic fling was fresh out of college when she dated a 2nd-grade teacher named Sean from Stillwater. Sean was a nice enough guy but had an unhealthy obsession with JFK assassination conspiracies. Newspaper clippings covered his bedroom walls, and a bookshelf was filled with books discussing various theories. Sean would also constantly mention how they should vacation to Dallas together to visit Dealey Plaza. It got so bad that he was eventually fired from his job after he taught a lesson over *Charlotte's Web* where he proposed that the government assassinated the outspoken Charlotte in a politically motivated effort to keep pork prices artificially low, all while attributing her death to a "short spider lifespan" to cover up the crime and ease suspicion from the rest of the farm animals. He also wasn't keen on showering.

This night felt different and, best of all, hopeful. They continued to make each other laugh as they dined on their entrees, learning that they had a ton in common. Everything from their mutual love for grunge music to their admiration for the bizarre antics of Dennis Rodman was a breath of fresh air for Jill. Maybe it was the wine talking, but she couldn't get over how handsome he looked. Anna really did me a solid with this one, she thought.

"Do you read at all?" he asked as he poured himself a glass from the Chianti bottle.

"I do! I'm actually quite the voracious reader," she replied.

"Me too. It keeps the mind sharp," he said. "Do you have a favorite author?"

"Oh definitely, Tolkien," she said, covering her mouth while finishing her bite. "I know I sound like a massive nerd, but I am absolutely obsessed with everything *Lord of the Rings*."

"You know, I can't say I'm super familiar with the stories themselves. I know of them, of course, and that they're the pinnacle of fantasy, but I just never got around to reading them, I suppose," Todd replied as Jill took in another bite. "Do you have a favorite character?"

"Gandalf," she said, wiping her mouth with her napkin as she chewed her last bite.

"Gandalf? What does he or she do?" he replied.

"Great question," she said with a coy smile as she sipped her wine. "Gandalf is this all-powerful wizard who befriends these little guys called the Hobbits —basically a jolly bunch of 3-foot-tall people who love to eat and drink."

"Sounds like my kind of people," he noted.

"Indeed," she replied with a wink. "Anyway, one of his Hobbit friends is in possession of this one ring to rule them all, which was created by the villain in the story, Sauron, who made it to bring darkness over the world for all eternity. And the only way you can destroy the ring is to throw it in the fires of Mt. Doom, where he made it. Long story short, they form this fellowship with all of the races in Middle Earth to destroy the ring and defeat Sauron. Are you with me so far?"

"I think so," Todd said with a laugh.

"Good," she said before grabbing the salt and pepper shakers from the middle of the table and placing them in front of her. "Now, what makes Gandalf such a badass is that he starts out as Gandalf the Grey —this wise, caring, powerful, inquisitive wizard who guides the group —and then he comes across this giant, monstrous beast called a Balrog, whom he fights to the death. And then no more Gandalf the Grey," she said, purposely knocking over the pepper shaker.

"But then..." she went on, grabbing the salt shaker and placing it directly in front of her, "he comes back. This time, however, he's transformed into Gandalf the White. He has an all-white robe, staff, and even an all-white trusty steed named Shadowfax. He's more powerful than ever, and despite this change in appearance, the new Gandalf still has the urge to fight for what is right deep in his being. He's an unexpected hero in this unexpected journey."

"Wow," Todd said, leaning back in his chair with his arms folded. "You...really are a nerd," he teased with a laugh.

"Oh, shut up!" she bantered back playfully.

"Hey, those were your words originally, not mine," he said with a smile as he took another bite of pasta.

"Okay, Mr. Accountant," she said with a playful eye roll, "because it's much less nerdy to crunch numbers all day."

"Well, I actually don't work at the accounting firm anymore," he admitted before setting his fork and knife down and wiping his mouth with his napkin.

"Oh," Jill said, with genuine surprise in her voice, "did you recently quit or something?"

"No, actually," he said with a heavy sigh as he folded his hands, "I ended up getting into some trouble...listen, I really hope you don't think less of me here..."

His head sank, and he started to slouch behind his plate of rigatoni. Jill saw the cheery spirit drain from his eyes as if he were on a therapy couch in the middle of the restaurant. She put her hand across the table and put it over his own.

"Hey, hey, I'm sure whatever happened is in the past, right? We all make mistakes. If I wasn't my own boss, I'm sure I would have been fired at some point too."

He looked across at her with hopeless brown eyes. Seeing the welcoming expression on her face made him feel safe and at ease. Todd smiled at her and then put his other hand over hers.

"I'm sorry. I know I should be more vulnerable; it just gets scary to let people in, especially on a first date. Yes, I was fired. I mean, with what I did, I not only ruined my career...I...well, I ended up serving jail time," he replied.

Jill jerked her neck in surprise. Firing was one thing, but she never anticipated he'd fess up to jail time. She leaned toward him and looked to her left and right.

"Jail time? Like prison?" she asked.

"Yeah...I just got out six months ago on probation. I've been in lockup for about seven and a half years," he said, sinking his head and staring down sadly at his plate of noodles.

Jill sighed as she looked at this man with pitiful eyes. She could only imagine the kind of ostracization someone in the accounting world must face when getting into trouble with the law. The poor guy probably didn't have a friend in this world, she thought.

"Well, that's not the end of the world, you know? We all make mistakes, and everybody deserves a second chance at life," she added, squeezing the back of his hand tightly. "White-collar crime happens all the time. Whether intentional or an unforced error, you've paid your debt to society, and you're holding your head high and putting yourself back out there. I think that's a very noble thing, Todd," she said.

"Oh, it wasn't anything white-collar. I was a fantastic accountant. Every number was in place, every 't' crossed, 'i' dotted, the whole nine yards," he said before taking a sip from the Chianti.

"It wasn't?" she questioned, "Well, what did you do, if you don't mind me asking?"

"Well, it's kind of a funny story, really. You know, one of those workplace situations that just gets a little out of hand. But, essentially, I strapped a bomb across my chest and held the entire office hostage for a few hours," he stated, with the wholesome face someone would make upon realizing they accidentally grabbed someone else's grocery cart.

Jill slowly pulled her hand back from him. She took a couple short breaths and sat with widened eyes as he began digging back into his spaghetti like a hungry, absent-minded teenager.

"You...you took hostages...with a bomb?" she asked, lowering her voice to a near whisper.

"Yeah, it wasn't my best moment," he said before taking in a mouthful of wine, the scarlet stain of it hanging around his lips. "You see, every day before I went to work, I'd buy one of those Zebra Cakes-you know, the little sponge cake things with the vanilla and chocolate frosting on them-for my midday snack. I'd stick it right in the breakroom fridge because I liked them nice and cool. I looked forward to that

Zebra Cake every day, right at two o'clock to help get me through the rest of my day. Hours of accounting work can be a terrible strain on a person, so this was my way to treat myself, you know?"

He slurped up a noodle off his plate, making a revolting sucking sound that sounded similar to a dentist's suction hose. Jill watched with minor disgust as it slithered into his mouth like a worm.

"So one day, 2:00 p.m. rolls around, and I walk over to the fridge. And lo and behold, my Zebra Cake is nowhere to be found. Poof. Gone. Vanished. And I'm like, 'Okay, that's upsetting, but I'm sure somebody must have thought the boss brought in treats or something. No big deal.' So the next day, I buy another one, get a sticky note, and write my name on it before it goes into the fridge. That should solve the problem, right? No!" he banged his fist on the table, making the glasses and silverware shake, turning the heads of the other patrons and startling Jill, "I go in there at 2:00 again to get my goddamn Zebra Cake, only to find it gone again, but the sticky note is left on the fridge shelf. They take the treat and leave the goddamn sticky note. That's a disrespectful slap in the face, is it not? It's like hot wiring someone's car and leaving the license plates behind so you knew that they did it!" he exclaimed, his voice getting louder with each sentence.

"I...I guess so?" Jill agreed, her voice trembling as she looked around at some of the other patrons still staring at Todd, whose face was now red with anger as the blood vessels in his eyes became visible.

"Exactly! And so now I'm pissed. And I'm saying to myself, 'This motherfucker. Thinking they can eat my Zebra Cake even though my name is stuck right to the label.' So I'll tell you what I did. The next day, I get my Zebra Cake, and I get two sticky notes, stick them together, and write 'PROPERTY OF TODD. DO NOT EAT.' in clear as day, big letters in black marker. And so I'm waiting...oh boy, am I waiting until 2:00 to roll around again. And finally, it does. I go back to the breakroom, I open the fridge, and do you know what I saw?" he asked.

"...no Zebra Cake?" Jill asked tepidly.

"No goddamn Zebra Cake!" he shouted, banging his fist on the table once more. "And that's when I snapped. I get in my car, and I drive home. At this point, I'm seething, and I black out. I don't remember much from here on out, but apparently, I went to my house and grabbed a sweater vest, some duct tape, and some sticks of dynamite I had left over from a college summer job I had working in a quarry mine. I attached it all to this little handheld switch and drove back to that office. And when I marched through those doors, I shouted, 'LISTEN UP! WHICHEVER ONE OF YOU LOWLIFE KEYBOARD JOCKEYS ATE MY ZEBRA CAKE BETTER STEP THE FUCK FORWARD RIGHT NOW, OR I'M BLOWING US ALL TO HELL!'"

Todd was now standing up and pounding on the table in his reenactment of the events. Jill covered her mouth in horror as the entire restaurant was now looking in their direction.

She could see their waiter reluctantly approaching their table, his arms shaking with every step. In a moment of realization, Todd looked around the restaurant to catch every eye in the building looking at him and that the violin music that was playing softly over the speakers had stopped. He turned to face the waiter, who looked like he was approaching a caged tiger.

"I'm good, I'm good," Todd reclaimed himself calmly, putting his hands up in a surrendering gesture.

He sat back down at the table and poured the rest of the bottle of wine into his glass. Twirling the wine in his glass like a sommelier, he took a long, interminable drink, nearly finishing it. Jill sat stunned, looking at her date as if he had just transformed into O.J. Simpson.

"Anywho, they ended up calling in a SWAT team and the bomb squad, who yelled through their megaphones, 'You've got your whole life ahead of you' and 'Think about the families.' Ya know, the typical shit. After about 4 hours or so into the standoff, I ended up caving. The snack thief ended up being the lardass in accounts payable named Mark. He claims to be a diabetic who just needed to balance his blood sugar, but I'm calling bullshit on that. Get your own snack if you need it that badly, am I right?"

Jill remained speechless as Todd continued to chow down on the remainder of his meal.

"So," he said, chewing down on a mouthful of noodles, "how did you lose the arm?"

Chapter 6

Can't Help Falling In Love

The clock on the truck dashboard read 8:11 p.m. as Colton sat alone in the truck he parked outside the stable. It was pitch black and barren, just as Vicky had described. In the dead of winter, not a soul would make it out to these fields until Friday to check in on Frosty, fill his automatic feeder, and make sure the heating inside his stall was functioning. When he arrived at Vicky's home after the retirement home visit, he and a non-conversational Grant attached the insulated trailer to the back of the truck. This wasn't out of the ordinary, as any attempt at bonding he made with Vicky's husband was usually met with one-word answers that never included eye contact of any sort.

Colton's suspicion was that Grant knew deep down about the ongoing affair. And although Vicky was guarded about the details regarding the relationship with her husband, Colton couldn't imagine her spilling the beans to him. They snuck around carefully, with Vicky always keeping tabs on Grant's whereabouts to avoid any catastrophe. The only time they were close to being caught was when Grant came home early from work during a particularly aggressive sexcapade. Colton, tied up with a rope and gagged, was bent over an old desk in their basement while Vicky paddled his backside and belittled him by shouting out insults and obscenities. She heard Grant running downstairs to the basement door and quickly had Colton hop and hide behind the water heater in the corner of the basement. When a panicked Grant asked what was going on, Vicky, dressed in her nightgown, lied and told him that she came down to look for a humidifier for her nap and saw some mice that startled her, and she tried beating them to death with the paddle. Grant seemed to have bought the excuse, noting that it explained why he heard high-pitched squealing. Vicky returned later in the middle of the night to free Colton, who had been trapped for several hours.

Colton imagined that, even if Grant ever did find out, he was too nice of a guy to end his wife's promising political career over it. At the very least, that was comforting, and a luxury he didn't get in previous affairs. He vividly remembered having to climb out of a fourth-floor D.C. apartment window in his underwear after being caught in the act with the wife of a former White House staffer, who proceeded to chase him eight city blocks with a machete. Colton escaped the machete chase by hiding in the dumpster behind a popular Chinese restaurant called Hunan Garden for two hours (and refuses to touch lo mein to this day as a result). But that just wasn't the type of guy Grant was, thankfully. A good man like him would discover an affair and probably head to the nearest watering hole to quietly drown his sorrows behind a stiff drink. The poor bastard, he thought.

The beige stable in front of him looked more like a guest house than it did a place to station a lone horse. It was walled and insulated, with two large garage doors closed off to the sizable fenced-off field of snow. He approached the side door with a crowbar in hand. Jiggling the door handle and pushing on it with his shoulder, he could budge it a half-an-inch forward. He saw that the only thing locking the door was a rusty latch on the other side. Taking the straight end of the crowbar, he gave several solid jabs to the latch and bent it until it broke off completely. The door slowly swung open, revealing hay-covered floorboards and a towering bronco as white as the snow outside.

He stood outside of the single stable in there, with the stable door removed for him to go in and out as he pleased. Above the stable was a hand-crafted wooden crest that read "Frosty" in a hand-painted font that looked distinguished enough to belong on colonial documents. A huge automatic feeder and water dispenser were on the wall opposite the stable, and inside were several dangling rubber toys for his entertainment. Colton noticed that the inside was heated and was a delightful contrast to the cold outside. The horse let out a loud, neighing grunt as Colton entered the building.

"Hey, horsie...how are you?" he said, tiptoeing toward the animal.

The horse respired a louder, uncomfortable groan and started kicking up his feet in place. Hanging on the wall near the side door were two saddles, one black and one a light mahogany color, and the black bridles to go over his face. Colton grabbed the reins, untangled them, and held them open between his hands. He slowly crept toward Frosty, who became more agitated with each step.

"Shhh...it's okay, Frosty...it's okay...be a good horsie for me, huh?" Colton said as his heart began to race.

Frosty started scraping the ground before him, kicking back hay behind him, grunting with each kick. Colton carefully reached the bobbing head of the Frosty and somehow managed to get the brindles around the horse's dome. He tightened it and fastened it snuggly atop his snout.

"See, that wasn't so bad, was it? Who's a good horsie?" Colton asked in a baby-talk voice.

Just then, Frosty bellted a thundering squeal and stood up on his hind legs, attempting to crash down on Colton's scrawny body and break him in two. Colton fell backward on his back and rolled over quickly to avoid the horse's massive feet. Though he avoided the blow, he rolled his torso and legs on top of a large pile of fresh horse droppings that caked onto his jacket and slacks. Frostygrunted as he trotted back into the corner. Colton picked himself up and looked down at the feces that now covered his entire front.

"You stupid son of a bitch," he hissed at the horse. "If I had it my way, you'd be turned into dog food, goddammit!"

He again started to tiptoe toward the horse, who was now bearing his teeth in a way that felt like a mocking smile to Colton. He extended his hand toward the horse as his fingertips inched closer toward the reins of the harness. Once the end of his pointer and middle finger touched the leather of the reins, he lunged forward and gripped them tightly.

"Got ya!" he snarled, pulling the horse toward himself. "You're not so tough now, are you, ya big dumb idiot?"

Frosty let out another dissatisfied grunt as he reluctantly followed Colton's lead. After hitting the top garage button on the wall, the left stall opened up to the howling winter wind outside, blowing snow into the building. With more negative neighing, Colton pulled the horse out to the side fence gate and walked him to the back of the trailer. Unlatching the door and swinging it wide open, he got up on the platform of the steel box trailer and yanked on the reins of the resistant horse.

"Come on, you bastard!" he yelled. "Get the hell in here!"

After having his neck jolted forward to an uncomfortable degree, the horse finally caved and entered the closed-off trailer. Colton quickly jumped out and closed the back of the trailer. He let out a heavy exhale with his back against the closed trailer gate, listening to the rustling noises of a frustrated Frosty. Colton ran back to shut the gate, made his way back into the building, and closed all the doors. The truck door flung open from the wind the moment he pulled the handle, forcing him to pull it back shut with all his might. He sat in the driver's seat, catching his breath before turning on the ignition.

The quiet Minnesota highway lay dark and barren as the truck returned to Rockdale. The heavy wind jolted against the side of the vehicle, slightly shaking the trailer as it passed by endless acres of open farmland. The smell of the horse feces was settling in as the heat from the air vents assisted in its odorous offense to Colton's nostrils. His only soothing thought in this situation was knowing that a seductive Vicky was waiting to jump his bones with a night filled with sexual rewards for his commitment. The fact that it would take place in the old apartment of the parents she resented meant it would likely be rough, too, which put an even bigger smile on his face.

His masochistic fantasy followed him back to Rockdale, going five miles under the speed limit the whole way. After cruising into town, he located Crosby Estates Apartments, parked the truck near the back of the lot, turned off the ignition, and took a moment to collect himself amongst the night's chaos. He looked at himself in the passenger mirror and realized he was still covered in horse dung. There was no way he could go up like this without instantly killing the mood, he thought. After looking in the truck's back seat, he realized he had left his luggage and a bag of custom-made marital toys he had ordered from China in Ethan's car.

"Shit!" he yelled as he slammed his hand against the steering wheel.

He did a double take to the back seat again, noticing the shine of fake leather reflecting the light of a nearby street lamp. The skin-tight, all-black sex suit Vicky had bought him for his birthday, equipped with a mask, red ball gag, and sex toy holster, lay across the floor. It was a better option than he was currently working with, and she mentioned bringing it for him. This unfortunate horse incident quickly turned into a pleasant surprise. Removing the stained clothes, he grabbed the royal pine air freshener that hung on the rearview mirror. He rubbed it all over his chest and legs, hoping it would help mask any leftover scent from the stable. After a struggle that lasted a few minutes, he worked his way into the suit until it covered him completely.

Forgetting about the keys in the ignition, he quickly grabbed the pile of clothes and ran toward the nearby dumpster to toss them in. He figured Vicky could retrieve some clothes for him in the morning or have Ethan bring over his suitcase. The suit was oddly warm against the cold winter breeze that shook the ball gag hanging around his neck. Without trying to be noticed, he quickly ran into the apartment building and made his way to the stairwell.

"What room did she say again?" he asked himself as he stood against the wall. "Let's see...it ended in 06...I think it's 206," he said, feeling primarily confident.

Quietly moving up the stairs, he poked his head out into the hallway to find no one in sight to see him in his lewd outfit.

He quickly tiptoed his way down the hall until he got to apartment 206. Putting his ear to the door, he heard faint music-something Vicky did occasionally to set the mood. Colton rubbed his hands together in excitement for the night that awaited him. He put the ball gag in his mouth, tightened it, and then zipped the headpiece to the top of his head, covering it completely.

"I'm coming for you, baby..." he mumbled in a muffled voice as he opened the door and walked in, shutting it behind him.

Chapter 7

Unchained Melody

The Starry Night Lounge stood like a lighthouse beacon as it sat atop the hill overlooking Rockdale. It was an older building that used to be a lodge before the town's founding in 1897. The logo on the sign that sat in front of the lodge shingles that hadn't been replaced for at least 20 years was an image of Vincent Van Gogh, with a bandage over his ear, extending an arm out that held a massive mug of beer. At the end of the bar was their pick-up station labeled "To-Gogh Orders", where the most popular item to go out was their loaded potato bites, which were ironically, but unintentionally, shaped like severed ears.

As the only local watering hole for the town's inhabitants and all of its degenerates, there was only one place for weary travelers to wet their whistles or get a bite to eat. Tonight, that traveler was Ethan Bile, who ponied up to the bar, placing the drawstring bag Colton left in his car at the bottom of the stool. The place had about ten other people, none sitting at the bar but in booths lined up along the sides. He noticed the blackboard that read "TUESDAY KARAOKE" in colorful chalk and a man with long golden-grayish hair setting up his sound equipment in the corner.

"Great..." he muttered, "just what I need. A bunch of drunks belting out 'Don't Stop Believing' during my dinner."

Stan Novotny, the 62-year-old owner and bartender, worked every day except Monday with his son, Daryl, who cooked in the back. Stan's general outlook on life was akin to that of a self-loathing tortoise who was administered a muscle relaxer. Every day at work was his personal purgatory, where he would sometimes subconsciously do things in hopes of getting fired, only to remember that he was self-employed.

When he opened this spot in 1966, it was simply named 'Stan's Spot' and was a place where people came dressed up. Walking in, the bar shone like a man who clearly took pride in the upkeep. White upholstered barstools sat along the length of a satin burgundy bar stocked with the finest liquors available. There were low-top tables with classic '60s leather lounge chairs with a dimly lit lamp hanging above them. But the crown jewel of the joint was a polished mahogany bar piano that his wife, Shirley, would play every night. Some days, he closes his eyes and still imagines her tickling the ivories, her bright red lipstick matching her dress, giving him a subtle smile and wink as he delivers a couple of lemon drop martinis to table 4.

Unfortunately, Shirley's claims of arthritic wrists made her call it quits with the piano a decade ago. She instead began staying home, watching daytime soap operas, and having an affair with the mailman while Stan was at work. He caught them in the act after the school called and requested Daryl be picked up after vomiting in Home Economics class after accidentally mistaking sink cleaner for baking soda in the cupcakes they were making. When Daryl and Stan got home, they heard muffled yells coming from the living room, where they found a pantsless mailman handcuffed and bent over the coffee table, receiving multiple spankings from Shirley with a paddle in her hands. After that day, Stan wondered whether she had arthritis or if a prolonged love affair with lousy spanking form had brought it on. He would never know the answer.

Regardless, Shirley left with the mailman to live in Ft. Lauderdale, Florida, while a devastated Stan stayed back to raise Daryl. The bar fell apart in the process, as the markings of a defeated man infested Stan's Spot like ants after a soda spill. The much more chipper Daryl, who would grow and end up needing income to support his dream of one day traveling to New York to become a puppeteer for Sesame Street, forced Stan to keep the place open despite his sullen deposition. And to the constant pleading of Daryl, Stan gave in to renaming his dream bar. It was only fitting that his son chose to name it after a misunderstood artist who, too, was at odds with his existence.

To make matters worse, Daryl would take food orders at the bar using a Vincent Van Gogh puppet he bought in a Dutch museum gift shop on a church trip his youth group took to the Netherlands. He voiced it in a way that could only be described as a raspy Kermit The Frog with a mediocre Dutch accent that was mainly just him putting a 'sh' after certain words. Without warning, Daryl would startle Stan by making the puppet pop up behind the bar to take the patrons' orders. Stan initially objected but eventually stopped correcting his son for this bizarre ritual. He was no psychiatrist but speculated on whether this was his son's trauma manifesting itself years after walking in on his mother spanking the man who delivered his grandmother's birthday cards. Yet every time Daryl brought out the puppet, a part of Stan contemplated the probability of getting away with arson.

"What can I get you?" Stan asked a hunched-over Ethan while wiping his hands on his bar rag.

"Yes, I'll start with a club soda with two lemon wedges. And for food—"

"—We don't have lemons. All I got are a couple of limes, but they've seen better days."

Ethan put his palms up in disgust as if the man had just told him he would have a 6-hour layover.

"You don't have lemons? I mean, I didn't have high hopes for this place, but I mean, wow. Just wow," he said, crossing his arms. "What kind of bar or restaurant doesn't carry a basic fruit for making cocktails?"

"A terrible one," Stan retorted, without a muscle in his face putting up a fight against gravity.

"Jeez...that sure is a glowing endorsement. The limes will have to do. May I please have a menu?"

Stan slumped over to the other side of the bar to retrieve a menu shaped like a painter's palette with individual colors around the edges. It was a small menu that had their specialties listed at the top. Ethan didn't trust this place enough to try the 'Seafood Medley' (he imagined it probably involved some stowed-away imitation crab that sat in their freezer for at least a decade). He assumed he couldn't contract salmonella or E. coli if he selected from the fried foods.

"Alright, I'm ready to order," he huffed impatiently.

"Sounds good. Hey, Son!" Stan shouted at the kitchen station window, "Come up here; we've got an order!"

A few moments later, the Vincent Van Gogh puppet popped up over the bar, looking back and forth with oddly accurate personified movement. It startled Ethan enough that he almost fell back out of his stool as the cartoonish eyes looked straight into his own, just a mere six inches from his face. The puppet of the stoic painter with red hair and a beard to match came equipped with a paintbrush in his hand, a deep blue shirt, and a bandage over his ear.

"Oh yesh! Vee have a cush-tomer to help sh-upport my career, ya!" the puppet said, as Stan's face remained unchanged. "I have only sh-old one of my paintings, which was s-very dear to me, yes? Oh ho, if only I sh-pent more time sh-elling and lesh time cutting off my ear!"

A tiny fabric ear was thrown onto the bar before a startled Ethan. He picked it up and stared at it as if he had been drugged and was in the middle of a wild hallucination.

"What in the world... what's going on right now?" he asked the gloomy Stan with angered bewilderment.

"I wish I knew. Believe me, I do," he replied, with the same blank stare in his eyes, placing down a club soda with a haggard slice of lime hanging on the brim of the glass before heading to another table to take an order.

"Perhap-sh, I might enlighten you?" the puppet said, pressing its cotton hands together. "I am zeh world famou-sh Vin-shint Van Gogh, v-ready to take yo ordah!"

"No, you aren't. You're just some weirdo with a doll!" he barked back at the puppet, pointing his finger at the puppet's chest.

"It take-sh one to know one, ya? I am zeh real deal!" the puppet replied tauntingly.

"No, you aren't."

"Yesh, I am."

"No, you aren't!"

"Yesh, I am."

"No, you aren't!"

"Yesh I aaaaaaaaam!" he sang out.

"Stop it! Stop it! Fucking stop it!" Ethan yelled, banging his fist against the bar, causing the place to go completely silent.

His face reddened with embarrassment as he realized his overreaction. He temporarily covered his mouth, remembering that his mother would chastise him growing up if she had ever heard him say a swear word, let alone in public.

"Oh, it look-sh like shum-one had a little meltdown, ya?" he taunted, bringing the puppet to the right side of Ethan's fuming face. "Perhap-sh we trade zis meltdown in for an $8.99 patty melt in-shtead?"

Ethan took a deep breath and closed his eyes, focusing on how hungry the long day had made him.

"No, thank you," Ethan replied.

"Ooooooh, are you sure? Vee have it on sh-pecial today, ya!" the puppet replied as its tiny arm pointed to the chalkboard that listed the daily specials.

"Yes," he insisted, seething, "I'm sure! Why the hell would you choose to take orders in some asinine voice? It's demeaning to your guests. We live in a society, and there are rules! What the hell kind of place operates by creeping out its guests like this?"

"Like I said, a terrible one," Stan replied, his facial expression still unchanged.

"No! Zeh only zing that ish terrible ish the underappreciation of my art! Oh, woe ish me!" the puppet said, putting the back of its hand to his forehead like an overdramatic actress from a 1920s noir film.

"You're ridiculous," he said, folding his arms again and turning away from the puppet.

"Oh ho, maybe so, vut at leash I don't look ridiculou-sh like you!"

"You take that back!" Ethan said, pointing a finger into the plush stomach of the puppet.

"I don't sink so!" the puppet mocked back.

"I mean it, you! Apologize, you overrated Dutch douchebag!" Ethan said, his face glowing red with rage.

"If I'm sho overrated, zen vhy do zey sh-till sh-ing sh-ongs about me?"

"What songs? That doesn't even make sense!" he said aloud, "Why are you arguing with a puppet, Ethan?"

Ethan leaned over the bar to see a well-upholstered twenty-something with unkempt shoulder-length brown hair. He was wearing a grease-stained Metallica shirt that was a size too small exposing his freckled gut. His big emerald eyes were magnified by the Coke bottle glasses that sat high atop his round nose. As he stared up at Ethan, the look of surprise was like one a cat makes when catching it cleaning itself.

"What the hell is wrong with you?" Ethan asked, scowling.

"I uh, I don't know what you're talking about," he replied as if he were the Wizard of Oz being caught behind his curtain.

"Yes, you do. Now stand up!"

The oafish boy stood up from his knees with the Van Gogh puppet hanging from his arm. The apron he wore draped over his waist, protruding over his ample gut. He was a whole head taller than his father and had two heads on the prickly political staffer. Yet fear radiated in his eyes as he looked down at the fiery Bile like an elephant near a mouse.

"Listen, clown, do you know who I am? Do you know who you've just pissed off?" he quizzed, leaning forward, extending his arm, and pointing a finger at the center of the Metallica logo.

"No..." the teenager said, puzzled and nervous.

"Oh? Then let me tell you," he offered, arrogance radiating off his face. "I work for one of the most powerful congresswomen in the country. And she is going to be President someday. That's right, President of the United

States. The same person with the capability to wipe freaking Tuvalu off the map if they wanted to. Which means, someday, I will have the power to make life for someone like you miserable. And because this is the only place in a miserable 30-mile radius, I have no choice but to eat at your little gimmick of an establishment. But I still don't appreciate this little schtick you're doing when I'm just trying to order food. Quite frankly, it's ticking me off. So why don't you save yourself some future trouble by going back into that kitchen and making me my fricken cheese curds and potato bites? Sound good, puppet boy?"

"Um...I guess so, yeah," Daryl answered, his mouth slightly agape as he stood and stared forward at Ethan.

"Good. Get on with it then," Ethan barked, taking a victorious swig of his club soda.

Daryl kept still. He continued to stare at Ethan like a giant, slouched ape who was entranced by a disturbance in his nature preserve. His hand reached up below his chin to scratch his neck stubble.

"Well? Go on, then. Don't just sit and stare at me like some mouth-breathing imbecile," he droned as he made a shoo motion with his hand.

"So your boss is running for President?" Daryl asked, unmoved from his previous position.

"Well, no, not yet. But mark my words: she will someday, and with my help, she's going to win," Ethan claimed, taking another vigorous swig from his club soda.

"But not right now?"

"No," Ethan said, pulling on his hair, "do you not know what *'someday'* means? She's not running yet, but she will down the line."

"Oh...got it," Daryl replied as he remained standing and blinking with the corner of his mouth hanging open.

An additional few seconds of silence passed them by in what now felt like a staring contest. Daryl slowly began to raise the Vincent Van Gogh puppet up until the red-headed replica of one of history's most famous painters was, yet again, face-to-face with Ethan Bile.

"Yoo-hoo! If dish ish true zen I sink I can shpeak freely, no?" the puppet taunted as Daryl had a smirk peering from each corner of his mouth.

Ethan's smoldering death stare had enough anger behind it to raise the global temperature two degrees. Daryl gleefully shuffled his way back to the kitchen as his disheveled father returned to the bar. The Van Gogh puppet popped up again behind the order station window, this time wearing a little apron.

"An artish never rushes hish work, but your food vill be ready shoon!" the puppet said, before plopping down and out of sight.

Ethan sighed and rolled his eyes. He squeezed the lime tightly into his drink, causing the citrus mush to fall into his glass. As he sat there looking over at Stan polishing another glass, he wondered what kind of father would let their son act that way in public. He wondered how a business owner could be so comfortable as to let one of his employees run amok like that. It was what was wrong with this country, he thought.

If more people raised their children the way his dad had raised him, then places like this would cease to exist. He believed the phrase 'the land of opportunity' was partially to blame. He believed that if you called yourself 'the land of opportunity,' you were opening yourself up to all of the freaks, freeloaders, and frauds who would come and ruin life for the rest of us. He'd fix that someday, he thought.

The front doors swung open as if an outlaw walking into a saloon was on the other side. Ethan turned to look as a teenager dressed in a slim black trucker jacket walked through the entrance. The shine of his tight black leather pants reflected off the dim lights of the bar. On his wrists were black leather cuff bracelets that bridged between his hands and the opening of the sleeves. Each step he took sounded like the clanking of a horse's hoof as he strutted confidently in his studded black boots. His voluptuous black hair was fashioned perfectly into a pompadour, with two strands dangling in front of his forehead. His sharp, determined look was a combination of fierce and utterly unafraid as he walked past Ethan and toward the designated karaoke area.

"Why is that guy dressed as Elvis?" Ethan asked Stan, who was pouring a glass of Nesbitt's Orange Soda.

"No idea. He does something different each week," Stan replied as he placed the drink in front of an open spot on the bar.

"Did I stumble into some sort of psych ward by accident?" Ethan muttered to himself, "I can't wait to get out of this godforsaken town."

The karaoke DJ, with long silver and blonde hair, stood up on the stage. He was wearing a beige t-shirt with the image of Leonardo da Vinci's *Vitruvian Man* playing an electric guitar. He began speaking into the microphone in his gravelly southern voice with the cadence of a monster truck rally announcer.

"Hello, everybody, and welcome to Tuesday Night Karaoke down here at The Starry Night Lounge! I am your master of song, dance, and fun, Joel! Come, sign up if you want to sing-don't be shy now-and I'll get your name into the rotation. Starting us off hot tonight, we have my man Randall-or should I say The King of Rock & Roll himself?-coming to us with a little ditty called 'Unchained Melody'," Joel announced before handing the mic over to Randall, who placed it back onto the stand.

"This ought to be a calamity," Ethan chuckled to Stan, who looked back at him as if he had asked him something in a foreign language.

Randall opened his lips to the mic as his eyes diverted to the stage floor. The bracelets on his wrists looked like two leather squares magnetically pulled together as he placed his hands in a praying pose. He looked up with his sharp cat eyes as they shot through Ethan like throwing stars. The recording of a piano blared, and his body jolted as if a bolt of lightning had zapped him. He began to recite the song's opening line in a voice so close to the real Elvis that, for a moment, you'd think you were transported back in time.

"Wooooooaaaaaah, my love, my darling," he looked up to the lights and grasped the air as if he were plucking something out of the air. "I hunger for your touch...a long, looonely time," he pointed at Stan, who, for the first time in the night, gave some semblance of a smile. "And time...goes by...so slowly, and time can do so much," he jumped off the stage and started walking toward Ethan. "Are you still miiiiiiiiiiiiine?"

He belted out the lyrics in a passionate cry, standing a mere few feet away from Ethan like a confident, leathered gladiator, unafraid of any foe that came before him. Ethan's jaw dropped as he watched this kid emulate all that once was a pop star sensation. Everything from the mannerisms to the singing to the androgynous poses was as if he were watching the original music stylings of Elvis perform in front of him. Ethan looked over at Joel, bobbing his head to the beat nonchalantly as if they were all witnessing a regular occurrence. During the ending piano solo and the final "God speed your love to meeeeeeeeeee!" he grabbed the mic stand and brought it down with him as he dramatically fell to his knees.

The song ended, and everyone in the bar erupted in thunderous applause as he held a final pose. He took a dramatic bow, throwing one arm out to his right as he brought the other across his chest for the downward crunch. He pointed at Joel, who smiled and pointed back, running up to the mic.

"Alriiiiiight! Everyone give it up for the Memphis Flash, Randall!" he shouted as the bar again began applauding. "Nice job, man. Up next, we've got Gayle. Come on up here, Gayle!"

A burly middle-aged woman with a pixie cut made her way to the stage to sing "Piece of My Heart" by Janis Joplin. It was horrendously out of key from the start. During her rendition, Randall strutted over to the barstool beside Ethan, his orange soda in front of him.

"Nice job, kid," Stan applauded.

"Thank you," Randall replied, in a soft voice that was almost a whisper, "thank you very much."

"Yoo-hoo! Who ish ready for shum ta-shty food?" the puppet of Van Gogh shouted through the order station window.

Stan retrieved the baskets and placed them in front of Ethan with some silverware and napkins. After taking his first couple of bites, he was surprised that it was pretty delectable for bar food. His only wish was that the puppet didn't have a hand in making it.

Ethan was struck by how this Elvis impersonator appeared to stay in character, even as he sipped on his orange soda, his hand sporting two gold and ebony rings. He looked at Ethan with a nervous-seeming side eye; the kind one gives when they know they're being watched.

"Sorry, I didn't mean to stare," Ethan said, with a half-chewed potato bite still tucked away in his cheek. "It's just not every day you meet someone who can pull off the look of Elvis. I mean, you were incredible up there!"

Of course, Ethan wasn't allowed to listen to Elvis's catalog or much of any rock and roll growing up. His father believed that popular music was a tool that was weaponized in order to corrupt children and dismantle the nuclear family. His only exception was Jimmy Buffet, given that many of his friends with whom he attended yacht parties were Parrot Heads.

Randall gave a half-smile to Ethan before focusing back on his drink, slowly twirling his straw in the mixture.

"I mean, Elvis is a legend. I suppose you can't go wrong with covering him," Ethan continued as Randall took another sip from his drink. "Are you from here originally?"

"I like to think I live in the world, but I'm not of it, brother," Randall said in a soft, calm voice with Southern twang.

Ethan looked as if he were an alien sitting beside him.

"What does that even mean?" Ethan asked in an ornery tone.

"It means I'm an admirer of the good Lord's creation," he said, completely cool and relaxed. "It's an image that the real legends know, and liars and snakes choke on...it's very hard to live up to that image, but it takes all kinds."

Ethan paused for a moment, reflecting on the words.

"You see, that right there is the mark of a good person," he said, popping three cheese curds into his mouth. "I was taught that you can tell a lot about a person's character by the spouse they pick and their relationship with the Lord."

"Take a look at you and me," Randall replied, still twirling his straw with his fingers. "Are we too blind to see? Do we turn our heads and look the other way?"

"Don't beat yourself up, man. We all have sins we have to overcome," Ethan replied with his mouth full, unaware that Randall was quoting an Elvis song. "My dad gets on me for mine all the time because he's such a hard guy to please. He's always going on and on about his legacy, the family legacy. It always feels like I'm walking on eggshells around him because I don't want to disappoint him, you know?" he continued, taking another handful of fried food and putting it in his mouth. "But, like, the thing is, I'm already making huge inroads all on my own. I wish he would just recognize it, you know? I've traveled across the country, working for some major players and decision-makers. People who will shape the political landscape for years to come. My philosophy is that you do what you can to win and don't look back."

Ethan caught himself rambling and looked over at Randall, staring at the bubbles fizzing up in his drink.

"Sorry, I know I'm rambling," he added. "What about you? Do you have a political philosophy?"

"Don't be cruel to a heart; that's true," Randall replied.

"Ah, I see what you're saying. We shouldn't let the establishment continue to silence the voices of the country's true patriots. Spot-on analysis." Ethan said, giving Randall a pat on the back, which was met with the same side-eye he had given before. "And I agree. We need to focus ahead at the next Presidential year and get our party on track to dominate in the future. The same old tactics and ideas ain't gonna cut it. I'm so thankful I'm finally working for someone who understands that like we do."

"A little less conversation, a little more action," Randall said.

"Spot-on, my friend! Vicky Veitch, a fighter who will be a ferocious lion for years to come-she backs up her words. Hopefully, one day, I'll see the inside of the Oval Office with her. That is, so long as her jerk of a chief of staff doesn't get in the way," he noted, looking down at Colton's drawstring bag. "I've hated the guy since the day he hired me. I don't know what she even sees in him, either. He's arrogant, careless." He looked around the room cautiously in case anyone was listening in. "And you didn't hear this from me, but I've seen him go into his motel rooms with...you know...ladies of the night," he said in a whisper. "That's crazy, right? I mean, you're a religious guy. How does someone like that, who reflects none of Representative Veitch's values, keep moving up in the world?"

Randall leaned forward and sipped the remainder of his drink. He looked up at the ceiling, lost in thought for only a moment. His sharp eyes returned, looking down at the bag and then at Ethan.

"Sometimes I think it's okay to intertwine, brother...sometimes a man needs the tender love of a woman to fuel his spirits high...love me tender, love me true," he said softly, adjusting his black jacket and his posture.

Ethan analyzed Randall's words as if they were the long-lost answer to an age-old philosophical question. He turned on his stool, looking at Randall with admiration and wonder.

"Intertwine, huh?" he said, scratching his chin. "So...what you're saying is that...by being sinful, he's actually learning to grow stronger in his faith?" he looked down at the empty cheese curd basket and single ear-shaped potato bite. "Of course...that's exactly what he's doing. And here I was thinking he was just some patronizing pervert," he smiled to himself. "You've got a sharp mind, uh...I didn't catch your name?"

As he turned his head, he saw nothing but an empty stool next to him with three one-dollar bills sitting by his empty glass. He looked around the bar to find nothing but the same patrons who had occupied the booths around him. Without even a word, Elvis had left the building.

Befuddled, Ethan asked Stan if this mysterious person had gone to the bathroom.

"He left," Stan said as he placed the bill in front of Ethan. "The kid usually sings a song and bolts."

Still perplexed, Ethan looked over at the entrance doors, which he didn't even hear open.

"He snuck out so swiftly," he said to himself.

Stan brought him his bill. Ethan reached into his pocket for his wallet and brought out a ten and two ones for the $11 tab. He only left a dollar for a tip, which he thought was generous given this place's aberrant atmosphere. As he zipped up his coat, out of the corner of his eye, he saw the Van Gogh puppet peering over the kitchen station window.

"Shtop by again shoon, ya!" the puppet yelled to Ethan's chagrin as he exited the building.

Ethan got into his car and put his keys in the ignition. His keychain charm of praying hands rattled against the side of the stereo as he turned the car on. He plopped the drawstring bag on the front seat. The contents made a loud rattling noise as he laid the bag down. He thought it best to find out where Colton was staying tonight and return it to him, just in case he needed whatever was inside. Temptation, however, was getting the better of him.

He stared at the all-black bag with wonder, thinking about what could be inside that would rattle like that. Pulling out of the parking lot and descending the winding road that led away from the bar, the continuous rattling taunted him with each cling, cling, cling. He kept looking over at it, eventually putting his hand around the outside to see if he could determine what was inside. Whatever was in there felt simultaneously jagged and round, as if he were feeling the contents of some sort of machine.

Pulling the car over, he gave in. He opened the bag and dumped everything out onto the passenger seat. A green metal thermos that looked like it had seen the horrors of World War II bounced on the seat. He smelled the inside, deducing that some sort of sweet liquor had a pungent gasoline burn to it. Some sort of black-laced whip found itself wrapped around the thermos; its ends frilled from use. A string of metal balls lay tangled like a garden house stuffed with golf balls.

However, the item that stood out the most was an object still in its cardboard package. The packaging was written entirely in what he assumed was Mandarin Chinese on the front, in bright red lettering at the top of the box. Inside was a large, dark metal ring shaped like an infinity symbol or chain link. It had a shine that glistened in the car despite the darkness of the evening sky.

Ethan was surprised it stayed in its package because it was loosely held by two prongs. He took it out carefully so it would be impossible to tell if the packaging was removed. His beady eyes examined it under the overhead light in the car as if he were Smeagol admiring the one ring to rule them all. On the back of the package was more Chinese writing with a close-up black silhouette of a figure with this ring around his genitalia.

"Intertwine..." he whispered to himself.

Chapter 8

If I Can Dream

Patrick Loveland pulled into Econo Foods with a twinkle in his beady green eyes. The 31-year-old bachelor parked his red 1990 Honda Civic with a hatchback in the 'Expecting Mothers' spot toward the front of the snow-covered grocery store. His thinning head of hair spread across his birthday balloon-shaped head like a couple handfuls of shredded sharp cheddar cheese. Patrick didn't have much of a neck, so his shoulders protruded upward, only sitting a few inches away from the ends of his patchy mustache.

On this Friday evening, Patrick's attire included slim khaki pants that would bust a seam if he makes any sudden movement when bending over, a crimson polo that hugged tightly against his sternum, and black orthopedic shoes for his plantar fasciitis. The silver Fossil watch he wore plucked a couple of hairs off his thick wrists every time he took it off. His outfit was completed with a gold chain necklace with a small medallion of a crustacean holding up two pinching claws embedded in his forest of red chest hairs. He entered the store, grabbed a red handcart at the entrance, and averted his path away from the produce aisle, opting straight for the cereal instead.

He went for his usual cereal purchase of Lucky Charms, which he would take home, sort through the box for all the marshmallow pieces to put into a separate bag and throw the rest away. In his mind, the cereal pieces weren't necessary for his breakfast experience. His other grocery items included a jar of low-fat mayonnaise, frozen dino chicken nuggets, five boxes of mac and cheese, eight cans of SpaghettiOs, Tide detergent, and two rolls of store-brand paper towels. Patrick typically turned his nose up at store-brand products, but Brawny was the only other brand on the shelves. He never bought Brawny because he found the unreasonable handsomeness of the Brawny Man distracting.

As he walked alongside the meat counter, making his way to the main event of his grocery store trip, his heart began to flutter. At the far end of the counter was a place of wonder. It was a mystical underwater landscape that not even the mythos of Atlantis could touch: the lobster tank. He stopped in front of it, bending over while putting his hands on both knees. He pushed his wire-brim glasses closer toward the top of his short, wide nose, a thick bead of sweat rolling down his forehead. Four lobsters of varying sizes pressed against the glass as the faulty water filter pumped into the teal water they lived in.

Patrick bit his lower lip, his eyes meeting the largest lobster. The behemoth slowly moved up his impressive right claw, which Patrick viewed as a direct invitation.

"She will be mine," he whispered to himself.

He began to rub his necklace through the opening of the collar of his polo, breathing heavily through the same airway that constricted during his nighttime fits of sleep apnea. A second bead of sweat fell down his forehead and onto his spectacles.

"Uh, can I help you, sir?" a meat department butcher asked after watching Patrick move through faces for a solid minute straight.

Patrick immediately popped up, wiped his brow with his hairy right arm, and removed his glasses to rub them dry against his shirt. He caught his breath nervously, acting as nonchalant as he could.

"Yes," he said, meeting the eyes of the butcher. "I would like to purchase two of the lobsters. I was just checking to see if they'd be enough to feed a family of four."

Patrick viewed this statement as only a half-lie. He didn't have anyone waiting for him back at his apartment but was also completely capable of consuming meals meant for families of four.

"Yeah, no problem. Two should definitely be enough," the butcher said, approaching the tank. "Do you have any preference, or do you want me to just—"

"—The big one in the middle!" Patrick exclaimed, noticing his excitement getting the better of him. "Uh, I mean, yeah, the one in the middle would be great. I'll also take the smaller one crawling up by the water filter."

The butcher grabbed his designated lobster gloves with steel wool inside (to avoid any pinching of the fingers) and began submerging his hand into the tank.

"So, lobster dinner for the family, huh? That's one way to score points with the wife," the butcher chuckled as he grabbed the more undersized lobster near the water filter and pulled him out of the murky tank.

"Ha...yeah...yeah, no doubt about that," Patrick agreed, unable to help himself from staring at the lobster held up in the man's glove. It began pinching the air while moving each of its toothpick legs individually.

The butcher smiled, unaware of the inner emotional journey Patrick was going through at this very moment. He leaned to the side of the counter to engage in more small talk, quietly frustrating Patrick for temporarily abandoning his promise of the behemoth lobster calling his name.

"Yeah, I remember a fella coming in here one time and saying, 'Mark, I got a third date with this gal and really want to impress her by cooking her something. What should I do?' and I says to the guy, I says, 'Say no more, buddy. Get yourself a couple of lobsters, and I promise she'll be tugging on your belt, if ya know what I mean.'" Mark began making a tugging motion on his belt downward with a chuckle. Patrick forced a nervous half-smile on his face while patiently awaiting his request.

"Ha...they sure do the trick," Patrick said, slowly losing the grip of his own forced smile.

"That they do," Mark replied, rolling up his leaves. "That they most certainly do...alright, enough chit-chat. Let's grab that big one for ya."

The euphoria returned to Patrick as Mark's hand submerged into the tank to retrieve the astounding arthropod. He started to rub his medallion once more as he watched her ascend her five-foot-by-three-foot ocean at his beckoning call. Mark held her in the air in front of them like an actor showing an Oscar off to the world.

"Alright, I'll take care of these back here and get them wrapped up for ya!" Mark said, grabbing the smaller lobster that he set aside with his other hand.

"Wait, wait, take care of them?" Patrick asked, his eyes widening with concern.

"Yeah. You know...clean them up and send their lobster souls to the great tank in the sky," he explained, turning his neck to one side to indicate the snapping of death.

"No!" Patrick shouted, nearly causing Mark to drop the lobsters in shock.

He was now staring at Patrick with an eyebrow raised and his mouth slightly agape.

"I-I mean, I like to take care of that part at home...you know, to impress the wife and uh, show off and stuff."

A new bead of sweat started forming atop his head as his face started to blemish, making him feel as if he were bare-naked and on display for the meat man in front of him. Without breaking eye contact or lowering his eyebrow, Mark took a step toward Patrick.

"You know what I think, buddy?" he said menacingly as the new bead fell down the bridge of Patrick's nose with a lump forming in his throat. "I think you're kind of a freak," he said, causing the lump in Patrick's throat to push up against the fat of his neck.

Patrick stood stunned. Surely, this man knew there was no family, no planned dinner, and no attempt at impressing a significant other. He was exposed and on the verge of nervous urination in the middle of the deli aisle.

"And boy, do I wish my old lady was into freaky stuff too!" he laughed as Patrick's blood pressure went back down in sweet relief. "I swear the only foreplay she's into is telling me to turn off the lights."

Patrick, once more, pretended to laugh along with the butcher and his remarks.

"I'll get these boxed up for you, big guy. Just be sure to be careful when removing the rubber bands. These bastards pinch harder than a great aunt around a newborn."

Mark returned with a big black container with Econo Foods brand tape wrapped around it like a Christmas present and placed it into Patrick's hands. There was a certain strut to his step as he made his way down beneath the fluorescent grocery store lights like a gambler who won big on the Vegas strip. He made his way to the register, got his items scanned by the bored teenager behind the counter, and sauntered out with his groceries in one hand and his prized mollusks in the other. The drive home was serenaded with songs on his burned CD labeled "HEAVY HITTERS" in permanent marker. The tracks mostly included female popstar hits of the 80s and German electronica.

The car pulled into the parking lot of the Crosby Estates apartment complex, which had an aged eggshell white paint job that was chipping away and a busted latch system on the entrance door that would only lock half the time. Patrick giddily got out of his car to retrieve the groceries in the back, slipping on the pavement and bringing him down to one knee. A slight tear formed at the bottom seam of his khakis that he likely wouldn't notice for at least a couple of weeks. He picked himself up, dusted off his knee, swung open his back car door, picked up the groceries, and waddled his way through the entrance and into the elevator.

Apartment 206 on the second floor was a collage of all things Patrick Loveland. The first thing one saw when walking into the studio apartment was a kitchen riddled with crumbs from chicken breading and a sink full of dishes that were placed there more than a week ago. His countertops were full of empty Pizza Lunchables boxes (he always opted for the Pizza Lunchables over the ham, turkey, and crackers, as he found the meats to be offensively rubbery).

He had two plates: a regular ceramic plate and a 1989 collectible McDonald's plate that depicted Ronald McDonald teaching a classroom of cheeseburgers with the Hamburglar peering through the window. He only used the latter on special occasions. His cupboard contained one singular 24 oz. plastic cup, a Muppets Show coffee mug, and his favorite cereal bowl that he lifted from his parents' cupboard when he finally moved out.

His living space included a full-size mattress with an indentation on the left side of a large human shape, where he preferred sleeping. His 50" Zenith TV sat atop his cabinet filled with VHS copies of alphabetized movies at the bottom, while the middle section contained his brand new Nintendo 64. In the corner of the room was his Dell desktop computer, the keyboard holding a spacebar stained with barbecue sauce.

Above the desktop were two movie posters, *Pulp Fiction* and *Jurassic Park*, respectively, which he stole from the Mankato movie theater where he worked as a part-time usher just two years prior. Hanging above his bed was a samurai sword with a golden encrusted design running halfway up the blade. A red bowstring on the handle hung down as the sheathed sword sat on top of pegs he mounted on the wall. His mother bought it for him at a pawn shop when he was 12 after swearing to her that it was for decorative purposes only. Now, he was a grown man, and it was his to wield for protection should the occasion arise.

Patrick quickly hopped through his doorway before quickly shutting the door behind him. He threw the two grocery bags on the kitchen counter without any attempt to put anything away and made his way straight for the bathroom with the container in hand. While most of his apartment was in desperate need of deep cleaning, Patrick kept his bathroom fairly tidy. It was a sacred place where he felt most at peace with himself.

Setting the container on the counter next to his Sony stereo system, Patrick threw the fish-designed shower curtain open and began to draw a bath. He removed his clothes, which he wadded up and threw by the door. He opened the medicine cabinet, which contained a CD case that was filled to the brim with every genre imaginable. Tonight's selection was Richard Wagner's "Overture to the Flying Dutchman," which he pulled out and placed gently into his stereo. He set it on top of the toilet and plugged it into the outlet above the counter. Opening the container, he stared at the mesmerizing crustaceans that were now his. Grabbing a pocket knife from the medicine cabinet, he cut the rubber bands on each claw, causing the lobsters to go into a frenzy of pinching the air.

"Get ready, you two," he announced, gently picking each of them up from out of the box. "It's show time."

Patrick gently placed them in the warm water that now filled two-thirds of the tub. After shutting off the faucet, he jiggled his way back to the sink and opened the cabinet below. He pulled out a pair of neon-red goggles, which constricted tightly around his pumpkin-shaped head as he put them on. Reaching down, he retrieved a fully finished LEGO Coast Guard boat he bought at Target last month. The blue and white "Coastal Cutter" was a double-decker boat with the steering wheel above and an open cabin below, with a solid white piece on the bottom to allow it to float. On the back, an orange lever attachment held up a miniature speed boat with a single passenger seat. The set came with two LEGO sailors: one with thick black hair and black swim gear and one with a hat, a lifejacket, and the same swim gear. Patrick named them Commander Ed Fitzgerald and Lieutenant Kevin Daniels, respectively.

Holding the boat tightly with his sausage fingers, he carefully climbed into the tub on the opposite side of the lobsters. Patrick began giving the two LEGO figurines dialogue as they ventured out into the open waters. He placed Fitzgerald on the deck below and Daniels at the top, behind the steering wheel.

"Commander Fitzgerald, we should be coming up on the distress call any minute! The water turbulence seems to be picking up! Are you sure you don't want your lifejacket, sir?" Patrick asked, giving Daniels a more concerned, higher-pitched voice.

Patrick, designated a lower, rugged voice for the Commander, who has been on the job for far too long (according to the backstory he just made up).

"Goddamn, Daniels. What do they teach you all these days down at the academy? I'm seven months away from my pension. Never once in my career have I thrown on one of those bitch-preservers," he moved up the Captain's arm to motion as if he was taking a long drag from a cigarette. "And I ain't changing today."

"Apologies, sir," Patrick moved his arm up as if he were giving a salute. "I'm just following protocol, sir!"

"At ease, sailor," he commanded, pretending to have him take another inhale of smoke. "I know you're just trying to do right by the uniform...I did once. But now, as I'm close to the end, I start to wonder if it was all worth it..."

"Worth it, sir?"

"Ah, it's nothing, kid. Some days, you just go through the motions, ya know? You get on the water and see the same currents holding you back, the same mechanical issues with the boat. You feel like there's nothing separating one day from the next," he inhales again and blows out a pretend cloud of smoke. "Then you go home to a wife who doesn't even look at you like she used to. The passion is gone; the conversations, the sex, hell, even the arguments feel completely stale. We go to cocktail parties, and she just rolls her eyes whenever I tell a joke or story to friends we don't even like. We both know that the spark is gone, Daniels. We both know it's gone." Taking the final drag, Patrick pretends Commander Fitzgerald flicks his nonexistent cigarette into the water.

"Oh man, Commander...that sure is heavy. I've been through a lot myself. You see, when I was a kid, my dad told me—"

"—Anchors up, Daniels! I see the distressed worker in front of us!"

Making sound effects with his mouth, Patrick swerved the boat to a screeching halt, picking out a LEGO construction worker from the cabin compartment and placing him in the water. The construction worker was gripped between Patrick's thumb and pointer finger and held half-submerged so the radio in his hand was above water.

"Help!" he yelled in a distressed voice.

"Don't worry, son," he said, leaning Commander Fitzgerald off the side, now with a bullhorn in his hand. "We'll have you picked up in no time. Daniels, look alive! Man, the rescue cruiser."

"Aye, aye, sir!" he said, placing Daniels in the smaller speed boat and, once more, making sound effects as he moved it toward the stranded LEGO figure.

Patrick reached out of the tub and hit the play button on the stereo. As Wagner's violins started, he grabbed the large lobster and slowly brought it down below the water-treading construction worker. He faced it upward, the claws pinching continuously.

"Grab my hand!" he shouted in Daniels's voice. "I'll pull you up!"

"Oh, thank you! Thank you! I'm so thankful to be—"

Patrick moved up the lobster, touching its claw to the LEGO figure until it gripped on (which took a solid 35 seconds). After gripping it, he pulled the lobster back down a few inches, completely submerging the LEGO.

"Oh my god! It pulled him under!" he shouted once more in Daniels's voice.

"Get back to the boat, Daniels! Now!"

The violins intensely started up again as he pulled the speed boat closer toward the main vassal. Still holding the lobster, he breached it out of the water, made it jump over the speed boat, and put it back under. The speedboat made its way to the back of the ship.

"Daniels! Grab on!" he shouted in the Commander's voice.

He linked his LEGO hand onto the arm of Daniels and pulled him onto the ship. Taking the lobster once more, he breached it on top of the rescue cruiser and against the back of the ship.

"Man the deck, Daniels! Take my harpoon and sit at the very front of the bow —we're going to give her the fight of her life!"

"Commander! It's too dangerous! She's twice the size of the ship, she is! I'll be a goner for sure!"

"Goddammit, Daniels!" he shouted, having Commander Fitzgerald slap him across the face with his LEGO hand. "Some sacrifices are worth making, son! And don't call me Commander...call me Ishmael."

Commander Fitzgerald took the steering wheel above the deck. Patrick extended his arm away from him, the lobster still in hand, and then pivoted him around to face the ship head-on.

"Alright, Lieutenant!" he had the Commander yell, "On my count, shoot her head on, right between the eyes!"

The two entities were now less than a foot apart, ready to collide.

"Three..."

The lobster started clawing and splashing in front of its face.

"Two..."

Patrick readied his finger on the button of the harpoon gun. The lobster was now mere inches away.

"One...smile, you great red bitch!"

The harpoon gun launched the tiny plastic piece at the lobster, which bounced right off his head. Patrick rammed the lobster against the boat and forcibly pulled it in half as if it were a major collision.

"Eeeeeeeecck!" Patrick cried out in another lobster noise of defeat while putting the completely unharmed lobster on the ledge of the bathtub.

Holding only the bottom half of the boat in his hands while the remaining LEGO pieces sunk below, Patrick held the Commander on top of the wreckage.

"Direct hit!" he shouted.

"What in the hell?" a muffled voice said from the open bathroom door.

Patrick immediately turned around to find a stunned, slender figure completely dressed in black and wearing a leather ski mask. He saw that the figure was holding handcuffs in their hands and some sort of twirled plastic item that looked like a purple nightstick—likely brought it for the purpose of bludgeoning him, Patrick thought.

"Ahh!" Patrick screamed with the pitch of an elementary school child.

He jumped up and threw half of his LEGO ship at the figure, striking them right in the face. Like a fullback attempting to barrel his way into the endzone, a naked Patrick charged the figure, completely bulldozing them over as he ran screaming into the main room of the apartment. The figure lay on the ground, holding their throat and rolling over in pain against the door frame. Grabbing the samurai sword from the wall, Patrick unsheathed it and took his battle position, still wearing nothing but his goggles and with water dripping from his body. The figure stood back up in the doorway, still holding the twirled purple object out in front of them for self-defense. Frightened, Patrick charged him again, raising the sword behind his head.

The figure jumped out of the way at the last second, got up, and struck Patrick in the face with the object. Patrick slipped on the floor covered in water, catching himself on the ledge of the bathtub with his left hand while nearly falling in. He picked himself back up and assumed his battle stance again. The two started dueling like medieval knights. Back-and-forth, steel meeting matted material proved to be surprisingly durable. It was a sword against mysterious purple plastic, and while Patrick had the size and weapon advantage, the figure was agile and repeatedly struck against his love handles. The two locked weapons in a stalemate as a naked Patrick had him pinned against the sink.

"Who do you work for?! CIA? KGB? That psycho, Ms. Melstad, on the first floor? The lease agreement doesn't entitle her to a parking spot! She can't have it!"

"Get off of me!" the muffled voice said as the figure kicked Patrick in his shin, causing him to yelp and cradle his leg.

Just then, the masked intruder grabbed the sword from his hand, held it up to his throat, and slowly started backing away. They laughed a muffled laugh, throwing the nightstick in the tub behind them. Patrick held his hands in the air, signaling his surrender to the would-be assassin holding the blade just inches from his chin.

"Now... you're going to walk out there and—" As the intruder took one more step backward, they stepped on the wet remaining half of the LEGO boat and started to slip. Flinging their left arm backward, they caught themself on the edge of the tub, directly in front of the larger lobster's face. The angry mollusk grabbed onto the fingers with an excruciating pinch, causing a muffled scream. The assailant flailed both arms and lost their balance, falling backward into the bath. While falling like a penguin trying to fly, the figure knocked over the Sony stereo on the toilet with the sword, flinging it directly into the tub with them. Massive electric shocks sparked across the bathtub as the intruder shook like a broken dryer. A spark flew out from the front of the stereo, sending a piece of burning plastic in front of Patrick's feet. The figure stopped shaking and lay silent in the bathtub.

A stunned Patrick took off his goggles and stared down at the masked person, whose non-responsive head was still above water. He grabbed the hand towel, wrapped it around his hand, and quickly pulled the stereo plug out of the wall with caution. With a large gulp, he slowly inched toward the individual, shaking as he dipped his pointer finger in the water to ensure his own safety. It was still. He took a deep breath and poked the figure in the shoulder.

"Hello?... Are you okay?" he asked, his voice quivering like a wet cat.

There was no response. Patrick identified a silver zipper on the back of the mask. Carefully, he pulled it upward, unzipping the leather around the skull. He reached the top and took another long, deep breath. He grabbed the front and began pulling it off slowly until it fell off the head and into the bathwater.

With a red ball gag tightened around his mouth, a lifeless Colton Lorenzo sat in Patrick Loveland's studio apartment bathtub. The now-dead large lobster was still hanging onto his fingers while the smaller dead lobster clamped to his pants.

Chapter 9

Stuck on You

Most Hennepin County Medical Center Emergency Room nurses believe that the strangest shifts always occur during a full moon. Tonight was a full moon, yet Theresa Mond was surprised by how tame the first four hours of the graveyard shift were. One man came in with a broken collarbone, two others came in with heart troubles, and the most exciting was a woman who came in shaking after receiving a bad cut of ecstasy at a nightclub. But at the moment, the waiting room was in a rare state of emptiness.

"Hey, can you cover me at the desk for a minute while I go pee?" her coworker Donna asked.

"Yeah, sure. Those Diet Cokes go right through you, huh?" Theresa agreed as she began to tie her braids behind her head.

"Hey, you know I ain't touching that Maxwell House shit they've got in the breakroom to stay caffeinated," she joked, laughing.

Donna was far from the pinnacle of professionalism, but Theresa loved the company of someone without a filter.

"I hear that." Theresa sat in the purple swivel chair as Donna walked down the hallway, adjusting her pink headband over her blonde hair. Her curves hugged her purple scrubs as the narrow space between her and the front of the dull gray hospital desk caused her to suck in her stomach. She wore a long-sleeve compression shirt underneath her scrubs to cover up her tattoo sleeve. A colorful portrait of the Greek goddess Aphrodite covered much of her upper left arm. In it, Aphrodite holds a dove on two fingers of her hand with ruby and sapphire rings while also sporting an olive wreath as a crown. She emerged from a bed of roses that wrapped themselves around the dark brown skin of Theresa's elbow. Her eyes were like green emeralds, with a seductive yet cunning look that Theresa found especially stupefying.

She read the Odyssey and Iliad in a literature class at the University of Minnesota and immediately became enthralled, with a particular fixation on the goddess Aphrodite. In her eyes, displaying her strength as one of the most powerful beings in the world through love and desire was exhilarating. A goddess who got her way by manipulating the other gods through seduction, beauty, and a full understanding of the lustful temptation she stirred up in them? That's one bad bitch, she thought.

Unfortunately, she found her own dating life to be far from goddess status. In the few dates she had in life, she found that most guys freshly out of college just wanted to "hit it and quit it" and never return her calls afterward. Despite attempting to channel Aphrodite, she found herself stuck in a world of douchebag men who acted like they thought they were Zeus, aka Zeusbags.

Theresa took a quick look at the top right corner of the desktop that read "Wed 4:07 a.m.," and she smiled. The time reminded her that in a few short hours, she'd be on her way back home to her parents' for her birthday. Feelings of nostalgia swept over her as she remembered hearing her dad get up at 5:00 a.m. every year on her birthday and frost the strawberry shortcake he had prepared for her the night before. He would always attempt to write a humorous message in icing on top of the cake, usually in the form of some sort of cheesy pun. She remembered as far back as his, "No cake for me, please. I already 8."

No matter what it was, she smiled at the thought of her father giggling to himself whenever it was revealed to her. Just one more shift, she thought. The front entrance doors of the emergency room swung open. A man in a black hoodie with a white cross in front of a yellow sun that read "Camp Owasso: Summers Over Sinners" with the letters "STAFF" in the upper right chest walked gingerly up to the front desk, where Theresa could finally see his facial features underneath his hood. His straight blonde hair and lanky frame reminded her of some sort of scarecrow. He stood in front of her desk, quietly shaking. Seconds went by, and he stood there silently.

"Umm...hello? How can we help you today, sir?" Theresa asked as she stared at his averted gaze as if he had just witnessed an unconscionable traumatic event.

"Yeah, well I uh, I have a p-problem...I don't know what to d-do," he stammered, trembling like a cat that had just gotten out of the bathtub.

"Okay, sir, can you please give me your name and date of birth?"

"It's uh, Ethan Bile, E-T-H-A-N, space, B-I-L-E. July 4th, 1971," he repeated, continuing to shudder and breathe heavily.

"Hey, I was born on Valentine's Day!" Theresa said in an attempt to calm whatever nerves this poor man was feeling, "Go team 'Holiday-Birthdays,' am I right?"

Ethan continued to stare blankly, not even acknowledging the words that had just left the nurse's mouth. Her concern started to deepen for this pale, skinny man.

"Alright, Mr. Bile, what seems to be the problem tonight?"

"I...I can't say," he mumbled, bowing his head.

Now, she was starting to really worry.

"You can't say? Sir, is everything okay at home? Are you having any thoughts of self-harm or suicide tonight?"

"No! No! Nothing like that," he squealed frantically. "I'm not going to off myself or anything. I just have a problem and need to show a doctor right now."

Theresa went from concerned to confused in a matter of moments.

"Mr. Bile, I need to at least know which part of your body the issue is occurring. Can you at least give me an idea?"

He finally looked directly into her eyes with a look that a child gives a parent the moment they're about to burst into tears.

"It's down..." he whispered.

"Down?" she asked, "Down where?"

His eyes looked away once more to check around the empty waiting room and then back to Theresa. "It's down there," he pleaded, pointing to his jeans. "Please...I need to see a doctor now."

At that moment, Donna had returned from the bathroom with a fresh Diet Coke in her hand.

"Thanks for covering," she said as she sat down in the chair beside Theresa. She looked up at Ethan, who was turning more ghostly white by the second.

"What's wrong with him?" she asked. "Sir, no offense, but you look like you just came straight out of a seance or something."

"Donna, he has an issue down below," Theresa whispered.

"What the hell do you mean 'down below'? Like he can't shit?" she whispered back.

"Well, I don't exactly know yet—"

"Can I please just see the fucking doctor already?!" Ethan screamed before immediately covering his mouth in shock that the words just left his mouth.

"Listen here, Bowl-cut Bill," Donna shot back with a fiery look in her eyes, "with outbursts like that, you're going to see a security guard pulling your ass out of here if you aren't careful!"

"Donna, it's okay. I think Dr. Park is available. Could you page him for me?" Theresa said as she got up from the desk.

"Yeah, I guess," Donna said with reluctance in her voice.

Theresa walked toward Ethan, who was shaking even more than before.

"Mr. Bile, could you please follow me?"

He nodded and gingerly followed Theresa down the east hospital hallway as Donna shot him daggers with her eyes.

They entered the second room on the left as she flipped over the door flag for the doctor and shut the door behind them. She quickly recorded his vitals and had him sit up on the patient's bed.

"Okay, Ethan, are you able to remove your clothing?"

He proceeded to take off the sweatshirt and tee shirt covering his scrawny body. Around his neck was a cross necklace with mini gold thorn crowns hanging on each side.

"Uh, Ethan...I meant the clothes that are covering the area of pain."

"F-fine...sorry, I'm just...you know," he studdered with a heavy exhale and the life drooping down from his eyelids.

"It's okay! I know it's uncomfortable."

He unfastened his belt and pulled down his designer jeans, revealing boxer shorts that had cherubs playing trumpet horns and harps. He sat still, staring straight ahead. Theresa sighed with pity and put her hand on his shoulder.

"Listen, Ethan. I know it's embarrassing to have a stranger examine your private parts. Trust me. I have to go to the gynecologist a few times every year, and it's always awkward. But I promise that whatever is going on down there is nothing we haven't seen or dealt with before." She stepped back and knelt to look him in the eye again. "So what do you say? Can you remove your underwear so we can get the awkward moment over and done with?"

For the first time since seeing him, she noticed that he finally had a small amount of relief in his eyes.

"Okay... okay, yeah," he said, exhaling once more.

He got up off the bed, straightened his back like a marine, and pulled the holy underwear to his ankles, revealing his genitalia.

"Holy shit!" Theresa shouted with the voice of someone who had just seen an oncoming eighteen-wheeler barreling toward them.

Theresa's eyes were fixed on what looked like a poor attempt at torture. A figure-eight-shaped metal ring contorted Ethan's genitals in a way that could best be described as a pulsating boa constrictor that was the same color as her favorite boxed wine attacking a blueberry-colored water balloon. Around the ring was a thick coating of Vaseline, where she could see his desperate attempts to free himself from the clutches of his metal prison. Never in her deepest fantasies and curiosities did she ever imagine something quite like this.

"I can't get it off!" he yelled. "It's been stuck for 2 hours, and I can't get it off me! Why God, why?!" Ethan started to hyperventilate as he laid his hands on his face.

Theresa collected herself while thinking of her mother. Though her mother had never seen the inside of an emergency room or taken one nursing course, she could teach a college-level class on managing even the most intense situations. She remembered her dad getting laid off from his I.T. job a few years back and how he couldn't bring himself to leave the basement. He spent his days wallowing in his recliner, watching his collection of old DVDs that dated back as far as 1958. She remembered the day her mom marched into that basement, threw on the lights, and said, "Daniel, I love and believe in you. But if you don't get that mopey butt of yours upstairs, shave that scruff of your face, and make a plan for your future, I'm going to call up my mother and tell her to leave that nursing home because you've got all the time in the world to take care of her."

He found a job just two days later.

"Ethan, look, I know that you're freaking out right now and scared. But you've gotta breathe with me, okay?"

Theresa took his hand as they both took a slow inhale followed by an even slower exhale.

"Good, good. I'm going to get Dr. Park, and we're going to fix this problem, okay?"

"Okay... okay," Ethan said as he tried to slow his shaking.

Just as she was about to track him down, Dr. Park entered the room, shutting the door behind him. He went straight for the sink, where he quickly threw on the hot water, applied the foam soap, washed his hands, and wiped them off with the disposable paper towels.

"Hello, I'm Dr. Park. What seems to be the issue tod—oh, good lord!"

Dr. Park's eyes met Ethan's genitals with the same morbid confusion the country had during the Kennedy Assassination.

Who did this? How did they do this? Why did they do this? A silence fell over them until Theresa spoke up.

"Dr. Park, this is Ethan. He has an issue, uh, down there," she explained.

"I can see that," Dr. Park said as he put on a pair of gloves. "Ethan, can you tell me what you were doing to get this um...contraption stuck on you?"

Ethan took another huge breath and drooped his head once more.

"Well...I uh...listen—I don't want you guys to think I'm some pervert or deviant here! I'm a man of God. I'm a man of virtue. I work every day to make the lives of the elderly pure before they enter God's kingdom. I'm not into weird, salacious stuff, okay?" Ethan was biting his lower lip with a grimace of pain that shot up his body.

"I am not here to judge you. I just want to help," Dr. Park reassured him as he examined the area of trauma.

"What happened is...I was...I was looking at," Ethan tapered off his sentence as if he was a prisoner of war debating whether or not withholding information was worth another round of waterboarding.

"Porn?" Theresa asked in an attempt to help him find his words.

"No!" he shouted back with disdain. "I don't do that! No...well, it wasn't quite... okay, I was alone and had found this thing that belonged to my boss, and I..." Ethan looked to the ceiling as if he was surpassing the conversation with Dr. Park and pleading his case straight to the almighty creator himself. "And—out of curiosity, of course—I used it...and well, it's stuck."

"It's stuck in your private area?" he asked.

"Y-yes," he replied.

"And there isn't any sort of mechanism or anything to get it off?"

"No," he whimpered with defeat on his face, sitting in the bags under his eyes, undoubtedly formed by a heavy amount of crying, "I just know I can't break it or move it or anything! It came from some company in China or something and didn't come with any sort of instructions on how to remove it."

"Okay, so we'll have to try to cut through it. How long have you had it on?"

"I tried for an hour to pull it off with Vaseline, but it wouldn't budge. I just got in the car and drove an hour and a half to get here. So just under three hours, I'd say."

Dr. Park took a few more seconds in silence to examine the genital stockade, tugging on it gently toward himself.

"Theresa, could you get me the cast saws, please?" he asked, sliding his glasses further down his nose. Theresa nodded and went into the utility room to retrieve two brand new Cryo cast saws. They had a thick, sea-blue-painted metal body with a sharp, serrated blade. She always wondered how quickly one could cut through something like a piece of fruit or a can of soup. It had to be a sight to see.

"Here you are, Dr. Park," she said, handing him the mechanical beast. He plugged it into the wall, pulled a surgical mask over his face, and said, "Let's give this a go."

The saw began spinning as he gingerly brought it toward the metal ring. He began to cut. Bzzzzzzzzzzzzzz rmmmmmmmm bzzzzzzzzzzzzzzzzz. The saw buzzed as tiny bits of metal shrapnel jumped up from the site of impact. Dr. Park turned the saw off to view the progress he had made. The serrated saw blade was smooth and completely dull, while the ring only suffered a mere scratch mark.

"Oh dear," Dr. Park said, wiping sweat from his brow, "Theresa, can you hand me the other saw? I think this one might have seen better days."

Theresa handed him the other saw as Ethan sat there, perched on the examination table, looking like a terrified cat stuck in a tree. Dr. Park plugged in the saw, started it up, and approached the ring again. Bzzzzzzzzzzzzzzz rmmmmmmmm bzzzzzzzzzzzzzzzzz. The saw roared on loudly as it clanked against the metal contraption for a solid ninety seconds. Dr. Park turned it off to check his progress once more. The saw suffered the same dulling fate as its predecessor, while the ring was, yet again, barely scratched up. Theresa and Dr. Park sat there, stunned by the durability of this ring. As a big fan of Lord of the Rings, he was starting to believe that even the lava in Mount Doom couldn't break through the material that had just destroyed $2,500 worth of medical equipment in under five minutes.

"One cock ring to fool them all," he thought to himself.

"Theresa, can you have Donna page the fire department? We're going to need something stronger," he decided, looking down at Ethan in his frightened naked state. "Much stronger."

Theresa ran out of the room and back to find Donna, who looked bored as she scrolled through the front desk computer and sipped from her water bottle.

"Donna, can you page the fire department? We need them with the guy who just came in."

"That little bowl-cut bitch needs the fire department to come help him out? What the hell is going on in there?" she asked, finally looking up from the computer monitor.

"No time to explain. Just please, do it fast!" Theresa said, slightly raising her voice as she now found herself gaining second-hand panic from the situation.

"Damn, okay. I'll page them. You doing okay?" Donna asked as she reached to put her hand on Theresa's shoulder. Theresa unknowingly shook it off and said, "Yeah. Yeah, I'm fine. Just make sure you call me when they get here."

Theresa went back into the examination room.

"The fire department has been paged, Dr. Park."

"Thank you, Theresa. Did you get an ETA?"

"I did not. Should I go check again with Donna?"

"No, that's fine. She'll call when they're here anyway."

The three began to sit in a deafening silence that cried out for anyone to say anything topical to distract from the elephant in the room (more specifically, the elephant's trunk). Ethan continued subtly shaking himself as Theresa hung her head and stared down at the white and beige Asics shoes she purchased at Shoe Carnival a few weeks ago. Dr. Park nervously wiped his glasses as he searched for something to say at the bedside of his patient.

"So, uh, you like movies, huh?" he asked.

"What?" Ethan asked with both confusion and annoyance in his voice.

"Oh no, it's just that, you know, I just figured that people who like to, you know, watch pornographic movies might, uh, enjoy regular films too," Dr. Park nervously laughed as he began to sweat at a more substantial rate than he was during the sawing. "You more of an action guy? Comedy? Horror?"

"I can't really think straight right now," Ethan stated.

"No problem; no problem..." Dr. Park said as they returned to a momentary pause. They continued to sit in silence, only accompanied by the buzzing of the fluorescent lights above them. Unlike the ring, the tension could be cut with a butter knife.

"Do you have a favorite actor, at least?"

Ethan sighed and muttered, "I don't know...Al Pacino, I guess."

"Awesome pick! One of the best to ever do it!" Dr. Park said, like a father who had finally gotten his infant to take a bite of baby food. "Say hello to my little friend!" he shouted in a Cuban accent to an unphased Ethan. Theresa put her hand to her forehead as if she was holding back the encroaching stress headache from taking effect.

"Not in reference to your situation, it's uh just, you know, the famous line," he said, stumbling over his words, "and not that your thing is little or anything, because it isn't... it's just, uh, just what he says in, uh, Scarface." The room returned to a monastery-like silence, Ethan going from panicked to defeated with each word coming out of the doctor's mouth. The silence was interrupted by a barely audible "sorry" from Dr. Park.

The examination room phone started to ring, and Theresa picked it up immediately.

"They're here," Donna announced on the other end.

"I'll be right there," she said before putting the phone back. "The firemen are here. I'll go grab them."

"Oh, thank Christ," Dr. Park muttered under his breath.

Theresa shut the door behind her and leaned back into it as if it were the couch in a therapist's office. Theresa saw something disturbing every shift—a guy with his fibula sticking out of his shin, an old woman with her face covered in bee stings, and even a guy with a Chia Pet stuck in his rectum. None of that phased her. But the shame in the eyes of this fundamentalist caught in a web of titanium just felt off.

Theresa closed her eyes, took three deep breaths, reminded herself of her job, and headed for the front desk. As she approached Donna, who was on the edge of her swivel chair, three firemen burst through the front doors. Two of the firefighters, a woman with a neck tattoo of a spade and a burly guy holding an extinguisher, walked in full gear —helmets, face shields, fire coats, and all —on each side of a 5'6" completely bald man with a thick black boomerang of a mustache that sat atop his lip. Instead of full gear, he had a way-too-small t-shirt that accentuated his biceps, with suspenders around his shoulders holding up his fire pants. He held an ax in his hands with a bright red head that sat above his shoulder, just above the "Hennepin Fire Station 6" on his t-shirt. The look on his face was reminiscent of an overly competitive little league coach who wanted his kids to humiliate their opponents.

"Alright!" he shouted to the two nurses, who looked dumbfounded. "What are we doing here? Where's the fire?"

"Fire?" Theresa questioned. "Donna, did you tell them what it was for?"

Donna threw up her hands to deflect blame. "No, because you never told me! You just said to page them, so I did."

Theresa exhaled heavily and approached the bald man, who made her feel like a giant by comparison.

"Hi, I'm Theresa," she introduced herself, extending her hand. The man grabbed it with the grip of five silverback gorillas.

"Captain Dan Grundle of Station 6. Where's the fire?" he said as the mustache on his face gave a subtle twitch of intensity.

"Well, so that's the thing. There is no fire…" Theresa admitted.

"No fire? Then what in the hell is going on? Why did we get the page?"

Theresa didn't know why, but she would bet almost everything she had in her bank account that this guy was a black belt in Taekwondo and loved smashing boards.

"Well, a younger gentleman has come in with some sort of metal device…constricting his genitals. We can't get it off. It's already ruined two of our cast saws."

Donna nearly choked on a chip as she stifled a laugh, finally understanding the situation at hand. Dan took a step back, put his hands on his hips, and looked at the ground with intense focus.

"My god, this country's going to hell," he continued, shaking his shiny cranium. "We used to win wars...now this new generation is fornicating with spare car parts. It's a goddamn shame." He folded his arms and turned to the woman to his right, "Deb, get the duffle bag. We've got a pecker to save."

"Yes, Captain," she said before marching back toward the entrance.

Dan turned back to Theresa.

"What room are we in?"

"102. It's the second door on the left."

"Affirmative. Seth, make sure to keep the door ajar for Deb as she enters the premises."

"Yes, sir!" Seth shouted as he ran back toward the door to hold it open for his fellow firemen, who barrelled in with an overladen duffle bag that appeared to be heavier than her.

"Lead the way, ma'am," Dan said, positioning himself forward in an upright position.

They walked down the corridor like a team of generals about to deliver the nuclear football to the President. Like the negotiations with a superpower, this would not be swift. It would, however, test the limits of humanity. They entered the room to the same awkward silence Theresa knew before she left the room.

"Thank you for doing that, Theresa. Hello everyone, I am Dr. Park," he said, getting up from his swivel stool and extending his hand to the Captain. The Captain took his hand and gripped it with the same gorilla intensity.

"Captain Dan Grundle of Station 6. Let's take a loo— oh my God!"

He looked over at the disheveled Ethan and his contorted package, which now resembled the eggplant that Captain Dan's mother used to make him eat as a child. The sight struck him, but he was intrigued by the chaos laid before him. He bent down to examine the damage like a crime scene.

"Christ on a cracker, son! You've got your rod completely tied up with your tackle box!"

"I know...Can you get it off of me? Please get it off! Please!" Ethan pleaded with newly formed tears in his eyes.

Dan examined Ethan's crotch intently, his mustache moving back and forth like a caterpillar as he examined the ring. He quickly tugged the ring to see if he could get it to move in either direction. His fingers slipped their grip immediately.

"Looks to be some sort of titanium; no wonder you quacks had trouble cutting through it. That shit's as sturdy as a fat kid stuck in a tire swing. And whatever lube Buster Balls here tried greasing it up with is making it slipperier than jellyfish diarrhea." Dan took a step back and wiped his brow with the handkerchief in his coat pocket. "Do you have a girlfriend, son? Did she talk you into this?" the bald man asked with his pronounced black eyebrows raised in disbelief.

"N-no, sir. I w-was just trying it on, and I—"

"—I don't want to hear it! Your generation is all about living through these goddamn sexual awakenings. It's no longer a question of if you like something in your ass, it's a question of whether you want it to have a turbo attachment! Am I right, Seth?"

"Uh, not me, sir. I don't have anything in my ass," Seth said, putting his hands behind his ass in a protective manner.

"No, Seth, I meant this younger generation. They like things in their ass," Dan said, pressing his fingers against his forehead.

"Wait, is there something in the anus as well?" Dr. Park chimed in.

"No, Dr. Park, just the—" Theresa was immediately cut off by the ramblings of Seth.

"—Sir, I'm confused. Do you think I'm younger than I am? Because I'm 39, and this guy is like, what? 19? 20?" Seth said, focusing his attention on the pale Ethan.

"22..." Ethan confirmed with a whimper.

"He's 22, sir. That's still quite a bit younger than me."

"I heard him, you idiot!" Dan yelled, turning crimson in the face.

"I wasn't saying that you liked things in your ass or that you are a part of his generation. I was just looking for validation from you! That was it."

"Oh..." Seth said, looking down as the hamster wheel in his brain slowly started to spin. "So, wait, if he's 22 and I'm 39, couldn't we technically be in the same generation? Like, what's the cutoff for when one generation starts and one ends, ya know?"

"Would you just drop it already?!" Dan exploded as Seth fell silent in the corner, his face looking the same as it did in the second grade when his teacher yelled at him for bringing a dead bird he found to show and tell.

Dan turned his flamingo-colored cue ball of a head back around to face Ethan and Theresa. "What I was saying is that you young people these days go on these goddamn Roman holidays where you stick your ding-a-lings into whatever inanimate object you can find until a third of my job becomes yanking every twenty-something in the metro area out of some head-ass contraption."

He stood back upright and looked directly at Theresa. "And the women are even worse! I can't tell you how many times I've had to—"

"Captain," Deb interrupted, saving the room from the remainder of his sentence, "which tool should I fetch out of here?" Her eyes met Theresa in a moment of unspoken understanding that they were the cool heads in the room.

Dan rubbed his mustache perplexedly as he looked at the items below, contemplating as if he were in a Wendy's drive-thru.

"Well... let's give 'er a go with the Aviator Sheers first. I think I can get the blade under the scrotum without snipping his nuts."

Ethan started to whimper at the fireman's words.

"I don't want to hear any whining, son! It's you who put your fellas in a two-half-hitches knot, not me!" Dan bellowed before slowly placing one of the shear blades under the ring and squeezing tightly against the skin.

It was in place, and Dan started to squeeze the handle with all of his might. His biceps flexed as the veins in his arm popped against the small sleeve of his shirt, to the point where Theresa couldn't believe they hadn't ripped right through the fabric. He stopped to exhale. As he looked down, he saw that the ring hadn't shown any signs of bending yet.

He started up again. This time, he stood up in a squatting position before audibly grunting into a strong effort. Sweat began collecting at the top of his head and brow like a washing machine dripping water during an intense rinse cycle. He gasped and looked down at the ring. Nothing. Not even a scratch.

"Shit," he said, wiping his brow, "where the hell did you get this thing from?"

"It was from an ad on this one site," Ethan admitted, his voice shaking more with each word. "I just know that the package looked like it was written in Chinese or something. I tried finding the instructions to take it off, but I couldn't—"

"Of course, it's the Chinese!" Dan shouted as he put his hands on his hips. "They've succeeded in taking our manufacturing jobs from our young men, and now they want to take their manhood too! What better way to ensure that we can't reproduce and secure global supremacy?"

Deb's eyes began to roll back into her head as she slowly sat back down with emotional exhaustion. Theresa could tell that this was a routine that required just as much patience as fighting fires.

"They know our boys these days are hornier than a rhinoceros from hell, so they take their cheap, indestructible Chinese metal and fashion them into some good ol' fashion castrating equipment. It makes me sick...to hell with China and everyone in it!"

Dan looked over at Dr. Park, realizing that he might have said something uncouth and insulting to the Asian physician.

"No offense, doctor. I'm sure there are some fine ones that come over here and become productive Americans."

"Um, I'm actually Korean," Dr. Park said, afraid to step on the land mines of this man's xenophobia tirade, "and from Rochester."

"Well, good. Then I stand by it even more!" Dan said, again wiping his brow. "To hell with those bastards and their plots to undermine American sovereignty! Deb, get me the angle grinder."

Deb got up from her seat and went back into the duffle bag, where she found two angle grinders, one with a red handle and silver blade that read "Milwaukee" and one with a magenta handle and black blade that read "Wu." Dan mistakenly called it the "W.U." blade instead of the actual name of the Mandarin manufacturing company that made it. She held both blades up in her hands.

"Which one do you want?" she asked.

"Oh, the W.U. for sure. It gives a much sharper cut," he said as he reached for the blade. "Son, you might be a goddamn moron for sticking your trouser snake in a bear trap, but you're still an American. And I'll be damned if I'm going to let those Beijing sons of bitches mutilate ya. Seth, can you give me some juice?" he asked, handing him the extension cord.

"Um, I can ask. Are you thirsty, sir?"

"No, you towering neanderthal— power! Plug it into the outlet!"

"Oh, right," Seth said as he sluggishly plugged the cord into the outlet behind him.

"Doc, I'm going to need you to push his stuff to the side so I can get a good angle. Nurse, can you hold him still so I don't slice him open?"

Dr. Park held the now royal blue genitals in place while Dan fired up the blade. Theresa held Ethan's chest while holding his hand with hers. She watched as his eyes raced back and forth in fearful anticipation. His mind went racing with the faces of every church camp counselor he failed and every broken pledge to not engage in sexual depravity he made at the Knights to Remember purity dances he attended growing up. Standing next to a portrait of Jesus and Ronald Reagan, he swore to his mother that he would be a gentleman, yet this was the furthest from gentle he could ever get.

The blade spun lightning-fast. Dan put on his safety goggles for eye protection and began carefully bringing them down to the exposed ring on the side of the shaft with the focus of a surgeon making a crucial incision. Metal contacted metal and the sparks began to fly like a swarm of lightning bugs in the night sky. Grrrrrrrrrrrrrrrrrnnnnnnnnnnnnnnnnnggggggggggggggggggg. The blade hummed loudly as Dan looked like a power welder constructing a metallic masterpiece. The other spectators in the room looked on in complete awe while shielding their eyes from the jumping lights below.

Ethan could feel the transfer heat from blade to ring rise to an unbearably hot temperature on the base of his member and yelped, "Hot! Hot! Hot! Stop!"

"Nurse! Can we get some ice?" Dan asked, momentarily releasing the blade from the ring.

Theresa processed the demand as if she had joined the military and this man was her drill sergeant. She ran out of the room and grabbed a large 64-ounce water bottle that was sitting next to the ice machine. She knew it probably belonged to one of her coworkers, but it had to be commandeered for the greater good. When she got back in the room, Ethan continued to wince in pain as Dan's drill continued to clash against the ring below. Grrrrrrrrrrrrrnnnnnnnnnnnnnngggggggggggggg.

"Okay, when I stop the blade, you go in and place the ice by the point of contact!" Dan shouted over the screeching sound of the blade. He finally turned off the blade and pressed up his goggles to sit on top of his forehead. Theresa jumped in with a clump of ice cubes and placed it on top of the red hot metal, but only for a few seconds, as she witnessed the ice quickly melt before her eyes. He examined his work below as beads of sweat fell from the top of his head. The ring was more scratched than before but with only a minor indentation. The sharp tips of his Wu blade disintegrated in the process. Dan looked at the blade and then down at the ring as if he were a renowned knight who had just witnessed his opponent disarm him in battle. He put the dull angle grinder on the counter beside Seth, sat back down, and sunk his head in his hands.

"Doc...I just don't know how it's coming off. I just don't know..." he said, with defeat echoing in his voice.

Dr. Park exhaled long and hard, and looked over at Ethan, who was now near hyperventilating.

"I'm so sorry, Ethan," Dr. Park said as he began to nervously wipe his glasses. "We're going to have to remove this from you via detachment. Theresa, can you make a call to surgery?"

"Detachment?! W-what does that mean?! What does that mean?!" Ethan barked at the doctor beside him.

Dr. Park sighed again and averted his eyes away from the sheer panic in Ethan's baby blue eyes.

"We're going to need to amputate..."

Just then, Ethan pulled down the curtain to his left with a single jerk, the rod narrowly missing Theresa's head. He began to sway back and forth on the examination bed like a tantrum-throwing child trying to contort his way out of a car seat.

"Please don't take my dick! Please don't take my dick! Please don't take my dick!" he yelled, tears falling down his cheeks like a leaky faucet.

"Ethan, it's going to be okay," Theresa said in the same soothing voice her mother used to calm them down as kids. "There are prosthetics, there's physical therapy, there's—"

"I don't give a flying fuck!" he screamed as he grabbed the blood pressure machine cord and yanked it out of the wall. "I'd rather die than lose my dick! Do you hear me? Please, do something! Anything!" he shouted as he grabbed Dr. Park by the collar, and the dumbfounded doctor quickly pushed himself back away. His chest started puffing up and down like a bouncy castle at a 7-year-old's birthday party.

"I'll never be able to start a family, I'll never be able to look my parents in the eye again, and I'll never be able to show my face on Capitol Hill ever again without everyone going, 'Oh look, it's that one guy who works for Vicky Veitch who has no dick!' I'm ruined, dammit! Ruined!"

"Goddamn, those Chinese!" Dan shouted as he threw his goggles to the floor. "So help me, I'm never eating another one of those goddamn crab rang-goons for as long as I live!"

Theresa surveyed the room during this intense episode of fright. She saw Seth frightened in the corner, his eyes looking down, knowing he wanted nothing more than to leave and bury his trauma at Denny's for some 5:30 a.m. pancakes. Dan had a scowl on his face as he sat there with his arms folded, likely associating the failure to remove the ring as a dereliction of duty for his country. Dr. Park was stunned and shaken, feeling the full burden of his medical responsibilities. But when she looked over at Deb, she saw someone deep in thought among the chaos. Her eyes moved back and forth, lost in thought, until her head popped up, her eyes meeting Theresa's. They both knew at that moment that maybe, just maybe, there was hope to be found.

"What about the diamond saw?" she asked, standing up from her swivel stool.

"What about it?" Dan asked as if she had just mentioned the name of an estranged relative that mustn't ever be talked about.

"W-what's the diamond saw? C-can you use it?! Please!" Ethan pleaded as he popped up and leaned forward, causing himself further pain to the wounded penis below.

"It's crazy!" Dan said, standing up with his hands on his hips, looking at an anatomic picture of the inside of a throat as if he were peering out of a window, lost in thought, "It's suicide, dammit!"

"Captain, we can bring it in and set it up on the edge of the bed. If Seth and the doctor hold his legs, you can hold up the saw while I carefully guide the genitals toward the—"

"It'll never work!" he said, turning back around in dramatic fashion. "That saw was only issued in the budget after a bunch of teenagers got their car stuck between a concrete overpass wall. It's a $4,000 stone-cutting juggernaut. The heat alone will scorch the poor bastard and render the effort useless."

"Exactly. That's where she comes in," she said, pointing each hand at Theresa and Dr. Park. "If she is able to periodically splash ice water between cuts, we can neutralize the heat enough to avoid severe burns. It's not perfect, but it's our only chance."

"I think it could work," Theresa chimed in, feeling as though she was the shy kid in class who was finally willing to speak up. "We have to at least try, right?"

"Yes! Please try it! Please!" Ethan begged the fireman.

Captain Dan sat back down and folded his fingers together, bringing them up to his nose.

"I just don't know...it might be too reckless. It might be too big of a risk."

Deb put her hand on his shoulder and looked up at Theresa, their eyes meeting in solidarity. Theresa understood where Deb was going to go with this high-strung jingoist before she even uttered her next sentence.

"Captain," she said firmly, "when has a risk ever been too big for the United States of America?"

Dan immediately thought of his father and WWII. The honor he brought to the family name as he returned home to receive a Purple Heart. Of course, the Purple Heart wasn't necessarily won in combat or in a heroic manner; his dad was the base camp cook who got distracted and accidentally cut off two of his fingers chopping onions while joining in a rendition of "She'll Be Coming Around The Mountain" with his brothers in arms. He was shipped back to the States the following week when his officers realized they couldn't reattach the fingers.

Dan's head popped up, and his chest puffed out, with visions of bald eagles flying above him. The honor of his forefathers coursed through his veins as he looked at the mangled genitalia in front of him. This was his moment. This was his duty.

"Never!" he proclaimed, standing upright like a soldier. "Our exceptionalism knows no limits! Doc, screw surgery. Make a call down to Tiananmen Square. Tell 'em Captain Dan

Grundle's gonna cut through their Great Wall when he's done with this."

He stood up and started making his way toward the door as a glimmer of hope shined in Ethan's eyes.

"Seth, come help me get it out of the back. She's a biggin'."

"Yes, sir!" Seth said as he followed his Captain out the door and to the firetruck.

Theresa looked at Deb as her sweating head caused the short, spikey highlights in her hair to droop down. The silence in the room was once again at an awkward standstill.

"That was a, uh, pretty cool how you did that," Theresa said, breaking the silence.

"Did what?" Deb asked back, adjusting her hair.

"Yeah, no, just the whole, like, the way you were able to convince him to get the saw and stuff." Theresa's eyes diverted back to the floor in embarrassment. She yet again felt awkward, even in the same room as a guy with his genitals in a bind.

"Oh, that? Ha! That's nothing. I used those same talking points when convincing him to install the A/C back at the station," she laughed.

"Well, regardless, it was some impressive quick thinking to get him to budge," Theresa replied, chuckling herself.

"Thanks," Deb said with a subtle, esteemed smile.

Seth entered the room and held the door wide open for Captain Dan, who was wielding what looked like a giant maize-colored flamethrower with a massive blade on the end of it. His arms were fully flexed while balancing the heavy piece of machinery and working his way into the room. He pivoted slowly, facing the blade between Ethan's legs, like a machine gunner preparing to open fire on a panzer tank. Ethan's eyes crossed in fear as he stared at the shiny beast before him.

"Alright, positions everyone!" Dan shouted as he locked his shoulders and legs into place.

Theresa grabbed the ice bucket and filled it with cool water in the sink by the door. Dr. Park held Ethan's right leg tightly while Seth did the same for the left leg. Deb placed

Dan's goggles over her own eyes. She gripped the genitals firmly in her hand, sending a gasp of pain out of Ethan, and flipped them up toward his lower abdomen, exposing the ring below his scrotum.

"Fire it up, Captain," she shouted with a nod.

"Here we go," Dan replied as he flipped the switch with his pinky.

The motor roared as the ensuing blade immediately rotated to a near-impossible speed. Deb held down with all her might as the Captain slowly inched forward with the blade.

"Get that water ready!" she shouted at Theresa, who quickly hovered over the water bottle of freezing cold water.

"Captain, about two inches to go!" she ushered him in like someone coaching an airplane pilot on the runway. "Steady...steady...and perfect!"

The blade kissed the surface of the titanium, which immediately produced intense sparks that shot down toward Ethan's backside, causing him to shriek and jolt in pain.

Rrrrrrrrrrrnnnnnnnnn! The two men were holding his legs still as if it were a spooked horse wanting to buck them off.

"It's burning my taint!" he cried out, with everyone in the room turning their faces away to shield themselves from the beads of flickering light.

"Ease back!" she shouted at Dan. "Water! Let's go!"

Theresa carefully poured water down at the impact site, which quickly evaporated into steam that shot back up in her face. Evaporated scrotum water wasn't exactly how she envisioned her morning would start. Ethan gasped in relief as the freezing cold water temporarily soothed the burning sensation below.

"Alright, ease back in, Captain!" she shouted again as she prepared to stare down the friction in front of her.

As Dan moved back in, he belted out, "Come on, you bastard! Give it to me!"

Sparks shot out once more down against Ethan's behind.

"Jesus Christ, my taint is on fire!" he shrieked, nearly fainting from the stray sparks that made their way behind him.

The sparks suddenly stopped.

"Stop!" Deb yelled while immediately throwing her hand out toward Dan. Theresa poured more cold water over the genitals, this time averting her face.

Dan backed away and flipped the switch with his pinky once more. The monstrous roar of the behemoth machine quieted into nothing. Deb pulled up her goggles and assessed the progress below.

"Well?" Dan asked, scared of the answer to follow.

"We cut through!" Deb exclaimed, followed by a collective cheer from the entire room.

"You're goddamn right we did!" Dan shouted at the top of his lungs.

Dr. Park high-fived Seth while Theresa fist-pumped in the air. The look of relief in Ethan's eyes produced tears that ran down his cheeks. Deb exhaled and assessed if any damage was done to the blade. The saw was seemingly unphased by the clash it had just endured. She pushed back her hair once more and pulled her goggles down.

"Alright, everyone, we aren't out of the woods just yet!" she looked over at Ethan, who was perched on his back and holding his weight up with his elbows. "You're going to need to sit up on your knees for me so we can cut the top part."

The scrawny Ethan popped up to his knees faster than an Olympian after a long jump attempt. She once more gripped his discolored genitals with her left hand, this time pushing them down as far as they would go. The tender pain shot up once more, creating another yelp from Ethan. Dan flicked the power of the blade once more as the blade sang another thunderous roar. Rrrrrrrrrrnnnnnnnnnnnnnnnnnnnn.

The sparks, this time, flew downward onto Deb's glove, shielding the penis from the confetti burst of light. The burning of the ring's metal was still incredibly painful as he continued to whimper with pain.

"Ease up!" Deb shouted. "Water!"

Theresa poured the remainder of the water out, creating the largest steam cloud yet.

"Ease back in!" Deb yelled, signaling for him to move forward.

The final clash of the blade saw its titanium foe create bedlam that would become a thing of legend in this emergency room. The blade sliced through the final bit of the figure eight ring, which fell clanking on the floor, forming almost a perfect black '33' with fire tips at the top. Ethan was finally free.

Dan turned off the blade, and everyone started cheering again. Theresa found herself hugging an unsuspecting Deb as Seth and Dr. Park high-fived once more. Dan looked up at the ceiling as if he were looking up to see his eight-fingered father smiling down from Heaven. Ethan laid back and covered his face in complete relief and exasperation. Theresa let go of Deb, feeling slightly embarrassed by the overreaction. Deb took off the goggles and smiled back at her.

"Seth, take this back to the truck," Dan instructed, handing off the machine to the burly man.

"Yes, Captain," he said before clumsily shuffling out of the room.

Dan picked up the two halves of the ring and held them up like the Pope holding up a split piece of wafer.

"This is coming with us," he declared, staring at the broken ring. "It's going on the board."

Deb followed Dan out of the room, rolling her eyes at the thought of her Captain putting a sex toy up on the 'Board of Heroes,' which was a glorified trophy case for responses that he considered a job well done paired with photos of the corresponding team members. Her headshot would now be forever associated with a broken cock ring. She supposed there were worse fates.

Dr. Park quickly attended to Ethan, assessing his lower half to make sure no major burns were sustained. Theresa felt still in time as her stomach began to feel like a butterfly sanctuary. She then returned to reality as Dr. Park asked her to get a handheld receptacle for Ethan to urinate into. She went into the cupboard above the sink and retrieved the two-liter plastic container.

"Alright, if you're able to pee, we'll know that you haven't sustained any permanent damage. I don't want to alarm you, but restricting blood flow for hours on end can kill the nerves in appendages...if the nerves are dead and discoloration remains, we, uh, will have to..."

Ethan gulped once more as his heart began to race again. All of that, and he could still lose his penis? The fear couldn't escape him no matter how hard he tried.

He closed his eyes and focused hard, trying to locate the flow of his bladder. He pushed hard with every fiber of his crotch, holding his breath and tightening his butt. All of a sudden, his stream began to pour out like a firehose, completely filling up the container to its brim.

"Wow," Dr. Park said, stunned, "you really had to go. Looks like everything is intact. Theresa will discharge you."

Ethan got dressed, and Theresa led him out of the room and to the front desk.

"I, uh, I just wanted to say thanks for, you know..." Ethan said as he put his hoodie up over his head.

"Don't even mention it," Theresa said as she finished his paperwork. "Crazy stuff happens in an emergency room. But it's alright now, and you can go home."

Ethan laughed nervously as he adjusted the top of his sweatpants.

"Yeah, I bet that was nothing compared to some of the stuff you guys have seen," he said with a cheeky smile.

"Oh hell no," Theresa shot back to his surprise, her eyes meeting his. "That was the craziest shit I've ever seen, dude. I'm never going to forget you. That's for damn sure."

Ethan's smile immediately sunk back down, his brow furrowing with disgust.

"Yeah, well, the bedside manner of this place could use a lot of work, you know? And I'm not your 'dude.' I'm a patient! No wonder 72% of Americans lack faith in our healthcare system. The unprofessionalism is astounding!"

Theresa peered over her glasses into his beady blue eyes. Without breaking eye contact, she tore the piece of paper from the clipboard and handed it to him.

"Have a lovely day, Mr. Bile. Make sure you ice your area for a good while when you get home. 100% of patients find that ice helps with the pain when they do stupid shit."

He snatched the paper out of her hands and scowled. Theresa watched as he stormed out of the front emergency room doors, looking like an angry scarecrow as he lumbered away. The sunrise peered through the automatic doors as they opened and closed behind him. Donna came back to the desk behind her, snacking on a bag of chips.

"What the hell happened back there, anyway?" she asked before licking the cheese dust off her thumb and index finger.

"Girl," Theresa sighed, "you don't even wanna know."

"That bad, huh?" she said with a laugh. "The crazies come out when the moon is full, Theresa."

"You're not getting any arguments from me," Theresa said as she watched the cantankerous Ethan scuttle through the parking lot.

"Hey," Donna said, with her mouth full of chips, "have you seen my water bottle?"

Chapter 10

Burning Love

"Hey...hey, buddy," Patrick asked the motionless man lying in his bathtub while cautiously removing the ball gag from his mouth. "Please, say something if you're okay. I-I won't be mad or call the cops, I swear..."

Colton remained unresponsive. Still naked and shaking from the reality of the situation, Patrick examined his face, which was now a new hue of red. His veins and capillaries looked like a roadmap of hell as they became more visible on his skin through the shock of the electricity. The mouth hung agape, propped up only slightly by the zipper on his mask. Patrick saw no signs of breathing from this still man in soaked black leather. He knew the man in his tub was most certainly dead.

Immediately slumping down on his wet bathroom floor, he began to sob uncontrollably. The disbelief of the situation was setting in as he began wiping his tears as they dripped down his plump, red cheeks. A random person broke into his apartment, presumably to either kill him or worse. And yet, he had no idea who this was. Had they met in passing? Did Patrick say or do something to provoke him? Why was he wearing a ball gag? Was this some weird spontaneous sex thing? A case of mistaken identity? Was this some sort of deep government plot to eliminate him as a potential threat? Everything was on the table.

He thought about calling an ambulance, but what good would they do? And beyond that, the cops would most certainly show up and want to know the whole story. What cop in the country would believe that he was role-playing with lobsters and LEGOs in the bathtub when an intruder with sex paraphernalia and accessories broke into his apartment, fought him, and accidentally electrocuted himself with a stereo? At best, he would probably be charged with manslaughter during a lover's quarrel. At worst, he would be charged with some sort of elaborate homicide. This guy probably had powerful lawyer friends who could send him away to federal prison for the rest of his life.

Visions of him spending the rest of his life in a prison cell were now racing through his mind. He would never last in the slammer; the other inmates would see him as a prized ham they could cut up for their own entertainment. He thought that after a judge rejected the ridiculousness of his alibi, he would sentence him to live the remainder of his days in a cramped 8 x 6 cell with some overgrown neo-Nazi named Big Bruce. He imagined that Big Bruce would probably brand him with swastikas and turn him into his personal ankle-grabber for him to take out all of his pent-up sexual frustration on. The tears began flowing once more.

"Oh god, what have I done?" he cried in agony. "I don't want to be Big Bruce's bitch!"

His teary eyes looked over at the body, still sprawled out in the tub like a tangled marionette. On his leather catsuit, just above his right pectoral, lay Commander Fitzgerald.

Patrick wiped his tears some more and waddled over to the tub. He picked up the small LEGO figure and flipped him around. He stared at yet another casualty of the night, as the Commander's face was now mostly melted.

"Oh, Commander Fitz...not you too," he whimpered, clutching the toy in his hand, "burnt to a crisp."

He paused for a second and opened his hand back up, examining the little LEGO man.

"Burnt to a crisp," he repeated as his eyes widened.

The charred plastic of the LEGO popped an idea into his head. He stood up and started pacing out of the bathroom and into his apartment, frantically chewing on his fingernails. This was an idea that, if done correctly, would become a secret he would take to his grave. He walked over to the bathroom mirror, put his glasses back on his head, and looked at himself in his bloodshot eyes. The reflection of the red-haired man staring back at him looked fearful–a fearfulness that would surely crumble under the heavy weight of the justice system.

"You have no choice, Patrick," he said, pointing at his reflection. "They'll come down harder on you than the goddamn Incredible Hulk. You have to do it if you want to stay alive."

He quickly pulled Colton out of the tub and drained the bathwater. After dressing himself, he grabbed a garbage bag from under the sink, carefully unplugged the stereo from the outlet, and placed it into the bag along with the lobsters, the man's handcuffs, the ball gag, and the twirled purple baton. He tied it tightly shut and gripped it with his hand. Cautiously creaking his apartment door open, he popped his head into the hallway, looking back and forth. No one was there.

Quickly locking the door behind him, he doddered down the hall with the trash bag, beads of sweat dripping down the back of his neck. As he got outside, his head was on a swivel, looking around to see if any witnesses or hidden cameras were in his vicinity. Yet again, he was in the clear.

He hustled to his car and tossed the trash bag in the back under an unwashed Ninja Turtles blanket he brought with him whenever he went home to his parents' place. He found his mother's choice of comforter blankets overbearingly hot and not conducive to his preferred sleeping temperatures. After locking the vehicle, he went back inside and ran faster than he had during the high school pacer test days he loathed. Patrick unlocked the door and immediately locked it behind him, leaning his back against the door while panting heavily.

His mind began to race again. What if this guy took his car here? Surely, the police would come searching for it if he went missing, opening up the entire building for questioning. He combed his entire apartment, looking for car keys lying around anywhere. Finding nothing, he frisked Colton thoroughly and aggressively as if he were a pillaging Viking looting a corpse. Yet again, he found nothing.

"If you have no car, how did you get here?" he wondered aloud.

There was no cab or shuttle service in a town as small as Rockdale, meaning he must have gotten a ride from one of his two associates. Were the associates in on this unknown plot as well? They'd have to be. No self-respecting person would give someone a ride in a mischievous, skin-tight black leather jumpsuit. Patrick imagined his partners would be back soon if that were the case. He had little time to waste.

If they were to make it downstairs undetected, he would need to disguise the man, Patrick thought. The pile of dirty laundry by his bed likely had items of use. Rifling through it, he found his maroon Champion sweatshirt with matching sweatpants.

"Perfect," he muttered to himself.

He laid the body down on his bed and struggled as he put the clothes over Colton's wet, leathery limbs. After tightening the drawstring sweatpants to their maximum resistance in order to fit Colton's slender waist, Patrick noticed that the slightly burned face was still too exposed. Digging further and making his way underneath his bed, he found a pair of yellow rimless sunglasses and a bucket hat branded with Sweet Martha's Cookie Jar, which he got at the Minnesota State Fair a few years ago. They would have to do. He put them on the body and took a deep breath. He stood back to look at him as if he were an art piece he had perfected to go on display.

"Alright," he said picking up the man, slinging his right arm over his shoulder and around his neck with a grunt. "We're going to have to *Weekend At Bernie's* this."

Patrick held Colton's wrist with his right hand while holding the rest of his body up by gripping his waist. Cautiously, he popped his head out again to check the perimeter. The coast was clear. Colton's body drooped like a ragdoll as Patrick struggled to lock the apartment door behind them. His sunglasses fell off his face and onto the ground, causing Patrick to drop the body like a sack of tools. The resulting heavy thud startled him, and he froze in shock, waiting for someone to poke their head out of their unit and discover his crime. The hallway remained silent and empty.

He picked up the glasses and then put them back on his head, this time fastening the frames tightly behind his ears. Picking him back up, Patrick staggered his way over to the stairs and carefully walked down. Colton's ankles hit each step with a thud as he was dragged along the old blue carpet of the staircase. The body bumped into the wall, nearly knocking over the generic apartment painting of a vase with daisies onto the floor. Steadying himself, he made it down to the landing and paced his steps one at a time.

Finally, he made his way to the lobby, his shoulder throbbing in pain from the unfamiliar exercise it was receiving. He slowly poked his head around the corner, looking out the front glass doors to see an empty parking lot. He took another heavy breath and took one step forward.

"Hello, Mr. Loveland," a familiar raspy voice said, startling him from behind.

Patrick was in disbelief at his bad fortune, for in a time when he was most vulnerable and in peril, wrath itself was there to face him before he even left the front doors.

"Ms. Melstad," Patrick replied, his voice shaking with fear, "what are you doing up at this hour?"

"I should be asking you the same thing," she said with a piercing glare while folding her bony arms. "Your friend doesn't look so well. Should I call for an ambulance?"

"No!" Patrick shouted before catching himself, "I mean, no. No, that's alright, Ms. Melstad. He just had a little too much to drink, is all."

"Just as I suspected!" she proclaimed, pointing her dagger of a finger at his chest. "I've always known you were a degenerate, and now I have the proof right in front of me. I have half a mind to report you to the property manager, you know? A debauchee like you, roaming the halls at night with your stumbling drunkard friend, terrorizing a building filled with frail seniors? I'll have you removed from this property faster than you can say 'eviction'!"

Patrick's glasses slid down to the edge of his nose. His sweaty forehead betrayed him as the fear of Ms. Melstad becoming the catalyst for his prison sentence overrode his desire to verbally assault her.

"Please, Ms. Melstad. This is just a night where my friend got a little carried away with the drinking. That's all," he said, pleading with the furrowed-brow figure in front of him, "I'm sure you had a couple of rowdy nights back in your day, huh?"

Images of her past entered his mind. He imagined that back in her day, she was gathering in some forest with her fellow witches as they boiled the innocent in their massive cauldron. Their screams would echo throughout the woodlands, along with their odious, witchy laughter. Her permanent grimace turned into a full-blown scowl at that suggestion.

"That poison you drink has never touched my lips in my entire life," she hissed like a viper secreting venom from its fangs, "judging by your, shall we say, amorphous shape, I'm sure just the opposite is true for you."

A combination of rage and trepidation sank deep into his stomach. He so badly wanted to tell her that the day she died, he would crash her funeral, walk up to her body on display, whisper, "I beat you," as he hovered over her corpse, and then belch in her face. But alas, he was but a pawn on the chessboard, put in check and ready to be trounced by a queen who would surely win the game. He let out a heavy sigh and pleaded with her.

"Please, Ms. Melstad. Please don't say a word to anyone about this. I'm sure that there's something we can work out, right?" he pleaded, with his shoulder pain starting to throb even more intensely.

The petite woman began stroking her chin, the sharp corners of her mouth producing a smile that could haunt the dreams of children around the world.

"Hmm...I suppose there could be some sort of arrangement. But what, oh, what could it be?" she jousted ,tilting her head to the side. "Perhaps you could water my plants...maybe clean my floors...feed Sprinkles when I'm at my bridge club," she barked, tapping her chin with her fingers.

"Whatever you want," Patrick said, a tint of agony in his voice.

She stopped stroking her chin and flared her nostrils like a dragon.

"I want my parking spot!" she hissed.

"Never, you old hag!" Patrick blasted back, nearly dropping the body once more.

"Fine! Then I guess it's straight to the property managers with me!" she shrieked, tilting up her chin.

She began walking back to her apartment before Patrick let out another sigh of anguish.

"Okay," he said in defeat.

"Okay, *what?*" she replied while turning back to face him with a victorious sneer.

"The parking space is yours," he whimpered, staring at the floor.

"Not just this week or month! I want it forever; do you understand?" she insisted, pointing her finger at him once more. "And you're also going to do all those other chores for me on Tuesdays and Saturdays. And don't you even think about overwatering my ficus plants because I'll know!"

"Done," he replied, "but you can't say a word about this to anyone, you hear me? You never saw any of this. If you rat me out, the deal is off!"

"Deal," she concurred, "you also can't have any more of those strawberry candies in the leasing office. I know you're the one who picks them out of the bowl."

"Oh, come on! That's not even fair," he replied, exasperated.

Ms. Melstad hated the taste of candy, but inserting her dominance over Patrick by taking away that which he loved gave her satisfaction.

"No candies or no deal!" she snapped back at him.

"Fine…but you better keep your word, you sadistic crone!" he grumbled.

"Oh, I will. Rest assured, I never betray a pact, especially one that suits me well," she boasted. "But one slip up, and you're as good as gone!"

He started making his way out the door before stopping himself to turn around and face the sneering beldam once more.

"Ms. Melstad, you really are pure evil," he retorted with total conviction in his voice.

She squinted her eyes and gradually formed her trademark haunting half-smile.

"And don't you forget it," she quipped back at him.

Patrick moved through the door with Colton's left arm nearly caught in the frame. His arm was starting to give out as he walked to his car. He dropped Colton onto the pavement and watched as the body sprawled out like a to-go box of pasta from an Italian restaurant. He picked him back up, this time on his opposite side, and dragged him to the passenger side. Somehow, managing to locate his keys in his tight front pants pocket, he unlocked the door and gently placed the body in the passenger seat, securing his legs underneath the dash. He shut the car door and, like a parent realizing their child wasn't fastened, opened it once more to buckle his seatbelt. The last thing he needed was a dead body flying through his windshield should he need to aggressively apply the brakes.

The engine started, and he began to drive to the funeral home. The clock read 12:51 a.m. on his dashboard in bright red numbers. He looked over at the body next to him, and a slight shudder went down his spine once more. With the sunglasses and bucket hat still attached, Colton's head and neck were leaning on his left shoulder toward the window. As the pasty ginger, yet again, wondered why this man attacked him of all people, he stared at the miniature figurine of the Hindu deity Ganesha, which sat atop his dashboard.

In the Hindu faith, Ganesha is the god who serves as the remover of obstacles and bringer of good luck. The deity is identifiable by his elephant head and four arms. Patrick considered himself to be a closeted Hindu in his beliefs – not because he studied or lived by any of the faith's lessons, but because he thought it was super cool that their gods could have animal heads and multiple limbs. He was also enamored with the idea that he could be reincarnated as an exotic apex predator, like a harpy eagle who patrolled the tops of the Amazon Rainforest. The guy at the record store who sold him the figurine and incense told him all about it.

Was he really a criminal target, or was this a random act of violence brought on by the fate of the gods? The idea that this was his damning punishment for past transgressions plagued Patrick's mind as he drove down Minnesota State Highway 23.

"Oh, Ganesha!" he shouted at the figurine with tears in his eyes, "What have I done to deserve this cruel twist of fate? Sure, I'm not perfect. I have fallen victim to pride and anger, and I don't return my rented videos to Blockbuster on time and purposely object to the late fees, knowing my crime. But I am but a mortal man on this planet! Why, in all of your wisdom, have you decided to curse me instead of bless me with your majestic trunk? Did Shiva put you up to this? That is just so typical of him!"

The light pink-colored figurine stared back at him blankly, with two of its four arms extended outward and the other two holding a hatchet and a flower. Patrick considered himself a loyal steward of the faith he knew so little about. He thought about all his personal sacrifices, like occasionally opting for chicken strips instead of a burger whenever he went out to eat to honor the sacredness of cows or holding the door for people to increase his overall karma meter. Surely, he was on the righteous path.

He then considered his own reincarnation and how accidentally killing someone would most certainly take him out of the running for becoming a harpy eagle. Now, he expected his post-mortem destiny would most likely have him transformed into an unremarkable three-toed sloth, falling to his death from the trees after mistaking his own arm for a branch. It didn't matter how many chicken strips he ate or the doors he held open; he was destined for the bottom.

After rambling on some more about his plight and the unfair inconsistencies of divine intervention, he saw a sign for the Rum River ahead. The Rum River flows into the mighty Mississippi, and the bridge going over it is the perfect spot for Patrick to pull over. He pulled over to the right side of the road in the middle of the bridge, flipped his hazard lights on for good measure, and bolted out of his front seat to the back of the vehicle. After grabbing the garbage bag, he struggled to open the top, which he tied too tightly. Using his teeth, he bit through the drawstring, releasing the tension and opening the bag. He waddled over to the side of the bridge and emptied the contents into the river below. The splashing gave him assurance that they were to be carried away forever. Littering would surely knock him down a few points on his karma meter, he thought, but it was a sacrifice that needed to be made to save his skin.

He got back into the car, flicked off his hazard lights, and took a deep breath. Doing another once-over in his rearview mirror, he saw no one coming behind him. The easy part of this cover-up was over. Now came the most challenging. Patrick started up the car again and continued driving down the highway toward Rockdale. His passenger was still dead, but Patrick's plan was still very much alive.

Normally, Patrick didn't mind his 45-minute commute to work every day. It gave him time to reflect, fantasize, and listen to music while mindlessly cruising down an open road. But tonight, this commute was soaked in the fear that his very existence could be threatened at any moment. It reminded him of the time as a teenager, during a trip to Chicago, when he had to take a frightening late-night ride on the L. He was harassed by a four-toothed man who mistook him for Hamilton Porter, the chubby, freckled kid from The Sandlot.

"Go on! Say the line! 'You're killing me, Smalls!'" the man shouted in his face, smiling and smelling of a combination of booze and gym socks.

"I-I'm not that actor, sir," a terrified Patrick replied.

"Sure, ya are! I saw the movie three damn times! Three!" he said, holding up three fingers with his torn mittens. "And you were definitely in it, boy!"

"Y-you're killing me, Smalls," Patrick said, on the verge of tears.

"Ha! There it is! I knew you were the guy all along. I can't be fooled! I've got that psychology in me," the man yelled as he twirled on one of the support poles. "Man, I hate that movie! It sucks!"

Now, instead of a crazy man shouting at him on a train, he was tormented by the deafening silence of a dead man in his car. While he collected his thoughts, lights flashed behind him in the rearview mirror, sinking his heart into the pits of his bowels.

"Shit!" he yelled before slowly pulling the vehicle back to the shoulder of the road.

Panicked, he threw the corpse forward into something that resembled a contorted pretzel, forcing as much of the body toward the floor mats as possible and quickly throwing the *Ninja Turtles* blanket over it. His heart was racing as if he were just forced to compete in a decathlon. Ms. Melstad must have double-crossed him and dialed for the police the second he left the apartment, ensuring he would be put away for life, he thought. The wrapping of two knuckles on the window startled him like a gunshot as the officer leaned down behind the window. He exhaled heavily, and rolled down the window with the crank on the door.

"Evening, officer!" Patrick said with a forced smile and fearful eyes. "What seems to be the problem?"

"License and registration, please," the hefty officer with a name badge that read 'Sheriff J. Jorgenson' said as his thick eyebrows curled downward.

Patrick dug through the center console to find the registration form, accidentally nudging the body with his elbow as it shifted underneath the blanket. Handing it over to the sheriff, he pulled his license out of the black wallet and handed it over. The man walked back to his patrol car. A few anxiety-fueled minutes passed as Patrick anticipated the officer would come back with backup to haul him away. He imagined that his mother would receive the news that her son was a murderer and have a heart attack on the spot. He would be responsible for *two* deaths tonight, he thought. The sheriff marched back, his facial expression unchanged even in the face of the cold winter night.

"What are ya doing out so late tonight, bud?" the man asked, the dimples in his face deepening.

Patrick gulped in anticipation of the man's reaction after telling him.

"I, uh...I work at a funeral home and forgot to get everything prepared for a wake we have going on later."

He felt ashamed at the pathetic attempt at the lie that just left his mouth. Surely, he could have thought of something better than leaving for work in the middle of the night. The man squinted his eyes as if he were trying to read an inscription written on Patrick's face.

"Just as I suspected..." he said, raising his chin, "please step out of the vehicle for me, sir."

Patrick's heart sank in his gut as if it had been gunned down by a battleship. The anticipation of arrest was all too real as he turned a shade of ghostly white that was closer to Frosty than it was a man. He slowly reached for the handle, opened the door, and stepped out.

"Follow me," the officer yelled upon seeing Patrick exit the vehicle.

Patrick followed him to what he assumed would be the squad car for questioning. However, Jorgenson stopped at the bumper. The pool of sweat under his armpits felt as if it was beginning to freeze in the cold air.

"Now, Mr. Loveland, do you know why I pulled you over?" the sheriff asked, leaning his arm against the trailer.

"I do not," he said politely as he continued to shiver.

"Well, ya see, I had a sneaking suspicion that I was going to see someone out tonight. Call it a premonition, if you will," he said, folding his arms as Patrick braced for the worst, "and it really frustrates me that I ended up being right about that."

Patrick's heart began racing again as beads of hot sweat dripped down his back and armpits, battling the cold of the night and winning.

"Why is that?" he asked in a frightened high pitched voice.

"Well," the officer said, putting his hands on his hips, "you've got yourself a busted tail light here. Now, normally, you'd think, *'Oh cripes, a bad tail light? Why the heck is Sheriff Jorgenson busting my chops over this?'* and I get it- no one likes a nitpicker. However, when you're driving out here in the dead of night with a busted tail light, someone might ram into the back of ya. We had a gal here not too long ago who was just minding her own business, cruising at night until she rammed into the back of a farmer's trailer transporting some big propane tanks. Boom! Up in smoke!" he said, waving his arms in the air to mimic the explosion. "Now, the farmer came out of it okay, but Little Miss Midnight Rider ended up looking like the bottom of your grandmother's oven. Now I can tell by the *Ninja Turtles* on top of your blanket pile and the *Pokemon* on your dash that you've got little ones at home. And it would just break my friggin' heart to see you or anyone with kids get into an accident at night because folks can't see ya."

Patrick felt relief wash over his body like a baptism. This lawman was either the most trusting sheriff in the state or so naive that he completely mistook the bent over shape of a body for a pile of blankets. Either way, Patrick knew he was in the clear.

"You're absolutely right," he asserted, "I am so, so, so very sorry. I should have checked before I left. That's my fault."

"Now, don't beat yourself up too bad there, Pat," Jorgenson said, patting him on the back, "listen, I'm gonna let you off with a warning tonight, but just get the thing fixed, alright? Jesus, Mary, and Joseph, I just can't have another Timberbox Tammy on my hands."

"Thank you, officer. And will do it! You have my word," Patrick said as he walked back to the truck.

"Good to hear," Jorgenson said, "drive safe now!"

The 45 minutes felt like an eternity, but the lit-up Rockdale sign shone ahead. He took the back roads to avoid Main Street in case anyone was awake who could identify him. The clock on the dash read 1:49 a.m. as he cruised down a residential street. Rockdale was characteristically tame during the daytime, but the eerie stillness of the night only added to the feeling that this was some sort of nightmare Patrick was having. After making it to the funeral home, he drove to the back lot, shielding his car from any view from the street. Putting it in park, he took another deep breath, looked over at the corpse next to him, and sniffled.

On the floor of the passenger side was a near-empty 44-ounce container of Nesquik with a missing lid. Typically, he had a tall glass of Nesquik every morning as his pick-me-up,typically mixing it with the half-and-half in the break room fridge. He felt as though the smiling of the chocolate brown bunny on the container was mocking him as he stared into the rabbit's eyes.

"Yeah, go ahead and smile at my misfortune," he said to the container, "you furry, chocolatey asshole!"

With his nail-bitten thumb, he pressed the button on the seatbelt, which disconnected and caught on Colton's lifeless arm. Patrick got out of the car, walked around to the passenger side, and freed the body from the seatbelt as he lifted him like a bride being carried over the threshold.

Colton's limp neck and head tilted back and wrapped around Patrick's right bicep. They made their way to the back door of the crematorium, where Patrick again struggled to open the door with his keys while simultaneously balancing the body. He opened the door and locked it behind him.

He flipped on the lights to the crematorium, greeted by a mundane collage of beige, white, and chrome. Many of Patrick's family members assumed that his work was daunting. The stigma of a funeral home in a small town is often synonymous with gothic fantasies where vampiric people with eyeliner and slicked-back hair ceremoniously handle dead bodies in a sinister manner. The truth of it, however, is that it's rather peaceful and relaxed. One of Patrick's primary tasks in his three years working for Jill was getting familiar with the cremation process (this was also a process where he had plenty of downtime to listen to music and read whatever he wanted).

Patrick became familiar with this large room, which contained a variety of essential equipment for a small funeral home to properly cremate the remains of the deceased. In the north corner of the room was a large cooler that housed up to eight bodies of deceased individuals before the proper paperwork got filed prior to any cremation. Alongside the east wall were multiple mobile racks with thick cardboard boxes used in the cremation process. The empty boxes all had a lid that read 'HUMAN REMAINS HANDLE WITH RESPECT AND CARE' on a white cover over the top. And in the very center of the room was the massive chrome-covered machine, known as the retort, where the cremation would take place. Jill had privately nicknamed the machine "The Ash Tray."

The machine was a large metal rectangle with a primary chamber that was encased in solid concrete. At the front was a solid metal door bordered with chrome paneling. Patrick turned it on and adjusted the burner control on the panel to 1800°F. Given the multiple repairs to the heating coils, the preheating process usually took about an hour before reaching its optimal temperature.

Patrick set the body, along with the empty container, on the ground and grabbed one of the mobile carts. He removed the top of the remains box, staring at the inscription with tears in his eyes. Temporarily setting it on the ground, he lifted the body and placed it in the box. He waited the whole hour with his face in his hands as he sat hunched over on a folding chair in the corner. The temperature gauge read: 1792 °F. It was almost ready.

A pale Patrick stood up and walked over to the cardboard container. His body began shaking as he looked down at the contorted dead man, who, for the first time, looked as frail as an old set of fine china. Gazing upon him, he decided it was only right for him to say a few words on his behalf while the retort continued to heat up.

"Well, first off, I'm so, so, super sorry for all of this. I don't know you personally or why you decided to attack me, but I never meant for any of this to happen. I don't know if you were some secret agent, an assassin, or if I did something to provoke you...I like to think I'm a good guy— I pay my bills, I mind my own business, and I don't cook fish in shared spaces. I like to think that if you had gotten to know me, we could have been friends," Patrick said as a tear ran down his pale, freckled cheek. "You would have been all, 'Hey Patrick, you aren't so bad after all. You're one heck of a guy, in fact. Let's go uptown and grab some pizza sometime! My treat!' and I would have been all, 'Hell yeah, dude! I fuckin' love that shit!'" he sniffled some as tears continued to fall down his face. He put his hand to Colton's cheek and caressed it.

"But now that dream is gone...cuz' you're dead." He gripped the lid of the box and held it to his side. "My mom said once that if you don't forgive someone, you hurt yourself more than they hurt you. At the time, I thought she was just trying to calm me down while I was calling my grandpa out for cheating at Monopoly, but it turns out she's right. I forgive you for what happened and hope you forgive me, too. You didn't deserve to go out like this, and I pray that the gods–Ganesha, Vishnu, Brahma, and hell, even Shiva-form a kickass superhero team and make your next life just so awesome and stuff... Amen."

Patrick placed the cover on the container and shut it tightly. Pulling the cart over to the retort, he opened the door and aligned the rack with the fiery opening of the primary chamber. He pushed the container forward and placed it inside, shutting the door behind it. The green 'DOOR SHUT' light lit up, as did the red 'DOOR LOCK' light. The clock on the wall read 3:01. Patrick fell to the floor and started sobbing in the fetal position.

Racing through his mind were images of this man's family crying as a search team looked for his remains. They would never know that his ashes would be at the bottom of a river, lost forever. The burden of his crime would likely weigh on him for the rest of his days. He thought about whether or not he could be traced back to the apartment, and if so, would Ms. Melstad rat him out to the police? Would his word be strong enough against hers if he denied it and claimed that she was a senile old lady? His apartment was probably crawling with DNA evidence that could place this man in the apartment. It would require a deep cleaning that would put laboratory standards to shame.

As he cradled himself, the adrenaline wore off, stress took its toll, and he drifted asleep. Two hours and fifty-five minutes passed before he was woken up by a loud hallway door slamming outside the room. Patrick quickly picked himself up and dusted off his shirt. In walked Jill, holding her forest green coffee thermos that belonged to her father during his military days in her hand. A surprised look manifested on both of their faces as they locked eyes.

"Well, you're certainly up bright and early, Pat," Jill observed with a delighted smile, "I don't usually see you until 9:00."

Patrick stood there sweating and frightened, yet trying his best to stay composed.

"Ha...yeah. I just thought I would get everything ready for the busy day today," he said, with a forced grin as he turned his back toward the cremator, the echo of the flames rattled in the machine.

"Did we have another cremation scheduled for today? I thought the only one we had this week was the Veitch one," she questioned, gesturing to the machine.

"No!" Patrick yelled, startling Jill.

He quickly collected himself and tightened his posture. "I mean, no. Sorry, we do not have another one scheduled for today."

Jill looked at the man as if his nose had just fallen off his face.

"So why is the retort running, Pat?" she asked pointedly.

He was trapped like a baby gazelle in the lion's den. Like the police, there was no way she was going to believe his story, he thought. And even if she did, he was using company property to get rid of a body. She would surely alert the authorities in order to clear herself of any wrongdoing. Potential lies ran through his mind like a world-class relay track team.

"I...I came back here to move a few things and had my coffee with me-because I'm not a morning person like you said-and well, I tripped and spilled it all over one of the cremation trays," he said, wiping his forehead, which was now caked in perspiration.

"Pat, you spilled coffee on an empty cardboard container, and your first instinct is to just burn it in the crematorium?" she replied.

"Yeah, well I...I figured that someone shouldn't be cremated in a coffee-stained cremation tray-at least, I know I wouldn't want to be cremated in a coffee-stained cremation tray-because it seems like someone would say, ya know, 'Don't go to those friggin' jerks down at Grinager Funeral Home! They're so sloppy that they burned my mom in a box covered in Folgers. She didn't even like the taste of coffee!' so I decided to get rid of it. But I didn't want you to find one just lying around in the dumpster either because, ya know, that would look wasteful and stuff. So, ya know, long story short, I just decided to burn it."

Jill walked past him and sat her thermos down on the end table. She took out a cigarette from the pack resting in her shirt pocket, placed it in her mouth, and lit it with her Zippo lighter. She sat down in the fold-out chair and peered over her glasses, giving a curious stare at Patrick.

"How would someone know that their mom was being cremated in a coffee-stained tray?" she asked before taking an inhale off of her cigarette.

Patrick continued to sweat as he stood with a nervous grimace, looking like a pasty snowman melting on the first day of spring. Just then, the machine timed out and gave a thudding noise, which meant the cooldown process was starting.

"The smell?" he asked softly, the words barely finding their way out of his throat to create an even more confused look on her face.

"The smell?" she asked with bewilderment, "Like a coffee smell? You think someone is going to jump to that conclusion because the ashes might smell like coffee?"

"Yeah, no, when you say it like that, I can see how I didn't really think it through all the way. I'm... I'm sorry. I just wasn't thinking, I guess," he deduced, feeling like, at any moment, everything would fall apart.

Jill paused and twirled her cigarette between her fingers while maintaining eye contact. She took another deep drag and then blew the smoke out of her nostrils. She leaned back in the chair, stretching her legs against the solid concrete floors of the cool, dull room.

"Alright," she said, shaking her head in disbelief, "just maybe tell me next time when something like that happens. Those boxes aren't cheap, but accidents happen, I guess."

"Will do," he agreed, as his rapid heart rate decelerated, "sorry about that; I just panicked."

"It's fine," she added, taking in another inhale, "one of the perks of this job is that the dead don't complain a whole lot when they see you mess up, right?"

"Ha ha ha ha, yeah," Patrick replied with fake laughter. "That's good. I'm going to start using that one!"

Jill smiled and opened the top of her thermos, the cigarette still between her fingers. She picked it up and took a hearty swig despite the fact that the coffee was still a little too hot, burning her tongue slightly. She set it back down and wiped the corners of her mouth with the back of her wrist.

"You can use it anytime," she said with a wink. "How were your friends, by the way?"

"Friends?" Patrick asked, flustered, initially forgetting the lie he told to cover up his lobster-LEGO entanglement. "Oh, right! My friends. Well...I canceled. I ended up just having a totally boring, non-eventful night at home."

"Ah, that sucks. I'm sorry, Patrick," Jill chimed, putting the cigarette in her mouth and patting his tensed-up shoulder with her hand. "Better no plans at all than the horrible date I had."

"Oh, did it not go well?" he asked as he nervously looked at the cooldown timer.

"It did at first, but the guy turned out to be a real psycho," she replied as she sat back down in the chair, releasing a defeated sigh. "Patrick, do you ever just get the sense that sometimes people aren't who they say they are?"

Nervous that she was on to him, Patrick took another step back toward the retort.

"Which people are you talking about, Jill?" he replied, silently gulping to himself, his eyes widening with fear.

She shifted in her chair, temporarily placing her weight on the knot in her shirt sleeve that rubbed against the bottom of her residual limb.

"All people, really. At least to some degree," she retorted, "I mean, it just seems like we all tell ourselves it's going to be okay, that we're normal, and that we need to just bury every flaw we have in order to appease others or capitalize on a big break. We do all of that instead of trying to fix what's broken underneath. No matter who gets hurt along the way, we keep up the facade because the truth is too real...and the worst of the worst will just about burn anybody in order to get ahead."

Patrick turned his back and pretended to tinker with the retort control panel. He wasn't sure yet whether or not Jill was on to him, but he would have to continue to act nonchalantly just in case. Jill took another long, slow drag from her smoke and stared out blankly as if Patrick wasn't even in the room.

"And maybe I'm to blame, too," she continued. "For Christ's sake, I allow my nephew to literally pretend to be someone different every day. How hypocritical is that? But then again, I still feel like I know who he is. I still know his heart is good, no matter how many times he struts through this building in one of his costumes. I still feel like there's truth to him in some strange, convoluted way. But then again, maybe it's better to be stuck with some strange, convoluted truth than live a convenient lie," she said, taking her last puff and then ashing the cigarette out on the table tray.

Patrick turned back to look at her eyes, which remained lost, deep in thought. He paused to think about his own lie, knowing that it would likely be one he would have to live with for the rest of his days.

"I don't know, though; I've just been thinking about it a lot lately. That's probably more than what you wanted out of a question about my evening," she said with a laugh, getting up from her chair.

"No, that's okay...I totally get what you mean," Patrick added, fully deducing that her ramblings weren't targeted at him.

Just then, the timer on the cooldown went off, and the green 'COMPLETE' light turned on. The cremator noise reduced from a dull roar to its idle, quiet rattle.

"Well, I'll leave you to it," Jill exclaimed. "Thanks for the chat, Pat. You oughta come in early more often! This felt like a good little therapy session."

"Ha...yeah...any time," he replied, "hey, I also forgot my dress clothes at home. Could I go and grab them real quick?"

"No problem, Pat," she said, giving him a friendly pat on the shoulder. "Just make sure everything is set up for the wake."

As she exited the room, the heavy door shut tightly behind her. In a panic, Patrick opened the chrome doors of the retort. Pulling out the metal catch tray at the base of the doors, the remains and brittle fragments lay bare. He brought the tray over to the cremulator, a large cylindrical machine that pulverizes the remains in order to reduce everything to ash. After inserting the tray, he flipped the switch and watched as the remains were quickly sucked in, listening to the spinning rattle of the machine as it compacted everything down. The cremulator only took about 90 seconds before the job was finished.

The remains would be collected inside a vacuum-sealed plastic bag after processing. After returning the tray to the retort, he ran to the other side of the room to retrieve the broom in the storage closet, just in case he needed to sweep anything outside the door. His heart began racing again as he leaned against the door frame. There were only a couple of times in his life where Patrick could remember being in this much of a panicked rush: once to the emergency room when he thought he was having a heart attack (which turned out to be bad indigestion), and once when he heard a rumor that the rare Bubbles the Fish Beanie Baby was for sale at Toys 'R' Us (it wasn't). Both occurrences happened last October.

Internally defeated, he walked over to the container of ashes and picked it up. Though he had been present for hundreds of cremations, the anomalous act of reducing someone into ash after accidentally killing them turned his stomach to knots. But soon, these ashes would be tossed into the river. They would be gone, there would be no evidence, and he could start to heal. After all, this wasn't his fault; this was a man who broke into his home and tried to kill him, followed by a series of bizarre, unbelievable circumstances that would have landed him behind bars for the rest of his life.

The retort timer went off, and the ashes were dispensed inside the plastic bag. He grabbed it, turned the machine off, and sprinted out of the building. Pacing toward his car, minding the ice below his feet as he tightly gripped the vacuum-sealed bag of ashes, he approached his passenger door and opened it. Just then, out of the corner of his eye, he saw Pastor Anna heading toward him from across the street.

"Well, if it isn't the lovely Mr. Loveland on a lovely Wednesday morning!" she exclaimed, walking toward him from across the parking lot with her scarlet parka coat bundled all the way up. "How's it going today, hon?"

A visibly flustered Patrick then slipped on an ice patch, causing his glasses and the bag of ashes to fly up and land against the pavement, tearing it open completely. The wind scattered ashes as Patrick frantically located his glasses and put them back on his head. He looked down to see that half the ashes were gone with the wind, along with the plastic bag, as the others remained in a clump on the ground. Still lying on the ground, he saw Anna's feet walking toward him from the view underneath the car. In a quick-thinking moment of consternation, he reached for the Nesquik container on the passenger side floor and clumsily scooped the remaining ashes into it, along with snow, gravel, and dirt.

"Are you alright there, Pat?" Anna asked as she made her way around the vehicle, "You took quite a tumble there."

"I'm fine!" he yelped as he picked himself up with the container. "It's all good; I just slipped. I better keep a better watch over this ice!"

The disheveled man squealed a nervous, high-pitched laugh as he put the container behind his back. She crept closer to him like a child who was unaware of the dangerous situation in front of her.

"Ain't that the truth? I couldn't tell you how many times I've fallen on my keister this year alone," she confessed, giving a pat to her backside.

"It's been that kind of winter, I 'spose," he quipped, shutting his car door. "Anywho, I gotta get going! Good seeing you, Pastor An—"

"—Before you do, I gotta tell you about my conversation the other day with Ruth Plaschke over at Willow Fields— who is just the nicest gal there is, by the way— and I says, 'Ruth, I know a really good guy in town who I think you oughta get sweet on,' and she says 'who's that?' and I says, 'Pat Loveland. He's a heck of a hard worker and a pretty great guy. And gosh darn it, Ruth, he's a catch if there ever was one.' And then I says, 'I know it's gonna be a good day in the church if Pat's around to help me,'" she explained, grinning.

Patrick, still faking a smile and digging for his keys, began nodding his head.

"Oh geez, that was awfully kind of you, Pastor Anna," he noted, trapped like an animal.

"And then she says, 'Well, I'll think about it some, Anna,' and I says, 'Look, there's no sense waiting on Prince Charming to swoop you off your feet,' and she says, 'Oh, I don't want ya to think I'm not happy.' and I says, 'Ruth, I don't want to put ya out or nothin', but he's quite a guy!' and she says, 'well, I'll think about it.' and I says, 'Well, I'll let him know you're thinking about it.'," she replied.

"That's very nice of ya, Pastor Anna. I'll be sure to give her a call sometime," he said, finally locating his keys and taking them out of his pocket.

"Oh Pat, that makes me so happy to hear! I think the two of you would make a better duo than leftovers and bingo night," she added, her eyes diverting to the container behind his back. "What's that you're hiding back there, Pat?"

"Oh, it's nothing," he said, sweating bullets as she looked around him.

"Well, I'll be a son of a gun, Patrick Loveland, you remembered!" she exclaimed, her voice reaching the excitement of a surprise birthday party.

Dumbfounded, Patrick looked down at the Nesquik container.

"My ashes for Ash Wednesday! You remembered! Oh, bless your heart, Pat," she exclaimed, taking the container from his hand. "Goodness gracious, I would've been in a pinch if you hadn't. The whole thing just completely slipped my mind! You can tell I've been giving sermons about the afterlife because, boy, have I had my head in the clouds lately," she said, grabbing the container out of his hands. "The palms must've been a special breed, cus' the color is much more gray than I remember...but I'll take what I can get!"

She began to rub Colton's ashes between her pointer finger and thumb as if it were talcum powder.

"P-Pastor Anna, those—"

She cut off Patrick's sentence before he could even drum up an explanation.

"—Pat, you're gonna be my first Ash Wednesday blessing of the day," she said, dipping her fingers further into the container.

With her two fingers, she took the remains and made the sign of the cross on the sweaty forehead of a stunned Patrick, whose mouth lay wide open.

"Remember, you are dust, and to dust you shall return," she recited as an ashy cross laid bare above his glasses. "Wow, what a great way to start the morning! Thank you so much, hon; I really appreciate ya!"

He stood speechless as he watched her cross the street and walk into the church. The keys fell out of his hand and onto the ground as if he had just been zapped by a petrifying bolt of lightning.

Chapter 11

Hard Headed Woman

The 7:00 a.m. alarm beeped like a cicada in apartment 306. A dazed Vicky woke up next to a half-empty bottle of merlot, dressed in her laced lingerie bustier set with adjustable garter straps and nylon stockings. Smeared makeup that she forgot to take off from the night before complimented the bed head that popped up to the sounds of the buzzing. She turned off the alarm and looked to her right to see that Colton still wasn't in the room. It was unlike Colton to pass up on a night of passion with Vicky, which left her bewildered at his whereabouts. He better have gotten that horse, she thought.

She didn't have time to waste dwelling on it. Picking herself off the bed, she walked out of the bedroom and into the living room space. The knick-knacks and travel photos that used to grace the walls and interior were gone, leaving nothing but a burgundy leather sofa that Vicky's parents insisted the leasing office dispose of on the claim of arthritis in Roy's knee. Conveniently, Roy would use the same excuse as a last resort when berating waiters for not applying a senior discount.

Vicky made her way into the bathroom, where she showered, reapplied her makeup, blow-dried, and curled her hair. She looked at herself in the mirror, parting her lips as she applied lipstick. The large yellow duffle bag on the bathroom floor contained her fur coat, which looked like two coyotes linked together to form a lapel on top of leather fabric. She put on her tanned leather chaps over her designer jeans, draping all but the toes of her white cowgirl boots. This was complete with a double holster belt, which held her .38

Special on her right side and, on the left, the crown jewel of the outfit: the Red Baron's gun. She put on her woven cowgirl hat with a leather band that was decorated with a golden cross and adjusted it in the mirror.

"You've got mass appeal, baby," she purred at her reflection.

As she made her way toward the door, she saw her red pickup and trailer sitting in the parking lot through the apartment window overlooking the parking lot. Breathing a sigh of relief at the sight, she grabbed the duffle bag and walked out the door. As she exited the building, Frosty's muffled neighing could be heard coming from the inside of the isolated trailer.

"Woah! Woah!" she said, running up to one of the small openings in the trailer, "It's okay, boy. It's okay."

The horse's eyes looked out of the slot at her, and he gave a dissatisfied snort but stopped neighing. After calming him down, Vicky approached the front vehicle and noticed that Colton wasn't inside, but the keys were. That's strange, she thought. Even more strange was the fact that the leather bodysuit she had dry-cleaned for him was also missing from the backseat.

"Why would he take that but not show up to the room?" she said aloud.

She deduced the possibilities in her head. He could have gotten arrested for stealing the horse, she thought, causing her heart to sink into her stomach. But as she dwelled on it some more, surely she would have seen and heard the commotion through the window. Surely, the horse would have been returned or at least inquired about. Colton would not be one to be arrested without shouting, and at the very least, she would have seen or heard police sirens.

Could he have been kidnapped? No, she thought. Even if powerful men in government wanted to track down his whereabouts to seek revenge for their destroyed marriages, it didn't explain the missing leather suit. There was also no other change of clothes in the car, so changing into the suit and then getting kidnapped seemed out of the realm of possibility as well.

There was only one explanation that made sense when it came to the disappearance of her sex-addicted advisor: he was sleeping with another woman, she thought. Maybe he picked up some trashy blonde at a local dive bar and recruited her help with Frosty, riding away in her car after the horse was delivered. Maybe he dropped off the horse and decided to visit an old hookup, thinking Vicky would never catch on. Or maybe, just maybe, he was inside the apartments right now, lying naked next to some lonely stranger he wooed in the parking lot after she was curious about the horse. All seemed possible when it came to the most likely explanations.

"That little weasel shit..." Vicky growled to herself as she seethed with jealous rage.

She revved up the engine of the car and hightailed it out of the parking lot, going so fast that the suspension on the trailer was being tested.

"Who does he think he is?!" she shouted alone in the pickup, "He would be nothing without me! Nothing!

Now he's trading a night with me for some big-haired, backwater floozy?"

Vicky gripped the wheel tightly, her gloves serving as a barrier between her fingernails and the leather. This fit of rage continued throughout the thirty-minute commute to the family cabin as she started to emasculate the man who wasn't there. She was so distracted that she didn't realize she was on the shoulder of the road. She immediately slammed on the brakes, nearly veering off into a ditch. Frosty neighed loudly in disapproval from the trailer. She closed her eyes, took a breath, and decided it was best to compartmentalize the situation for now.

The turn into the Chengwatana State Forest from the highway meant entering a narrow gravel road that went on for five miles before one reached the cabin's driveway. On each side of the road, barren white cedars looked like the landscape pulled straight from the mind of Edgar Allan Poe. Half the ground was covered in snow mixed in with hard, blackened soil. The cabin itself, however, was a warm hug by comparison.

When pulling into the driveway, the lights of the timber frame cabin greeted visitors from its wraparound porch. The trees left spacious room in the front yard, decorated with polished stones that served as a border for the front garden. The charcoal shingles on the roof complemented the light brown of the surrounding wood. Chimes hung next to an engraved wooden plaque that read "Veitch." To the right of the front steps, a pile of firewood sat covered with an ax leaning against the front. Fifty meters behind the back patio was the hideaway, frozen-over Pokegama Lake. It stretched for roughly a mile, with cedar-covered hills on its horizon.

Vicky made her way down the driveway and watched as Ethan and Peter waved at her from the front of the porch. The reporter stood about 5'5" and wore an unbuttoned red and black plaid shirt with rolled-up sleeves. His thick black hair had a middle part that formed an 'M' shape with his bangs, a pencil poking out from atop his ear. Draped over Peter's shoulder was his camera strap, with a lens attachment that looked like a small telescope. Tucked away under his right arm was a thick red spiral notepad with a pen clamped to the front. Remembering her compartmentalization, she took a breath, put on a smile, and waved back.

"Well, if this isn't a Minnesota morning, I don't know what is," she remarked as she exited the truck.

"Representative Veitch. Peter York, *Time Magazine*. My condolences about Bud," he said as he walked toward her and extended his hand.

Meeting it with her own, she calculated the firmness in her mind. This was a coaching exercise she went over with Colton (something they incorporated into their foreplay routine). A dead fish handshake conveyed weakness, but being overly aggressive could lead his writing to present her as too hawkish, she thought. She settled on firm enough to crunch a pop can but brief enough to avoid awkwardness.

"It's a pleasure to meet you, Peter. And, thank you. Bud might be gone, but his memory lives strong in this rancher girl," she said, counting to three in her head before letting go of his hand, "and welcome to the wild, winter wilderness of Minnesota! I hope the cold isn't getting to you already."

"Oh, trust me, I'll take the cold over the humid D.C. summers any day," he replied.

"Well, if that isn't just the god's honest truth," she concurred, putting her hands to her hips, "my apologies for being late, by the way. I'm sure Ethan here has told you that while I am a morning person, I'm also a bit of a perfectionist and have to make sure every little detail is checked off my list before diving into action."

Ethan perked up like a prairie dog popping out of his burrow.

"Representative Veitch is the most detailed person I've ever known. She leaves no stone unturned, no detail unnoticed, with energy that would put marathon runners to shame. She—"

"—Thank you, Ethan," she inserted dismissively. "That's quite the camera you've got there, Peter!"

Peter pulled down on the strap and held the camera in his hands. He twisted the very front of the lens out of habit.

"Thank you. I think we're going to get some fantastic photos out of it today!" he said bashfully. "Is that guy in the trailer the trusty steed Ethan was telling me about? I think getting some shots of you trotting around on him is a fantastic idea."

"It sure is!" she belted, forcing a smile. "I hope old Frosty isn't too cranky about the commute this morning."

Vicky walked over to the back of the trailer, genuinely hoping with all of her heart that the horse had finally calmed down. This entire facet would come undone if the stallion decided to barrel her over. She quietly hushed him from the opening in the back, holding out a Werther's caramel she had in her pocket. The horse sniffed it and then collected it in his mouth. Frosty grunted and then dipped his head down. She opened the back of the trailer slowly, bracing herself to be trampled.

As the gate opened, Frosty stood still and calm. He walked out slowly, allowing Vicky to take the reins in her hand and lead him over to the reporter.

"That's a good boy," she said, "say hello to Peter...you can go on and pet him if you'd like."

She completely gambled on that assumption but decided that she chose right after Peter gave a pat on the side of the horse's head without any trouble.

"Man, what a pretty coat," he noted. "I can tell you take great care of him."

"Oh, yes," she replied, "when you live the ranch life like we do, you have to treat your animals as if they are extensions of ourselves."

"That's a great sentiment to have," he replied. "If you don't mind, could you ride with him some? I hope there's enough space here."

"Oh, it's no trouble at all, Peter," she said, putting her boot in the left stirrup and nearly losing her balance, given the weight of her outfit.

She wobbled noticeably and nearly fell straight onto her back before correcting it and positioning herself atop the horse. Frosty began a gentle trot like a well-trained equestrian, demonstrating its capabilities for the judges. It was as if she herself was manifesting the movements within the horse. Peter began squatting into position to snap photo after photo, a shuttering sound made with each press of the button. Though she knew nothing of photography, the premonition she had told her that these shots were as good as gold.

"Fantastic!" he announced as he relaxed the camera once more. "Those are going to look stunning."

"I love to hear it!" she said, getting off of the horse and gripping the reins.

She walked it over to Ethan while handing the horse over to him.

"Do you have my talking points?" she asked in a sharp whisper.

"I'm so sorry, ma'am," Ethan replied in a whimpering whisper. "I...had something unexpected come up last night. But I can—"

"You don't have them?" she quipped, her eyes glowing like hot coals.

"No, but I promise that I can—"

She cut him off sharply, her voice in a quiet, piercing whisper, but her face reflected a sharp scream.

"—So now I've got to *wing* this whole thing and put on a show like I'm P.T. goddamn Barnum?" she hissed, "Typical."

Peter was still off by the trailer, patiently waiting for Vicky to return. Although he couldn't hear them, the deductive investigator could sense a bit of tension between the staffer and the office holder.

"We can take a quick break if you two need it," he offered.

"Oh, nonsense!" she suspired with a fake laugh. "We were just going over the...history of one of Bud's prized possessions."

She went to her truck and pulled out the duffle bag containing the container with Bud's antique pistol. She carefully took it out and held it in her hands as if she were presenting him with a fragile baby chick.

"This pistol belonged to the Red Baron during World War I. It was gifted to him during his time in the White House. Bud was definitely a champion for the Second Amendment, and I believe in my heart of hearts that I match that same ferocity he had for one of our most sacred rights."

His eyes widened as they zeroed in on the German firearm. While it took him off guard, it was certainly a pleasant surprise in terms of content.

"Oh wow," he said, "that's...something for sure."

"Maybe we could get a few photos of me holding it? You know what they say: side arms are a girl's best friend," she proclaimed.

"I think we could definitely tie that in–especially given its historical connection. Sure," he said, readjusting the camera lens.

"Fantastic!" she exclaimed proudly as she held it up.

"Alright, if I could get you to turn your back away from the cabin and more toward the East," he instructed, holding the camera up to his face and directing her with his free hand.

She turned her body around and held up the gun in her best James Bond pose, with all the look of Grizzly Adams. A frown would be too heartless, but a full-blown smile would look psychotic, she thought. She settled on a subtle, soft grin out of the corner of her mouth with one raised eyebrow. It said, *"I probably won't shoot, but I definitely could,"* she thought.

"Perfect," he said. "Excellent shots all around."

"You're a natural, Representative Veitch!" Ethan chimed in.

She ignored him while maintaining a look that exuded distilled confidence. Peter went back to his notepad, crossed something out with his pen, and ran his hand through his hair.

"Now for the hardballs," he said with a diffusing laugh.

"Bring 'em on, Pete," she replied, "I'm ready for ya!"

Peter made his way to the top of the note page. He licked his lips and rubbed his nose to counteract the itchy feel of the dry winter air.

"So Representative Veitch, your name has not only been tossed out there for a potential Senate run but is also on some short lists for Vice President in the upcoming election. What makes you stand out in either field?" he asked.

"Well, Peter, first off, I'm focused on my current position and my duty to those who voted for the principles I bring to Washington. I remain focused on the present, and that hasn't changed since day one," she admitted, brushing one of her hair extensions off the shoulder of her coat. "But the reason I think these rumors are happening is because people want someone who is going to speak the truth. They want someone who will fight for them at the highest levels of the government. Someone who holds the same family values as they do and wants to put more money in their paycheck. It's called freedom, and it's worked for us since the very founding of this country."

Peter quickly scribbled down as much of the quote as humanly possible before licking his fingers to turn the page.

"Excellent. So you are previously on record saying that you want to see Congress pass a nationwide law banning free and reduced school lunch— this is also corroborated by a concerted effort by you in the legislature— do you believe that a policy idea like that will resonate with working families, not only in Minnesota but throughout the country?"

A trembling occurred in her stomach. Colton's absence was not only a blow to her ego but a strategic error. Now, she was forced to resort to her own political instincts-a gamble as risky as trusting an unfamiliar horse. She was nothing if not coachable, but winging it was not her preferred method. Nevertheless, she pushed on.

"Well, like the great Milton Friedman once said, there's no such thing as a free lunch. Someone's gotta pay for it. And that someone is often the everyday worker who is getting money taken out of their paycheck to pay for some welfare queen's child to get fed at school. My bill simply takes an extra burden off of families who know it's a myth that it takes a village to raise a child. It takes responsibility, Peter. Personal responsibility. And personal responsibility can't happen if you don't have personal freedom over your own money."

Nailed it, she thought. But the test wasn't over yet. As she watched him scribble down the words on his pad, she looked over to Ethan with concerned eyes needing affirmation. He gave her the thumbs up out of Peter's line of sight. She smiled to herself.

"So, to follow up with that, what is your replacement plan for these programs? Do you think forcing children of low-income families to go hungry is ethical?" he pressed on, looking directly into her eyes.

Deflect. That's the word that immediately came to her mind. Colton always said that the best strategy when facing a pressing question was to deflect, attack, and turn it back on its head. It was the key to never having to answer anything while simultaneously addressing everything.

"Now, Peter, I think that's making a mountain out of a molehill here. I know you folks in the media like dressing up your stories, but there's no reason to push your own conclusion off a slippery slope," she retorted, buying herself time to think.

She made eye contact with Ethan, standing behind the reporter, waiting for him to speak or signal anything to her. Seeing the distress in her eyes, he shrugged his shoulders and looked around as if he were being chased. The only thing he could think of doing popped into his mind, and he made a pretend sweeping motion with his arms. Confused at first, Vicky took a moment to put it together. Then, it hit her.

"...What I'm simply proposing is instilling the value of hard work in our kids. The American people have been pulling themselves up by their bootstraps for generations. Why can't our children follow suit? My solution is this: any child who cannot afford a meal will assist the janitorial staff in cleaning before school in order to receive a meal. We'll call it "Sweeping the Nation." That way, our youth will develop an appreciation and understanding of hard work. Not government handouts," she responded, folding her arms to nail the dismount.

Vicky felt as if she had snapped the tape across the finish line of a track race. Like a prized fighter telegraphing the moves of the champion across from her, she felt as if she could go as many rounds as it took. She pulled no punches and stood squarely on her feet. Luckily for her, she had gotten through the worst of it. Peter rounded out the interviews with questions about her upbringing, her relationship with her family, and all she envisioned for her time in office. She proceeded to embellish all of it in a masterclass of political theater.

"Sweeping...the...nation," he mumbled as he finished scribbling in his notebook. "Well, that's all I think I have for you, Representative Veitch. I think this is going to turn into a remarkable profile piece."

"Well, that was quick and painless!" she trumpeted, giving him a friendly pat on the back while giving Ethan a discreet first pump.

He opened the car door to his airport rental car to stow away his camera. "As I let you know when we first made contact, this piece was originally going to be about dynastic politics, given your relationship with Bud. Although I would have loved to interview him as well, I think getting a feel for his life and legacy from his friends and family can still really piece that together. It's still not too invasive to have me at the wake, is it?" he asked tepidly.

"Oh, not at all!" she exclaimed. "Bud would have insisted on it, Peter. I just wish he could have seen what you ended up writing."

"Me too," he said with a smile. "I'll see you over at the funeral home then?"

"You sure will," she replied.

As Peter drove away down the narrow driveway and onto the road that would lead him back to the highway, Ethan and Vicky continued waving until he was out of sight. Once the vehicle was no longer visible on the horizon, they embraced each other and started jumping joyously. The victorious hollerings they shouted out echoed amongst the trees.

"That's how you do it! That is how you do it, Representative Veitch! I just witnessed a masterclass, ma'am," he said, sucking up to feed the ego in front of him.

"No, Ethan— that's how *we* do it!" she said, gripping him on the shoulders like a proud coach of her little league star player. "When Peter York puts me in Time Magazine, and our movement takes off like a rocket, I want you, Ethan Bile, to remember who helped make it happen. I can't do this without your help."

It was at this moment that Ethan Bile felt a sensational rush of pride so foreign to him that he would try to deny it citizenship. He would buy more copies of Time than all of the dentist's offices in the state combined. Visions of it hanging framed in his future office (next to his degree from Hillsdale and a signed photo of him and Newt Gingrich) became a thought he wished would stay forever. Finally, he could go home for the holidays and proudly show his dad evidence of his achievements. He smiled as he imagined his dad patting him on the back and bringing out the fine glassware to treat themselves and unwind with some sparkling soda.

"You're too good to me, Representative Veitch," he chirped, nearly choking up. "You have my solemn word that I will always give you everything I've got to fight alongside you and stop this new wave of cultural communists from taking over our way of life."

"Yeah, that's great, Ethan. Thanks," she said dismissively, like someone wanting to get off the phone with their rambling grandparent. "But did you see his eyes when I told him this gun belonged to the Red Baron? It was like I pulled the Holy Grail out of my holster! The moment he writes about that, we're going to have more campaign contributions from the NRA than we know what to do with."

She pulled out the antique pistol and held it in her hands, looking down at it like it was a newborn infant. Gratification poured over her, knowing that her political instincts were correct, withholding the gun for this moment.

Bud would be so proud. He would most certainly applaud her for shoring up a demographic of voters with a simple move.

"A beautiful woman on a horse who arms herself and proudly shows off a gun collector's dream?" he'd say. "That's the kind of woman who can get votes from a guy like me!"

She smiled as she ran her fingers along the grooves of the barrel.

"It was a brilliant call, ma'am! Beyond brilliant!" Ethan said, clamping his hands together like a scheming rodent. "I have to hand it to Colton on the horse idea as well. I think those photos are going to look monumental!"

"To hell with Colton," she sputtered, scrunching her face in an annoyed grimace.

"Ma'am? What happened?" Ethan asked, faking concern but feeling as if his fortune just kept getting better.

"Don't worry about it," she said curtly. "Let's just say he's no longer welcome to serve in our vision."

The raw pain in Ethan's crotch temporarily subsided as he found himself gaining favor with the person he coveted the most. In 24 hours, he had experienced the lowest of the lows and was now riding the highest of the highs. The serendipity he felt was almost too poetic to feel contrived. It was as if he was a pencil-necked Bolshevik grunt who just got to witness the execution of a superior who pissed off Stalin, raising his status. The sly grin of a cartoon cat overtook his face.

"But yes," she concluded, holding the pistol at her left side while approaching the unhitched, subdued Frosty, "I will give Colton credit for setting us up for a perfect photo-op."

"Isn't that right, sweet boy?" she said in baby talk as she gave an open-hand pat on the horse's side.

Like a firework going off unexpectedly nearby, when a horse gets spooked, one is immediately made aware of it. Frosty, the snow horse, was no exception. With a piercing screech and his front legs raised, the horse stood tall, looking to squash Vicky right then and there. The congresswoman began to fall backward; her limbs extended, falling away from the horse's bodily trajectory. As she hit the ground, the Red Baron's pistol discharged, letting out a thunderous bang that echoed throughout the woods. The noise caused Frosty to shriek once more and then sprint southbound at a lightning pace until he vanished entirely.

Vicky lay on her back atop the snowy ground, dropping the gun that felt hot in her hand. Disoriented, she stared at the sky as her ears rang from the unexpected shot. She started to collect herself, reaching for her cowgirl hat on her right side.

"What in the shit?!" she shouted, grabbing the gun again. "This damn thing was loaded this whole time?!"

The eeriness of the silence that followed her shouting crept in on her like the freezing touch of an unexpected hand. It was odd that she didn't hear a reply from Ethan. Even more odd was the fact that her token suck-up wasn't rushing to help her up. He was there with a box of tissues if she had so much as a sneeze and a sniffle. A cold, pale feeling rushed over her body as if her blood flow had halted entirely. Before she turned her body over, her instincts delivered a premonition to her mind that spelled out what she was going to see. She rolled over to see the boots of the staffer and a pool of blood forming around him.

"No, no, no!" she screamed as she picked herself up and dashed over to him. "Ethan!"

She looked down to see a perfect circular bloody bullet hole, just one inch below the bangs of his bowl cut, between two open eyes that stared off into nothingness. She fell to her buckling knees beside him, fear filling her empty stomach. As cold beads of sweat momentarily dripped down her neck, she looked around at the trees surrounding her as if they were witnesses judging her. Vicky put her hands together on the center of his chest and started hopelessly performing compressions to the tune of "Stayin' Alive" by the Bee Gees.

"Ah, ah, ah, ah, stayin' alive! Stayin' alive! Ah, ah, ah, ah, stayin' alive! Stayin' alive! Don't do this to me, Ethan! Don't you fucking die on me! Ah, ah, ah, ah, stayin' alive! Stayin' alive!" she yelled as she continued to push down on the corpse that was growing paler by the second.

Reality set in. The insides of Vicky's gloves were drenched in sweat and shaking uncontrollably. She looked down with a whimper and looked at the lifeless face of the staffer she once knew.

"Fuck!" she screamed at the top of her lungs, rivaling the gunshot, as she beat her fists on Ethan's chest.

Heavy tears began to flow. With a shaky inhale, she covered her face with her hands. Vicky tugged hard on the front of his shirt with both hands, the dead body flopping helplessly in the air. Letting go, the corpse hit the ground with a thud, the eyes still with an unwavering stare. She began to collect the surrounding rocks, stood up, and began throwing them at the nearest tree, crying hysterically.

"I'm ruined...oh, God, I'm so fucking ruined!" she shouted as she heaved one of the jagged rocks against the trunk. "Why the hell is this happening to me?!"

She looked over at the corpse through her teary eyes, wiping them off her face with her glove. Like a rapidly rising thermometer, she became heated as her eyes transformed from sadness to rage.

"This is all your fault, you sneaky son of a bitch…" she affirmed, slowly taking a couple of steps forward. "After all we worked for…you had to get in my way and do this? You bumbling, bowl-cut bastard!"

Vicky picked up more of the rocks and began launching them at Ethan's lifeless body, exhuming an exasperated grunt with every throw.

"They're going to make me resign! And-and I'll have to do a fucking press conference, and instead of a profile, they're going to write about whether or not I should be in jail! All because of you!" she said, making contact against his right shoulder with a gray stone.

"You hear me? I'm fucking ruined!" she yelled, whipping another stone but missing the body entirely.

Instead, the rock hit the hilt of the ax leaning against the pile of chopped firewood by the deck, causing it to fall over. Dropping the rocks in her hand, she walked over to the ax and picked it up. It still had a shiny red shimmer to its sharp blade; Vicky remembered that Grant had just gotten a new one last August when they treated NRA Chairman Wayne LaPierre and his fiancé to a weekend getaway-a connection Bud arranged himself. How she wished Bud was still here. She knew that, unlike his son, a man like Bud would know what to do in this situation in order to salvage everything they worked so hard to build. Nothing was more important. Nothing could supplement the feeling of a promising future.

An epiphany came to her like a beam of sunlight on a cloudy day. It was one that would allow Bud to invigorate her political career one last time. The procession. Looking down at the ax, she thought of all the episodes of Dateline that she watched while snuggled up to Colton in a hotel bed. The show was never meant to be an instructional video, but the circumstances necessitated it. Knowing there was no time to waste, she walked up to the body. She removed her boots and socks and rolled up the bottoms of her pants as she tip-toed around the pool of blood and to the left side of his leg. She pressed the blade against the left arm and took a deep inhale.

Chapter 12

Are You Lonesome Tonight?

Through the woods, three and a half miles to the east, Randall practiced a fusion of sword swings and karate. He snuck into Jill's late last night after karaoke and left early in the morning, both without saying a word to her. Randall's current Elvis attire was the famous white rhinestone jumpsuit. The skin-tight spectacle came bedazzled with golden suns, golden studs on the shoulders and arms, an open-button scarlet dress shirt, a golden eagle belt, and a cape with red velvet on the inside fabric. It all came together with his white leather zip boots, which he was remarkably agile in.

While it was hard to know exactly what he was thinking at any given time, a certain gloominess over the chastising he received from his aunt would surface periodically. Although he had gotten used to that rejection, he never anticipated it would come from the person he trusted the most. It wasn't the first time she got upset at him, but it was the only occasion where it felt like she rejected who he was. It was also the first time he actually attempted to run away or, at the very least, separate himself.

Neeeeeeeeeeeeeyaaaa heeeeee!

A shrieking cry called out from a distance. Randall crouched into a battle stance, wielding his blade like a baseball batter waiting for a pitch. Through the timber that surrounded him echoed the thunderous thudding of galloping feet. The fog of the winter's morning clouded all he could see beyond twenty meters. The thudding continued to creep up, closer and closer.

Suddenly, out of the cloudy white air in front of him, he watched as a snow-white stallion barreled straight toward his body. In a flash, he instinctively dropped his sword and rolled into a diving somersault to the right, avoiding the steed like an oncoming locomotive. As he picked himself back up, he watched as the animal maneuvered its way around the trees and looped back to face Randall once more. The teenager leaped for his sword and resumed his battle stance.

Instead of charging forward again, the horse let out a muffled neigh and approached the guarded Randall slowly. He could tell in the animal's eyes that he was spooked beyond all belief. Cautiously, Randall slowly stood up and sheathed his sword while extending out his hand toward the horse.

"Woah, buster... woah," he said, with a slight tremble in his voice, "there ain't nothin' to be afraid of... I'm not out here lookin' for a scruff with a stud like you."

While hesitant at first, the horse continued to move toward him. Frosty lowered his head and stood still as Randall gently rubbed the side of his head. The horse's eyes started to subdue into a calming state as Randall continued to stroke behind his ears.

"I bet a big fella like you is hungry," he decided as he reached inside his jumpsuit and pulled out a ziplock baggie with a half-eaten sandwich in it. "Ain't a soul on God's green Earth that's ever stayed mad after enjoying a peanut butter & nanner sandwich."

Frosty sniffed the sandwich three times before biting into it. Randall held it in his hand and watched as the horse consumed all of it in a matter of two bites. The horse raised the front of its lips to reveal what looked like a delighted smile.

"Well, there you have it, big boy," Randall said as he began petting the horse again, "looks like that fixed ya up real nice."

A few flurries started to gently fall from the sky. Randall looked at the handcrafted pattern of the saddle that sat atop the large animal. He could tell that he was meticulously cared for by someone. Perhaps the horse escaped its stable or got separated from its rider. Either way, it probably wouldn't fare well in the blizzard.

"Are you lost, chief?" he asked the horse, who flapped his lips in enjoyment at the fake southern accent. "That's alright. Everybody gets lost sometimes–even the King. But no one should ever have to stay lonesome...no matter what's been said or done."

Randall took a few steps away from the horse, who immediately followed him as if it were attached. Leaning against a tree, he reflected some more. The faces of his mother and father appeared in his head for the first time in a long while. The memory came in the form of a 7-year-old Randall watching his mother's soft hands work as she sewed a white sequin jacket for him while his dad tinkered with the record player. The song "Hound Dog" blared in their tiny Chicago apartment living room. Randall sang along with the lyrics as his legs would shake with precise choreography. The two parents, so obsessed with their baby boy, laughed and cheered joyously as they watched him perform a concert that they never wanted to end. But it did end. And although Randall so desperately wished he could bring it back, at this moment, he realized that he couldn't. A single tear fell from his eye and ran down his cheek.

"Oh, sweet horsie," he whispered, wiping the tear from his face, "I think we both got ourselves lost, huh? I bet my auntie is worried sick."

The horse gave a gratified grunt as it positioned its body for Randall to climb onto the saddle. As he hopped on, he carefully positioned his feet and took hold of the reins. With a kick to its sides, Randall made a clicking noise with his tongue.

"I guess we outta get ourselves back home, then. Let's go, big fella," he said as Frosty started to trot toward Rockdale.

Chapter 13

A Little Less Conversation

Bud looked like a bloated baked potato as his body lay underneath dimmed lights. Eye clamps were applied under the lids to keep them shut, his mouth was securely tightened and wired shut, and Jill applied the finishing touches to his makeup. However, there was nothing she could do about his protruding gut underneath the brown suit Grant had picked out for him. Luckily, it was covered mostly by the bottom, closed half of the casket. Besides, it wasn't like she could say,

"Hey, I'm going to need a bigger jacket because your dead dad is too fat."

Jill unlocked the front door with one of the many keys on her black lanyard. The sanctuary of the funeral home was like its own miniature version of the church across the street, except with fewer pews and less religious decor. The casket was raised on a platform on top of a bed of flowers. Next to it was a podium and a wreath on an easel that contained his portrait. In the portrait, the hefty man wore an Armani blue suit with an all-red tie and an enormous gold pinky ring on his right hand, which gripped the chair he stood behind. Just by looking at the portrait, you would assume this man was either in politics or a fourth-generation owner of a pork processing company, she thought. As she lit candles, Anna marched in the front door, wiping the snow off her shoes on the doormat as if it were glued to her feet. She checked her watch to see that it read 10:42 a.m.

"Cripes, Jill. It's snowing like Old Man Winter has a bad case of dandruff!" she noted, as flurries covered her creamsicle-colored puffy coat with her white robe poking underneath.

"You bet," Jill agreed without averting her eyes from her work.

Anna walked down the short aisle like a giddy kid, excited to go on a rollercoaster ride. She stood at the other side of the altar and faced Jill, who was still not making eye contact with her. Jill rested her key lanyard on the inside ledge of the casket as she reached for her makeup and brush to apply the finishing touches to Bud's face.

"So," she said eagerly, "how did it go? Tell me everything!"

"How did *what* go?" Jill replied as she brushed the foundation over the right cheek.

"Oh, for Pete's sake, the date! How did it go with Todd? Was he all that and a bag of chips or what?" she inquired, feeling as if she was reliving the prime of her teenage years.

"He was more like all that and a Zebra Cake," Jill smirked as she continued to work intently on the final decorations.

"A *Zebra Cake*?" Anna replied, unfamiliar with the phrase, "Is that good?...Oh, cripes, Jill, that's not a sex thing, is it? Ya know I love girl talk, but I'm still a pastor, hon."

Jill finally raised her head, her eyes showing the peeved emotion behind them.

"No, it doesn't mean anything, Anna!" she exclaimed bitterly. "Ya know, I wouldn't want you to think I'm not grateful, but did you or did you not know that your friend's cousin spent time in prison for holding his workplace hostage with a bomb?"

Anna's jaw dropped as if it had broken through a flimsy grocery bag.

"Well, that's different," Anna replied, nervously clamping her hands together as she rocked back and forth. Jill could start to see the guilt resonate with the typically jovial Minnesota woman.

Even when tempers were flaring high, the small-town residents of Rockdale, Minnesota, tended to express their disapproval of a situation with phrases that neutralized the strong feelings for the sake of being polite. But rest assured, the message is heard loud and clear.

"It certainly could've been better, Anna," Jill said as Anna followed her through the luncheon area through the west side doors of the sanctuary.

The room had eight gray tables with white tablecloths and two small pictures of Bud and his family in the center. The walls were an eggshell yellow with a pale blue carpet. The walls had portraits of Minnesota lakes (which Jill thrifted for just under forty dollars), the biggest of which sat underneath the fireplace. Floral-accented sofa chairs, a grandfather clock, and a coffee table in the back right corner.

Personally, Jill found the chairs to be ugly, but they were gifted to her by the previous owners of the funeral home, and she didn't want to be impolite. An assortment of cookies, bars, and finger sandwiches sat on a fold-out table toward the entrance, with the kitchen hidden away on the right. Plenty of space was reserved, of course, for the inevitable array of hot dishes that would pile up toward the front of the tables. Jill pulled the saran wrap off of the sandwiches and desserts.

"Ya know, now that you mention it, she did say he had gotten in a little bit of trouble with the law," Anna admitted.

"Oh, for crying out loud, Anna," Jill quipped, her eyes piercing through the pastor like daggers, "I really wish I could've gotten a heads up there. That's the kind of information you normally warn a gal about before she goes recklessly into a blind date."

"Cripes Jill, I'm awfully sorry," Anna replied sincerely, "when Ruth told me he got into some legal trouble, I didn't want to make it my business, ya know? They always told us in the seminary that ya can't be judgemental when people confide in you. 'Turn that cheek and shut that beak,' they'd say. But Heavens to Betsy, I didn't think he was a maniac. I just assumed it was small potatoes, ya know?"

"Well, no offense, but I'm not rearing to go on another date anytime soon after that calamity. I mean, yelling in the middle of the restaurant might be fair game in Connecticut, but it felt like pure torture to me," Jill said as she scratched an itch on her neck from her black turtle-neck sweater.

"Oh, dear lord, he's from out East?" Anna asked in shock, "Hon, I had no idea. I swear!"

Oddly enough, the idea that she let her dear friend come into contact with someone with rude and pushy East Coast behavior eclipsed the fact that he nearly blew up his coworkers over a preservative-filled snack cake. Jill sighed heavily, realizing that Anna would likely spend the next 24-48 hours beating herself up for the incident. She would likely show up at her house with a freshly baked pan of bars as a sincere offering for her negligence and transgressions.

"It's alright, Anna," Jill relented as the two women started to walk back toward the entrance of the funeral home. "I don't want you to beat yourself up over it. Lord knows I'm not perfect either. I took the whole thing out on

Randall when I got back, and now he's run off again. I think I really hurt his feelings this time."

"Oh, I'm so sorry, hon," Anna apologized, touching her shoulder. "You know he'll come back. He always does."

"I don't know, Anna," Jill said, her head hanging in shame, "I worry this time might be different. I deserve to work this wake solo."

"Solo? Where's Pat?" Anna replied.

"I think he's caught a bug," Jill answered, "I sent the poor guy home after he started hurling like a reverse garbage disposal in the parking lot this morning. It must have taken hold of him fast because he seemed just fine and at it this morning."

"Yeah, I saw him earlier too. There's definitely something going around. It's that time of year, I 'spose," Anna agreed, shaking her head. "Do you need any help around here? I was gonna take the truck and check in on my folks and maybe watch a taped episode of *Law & Order* with Mom. They're just a few blocks away, so I can wait until after things get wrapped up here."

"Thanks for offering, but I've got a good handle on things. I appreciate it, though," Jill replied, knowing that letting Anna help out would unnecessarily extend the whole affair by at least another hour due to the rambling conversations she would likely initiate.

"Are you sure, hon? It's really no biggie at all. Mom can fly this episode solo without any complaints from me. The killers on that show are becoming just too gosh darn predictable. I swear we only watch because she has a crush on Jerry Orbach," she said.

"No, no, no, it's all good," Jill assured her as she shooed her off with her hand, "Go see your folks, and then we'll get this show on the road later."

"It's really no trouble, Jill. I wouldn't want you to think I'm not happy to help. I'll just think of it as an extended church service."

"Oh, don't sweat it. You don't need any more of a burden today with Ash Wednesday going on."

"Well, if you insist, I 'spose I'll get headed over to the church and finish setting up. I'll see you later for the procession, then?" Anna said as she made her way out the door.

"Sounds good to me," Jill responded, "Give my best to Paul and Ava."

"Will do, hon."

Forty minutes passed by as Jill finished setting up the eating area. She grabbed a stack of her homemade pamphlets, which she spent hours into the night making on her slow dial-up internet, that went into detailed fashion regarding Bud's life. She could hardly focus on the research on the political figurehead's achievements as the grueling guilt and worry set in over Randall storming off. A horrible pain sat in her stomach just thinking about the way she chastised him, a pain only rivaled by the one Patrick must have had in his body.

As she walked through the door into the sanctuary lobby, placing the pamphlets on the main table, she saw a figure in her peripheral vision standing by the casket. Spooked, she turned cautiously to see a disheveled-looking Vicky dressed to the nines in what looked like some sort of rodeo cowgirl getup and the casket, which had now been completely closed. The eyeshadow on her face was smeared as if she had just spent the last hour bawling.

"Hey, Vicky," Jill said, approaching her softly, "is there anything I can do for you?"

"No, sorry, Jill," she said, wiping her eyes, "I know I'm early, but I just wanted to spend some time with Bud alone before anyone else got here."

Jill never took for Vicky as someone with a heart, but maybe she was deeply attached to Bud in ways she never knew. Perhaps the world of politics really does connect people in deep ways, she thought.

"It's no problem at all," Jill said, placing her hand on Vicky's shoulder as she rested her side on the front pew. "I understand that grieving takes many forms. If you want some time alone with Bud, I will absolutely honor that."

"Thanks, Jill...that really means a lot," she uttered with a sharp sniffle.

"And I understand that seeing the body up close can be haunting for many," she said, "so I'll wait for you before we open it back up when your family arrives."

"I want this casket closed, Jill," she instisted, without turning around, in a sharp tone that could slice through steel.

"Oh...okay, well, Grant stated to me that he preferred an open casket. He also approved the embalming, so I am just going off of the arrangement," she explained as if she were approaching a wounded wild animal.

Her head whipped up, revealing eyes that would make Sauron blush. The angry look invoked an erstwhile fear in Jill that she hadn't felt since her school days. It was like a geyser connected to the bowels of Hell was about to be released on her.

"Listen here," she barked, taking an intemperate step toward Jill. "My mother-in-law has dementia that gets worse by the day. And not that you care, but I know for a fact that when she sees her husband lying in this casket, she will have a meltdown, the likes of which will ruin everything, Jill. *Everything.* It will not only make a fresh hell for my family and me but also cause her weeks of stress and despair. So whatever arrangements you made with that *ball-ess wonder, Grant,* can go ahead and get scrapped because the last and final spot for *this* casket is fire and ashes."

"Vicky, I'm so sorry, and I didn't know all of this," Jill said, backpedaling away from the demonic woman. "However, the arrangements are already lined up through the next of kin. Grant approved the embalming, which allows us to make the body presentable for viewing and—"

Vicky held up her pointer finger to Jill's lips to shush her. Jill looked down at the red polished nail on the boney finger that sat over her mouth.

"I don't think you're getting it, Jill," Vicky remarked softly. "If you open this casket at all, your other arm is coming off...do I make myself clear?"

The grandfather clock chimed in the other room, echoing in the eleventh hour. Jill stood frozen, her chin tucked into her neck, as she stared into Vicky's eyes. Slowly nodding, Jill backed away as Vicky turned to face the casket. A fear sat inside Jill in the pit of her stomach; it felt as if she had just been presented with a life-or-death ultimatum by a mobster. With that threat, the Vicky she knew was back.

Walking away and shaking off the interaction, she made her way toward the entrance. She stared out the front window as the snow began to pour down in heavy droves that covered the parking lot. She watched Julio's Willow Fields van drive away, loaded with the few seniors who braved the Ash Wednesday service. None of them looked intent on attending Bud's send-off.

With a cold, snowy draft coming in through the front door, the first two attendees of the wake entered the funeral home, wiping their feet on the rug and carpet as they walked in. Rose and Roy Turner, with ashes still on their foreheads, steadily took off their coats in the entryway. Rose was holding a tinfoil-wrapped casserole dish. Jill recognized them from previous church services, particularly remembering Roy as the only person to harass one of the ushers to let him exchange the bill he put in the offering plate for a smaller one. Standing in the lobby next to her pamphlet table, Jill approached them and greeted them as they hung up their coats.

"Hello, Turners," she said, approaching them gently, "I am so sorry for your loss."

Roy gave a squinted glare at her through his bifocals like an angry cartoon owl.

"Loss? Ha! I haven't lost anything but something to laugh at," he sneered as he grabbed a pamphlet and walked past her. "I mean, just look at this picture of him! The homunculus looks like he belongs on a bottle of barbecue sauce."

"You're the homunculus, Roy. We promised we wouldn't insult the man in his own wake," the old woman ordered.

"Yeah, yeah... don't remind me," he muttered.

Then she, too, picked up a pamphlet, looked down at the cover, and raised an eyebrow.

"Hmm...ya know, I kind of see your point, though. He does look like he could be on a bottle of barbecue sauce," she said.

"Vindication! That round pink noggin looks just like a hog who won the blue ribbon at the state fair. Just put a chef's hat on him, and it's perfect," he exclaimed, waving his arms in the air.

Jill was taken aback by the brazen exchange between Vicky's parents as the couple continued to examine the picture together. Despite being just feet away, it was almost as if she wasn't even in the same room as them. It was clear that whatever connection they had in their marriage was propped up by the need to degrade other people. Like a stealthy vampire, Vicky popped up behind Jill, causing a chill to shoot down her spine.

"Mom, Dad," she said coldly, "you decided to come."

Her mother stepped forward and lowered her head apologetically.

"Vicky, we felt bad about the other day and wanted to apologize and show our support for you and Grant. It was wrong of us to be so short with you," she said.

"I see," Vicky said, still looking as if she was seething underneath.

Like a heated-up tea kettle, Roy's anger started to steam at that response. Jill watched as a vein became visible on the old man's forehead.

"I see?" he mocked, crossing his arms. "I see?! That's all you have to say? No 'thank you for coming,' no 'I accept your apology,' no 'I'm sorry for trying to exploit your prized horse for political influence'? The nerve!"

"Roy, stop it," Rose insisted, grabbing his arm.

"Your mother comes to you—tuna noodle hot dish in hand—and you show her nothing but contempt? Well, Ms. Too-Good-To-Show-Up-To-Ash-Wednesday, I can see that whether it's the person who gave birth to you or your lord and savior, you've got no respect! None!" he bellowed, wagging his finger so hard you could hear the rattle of his watch.

Jill looked at the unphased Vicky, who looked as though whatever she was feeling deep down provided a cloud over her current reality. She stood unphased by her father's words for a moment. Then she leaned forward.

"Well then...why don't you fucking leave, Dad?" she asked in a poisonous tone.

A stunned Roy couldn't find the words as the room fell into an awkward silence. Jill shuffled the pamphlets on the table in an attempt to look preoccupied. Just then, Grant opened the front doors, escorting his mother, who had both of her arms secured tightly around his left and a casserole dish in his right. After helping his mother take off her coat and sitting her down in a cushioned chair, he approached the three of them with the dish resting in his hands.

"Rose and Roy! I'm so glad you decided to come. Vicky told me that you were concerned about the weather and weren't able to make it," he said, genuinely excited to see his in-laws.

"Oh…right, we were a little worried, but we would feel just awful if we weren't able to support our Grant," Rose said, giving him a side hug. "How are you holding up?"

I'm not going to lie, Rose, it's been tough," he admitted, with sincere sadness in his voice, "but it just makes me so happy to know that I have an extra set of parents by my side with you two here."

"That's so sweet of you to say. Isn't it Roy?" she said, giving her husband a nudge.

Roy was still stunned by his daughter's downright aggressive response. They'd had their fights before, but for some reason, she had the look in her eye of an enemy with nothing to lose. Trying to shake it off, he addressed his son-in-law.

"We, uh, feel the same way, son," he said, giving him a pat on the shoulder.

Roy despised hugging and most forms of showing affection. A handshake was as far as he would normally go, but he was known to very rarely give out a pat on the shoulder or hand. Rose received a total of three pats in her life from him: once when they got married, once after she gave birth, and once during the series finale of *M*A*S*H* (the last one being one of the only occasions where she witnessed him crying).

During this exchange, Peter York quietly crept into the building, dusting the excess snow off his jacket. He immediately spotted Vicky and walked over to her, his notebook tucked under his arm. The panicked woman put on a smile and turned on the persona.

"Representative Veitch, you didn't make it to the Ash Wednesday service," the reporter said, with an ash mark on his head. "Did you get caught up in this weather?"

"I did, I did," she answered while shooting her father a look to fend off any oncoming commentary. "I'm so sorry, Peter! As you know, faith is the biggest pillar of my life, but the good Lord stepped in today and said, 'Vicky, I'm going to test your resolve with this storm today,' and well, I got through it."

The hope of getting pictures of her praying with ashes on her head to appease the evangelical demographic was lost, but it was the least of her worries now. Still, in this specific arrangement, she and Colton took an ax to a pivotal part of the narrative she wanted out there.

"It's not a problem at all!" he said, attempting to comfort her. "You Minnesotans sure are a tough bunch to be able to withstand such harsh winters."

"It's our way of life, but we're happy to endure it!" she said, feeling as though she was finding her groove again.

"It's quite impressive," he said with a smile. "By the way, where's Ethan? I figured you two rode back together from the cabin—"

"—Flu!" she interjected like someone desperately trying to get a bid at an auction, "Yeah, he has the flu...the poor guy toughed it out for me, but I relieved him of his duties after seeing how sick he was."

Peter raised an eyebrow and gave her a perplexed look.

"Weird," he said. "He seemed totally fine before and during the interview. Chipper even."

"Yep! That's my Ethan," she said, a hot flash falling over her. "The guy is just such a trooper. You wouldn't know something was bothering him unless you shook it out of him."

"Poor guy," Rose added. "That's how all the men I grew up with were. Work always, complain never."

"We've *clearly* lost our way!" Roy exclaimed.

For the first time in years, Vicky gained admiration for her parents. She could never get them to do her any sort of favor if she asked, but their curmudgeon nature at this moment became an asset.

"Exactly, Dad," she affirmed, giving him a nod. "It just seems like people don't want to work these days. We're teaching people that it's okay to choose the hands of a taker over the hands of a worker. It's truly destroying us."

Everyone made their way into the sanctuary. Jill found herself a good distance away from the group, silently wishing she could forever be separated from a family that had no clue what it was like to be on call every day of the week. They would never know a life outside of the narrative they've concocted and believed to be true. Vicky stepped up to the front of the pews, facing the few in attendance. Jill watched on, hoping that time would accelerate.

"Thank you, everyone, for coming today. I know that the weather is less than ideal, but no day is too treacherous to celebrate an icon," she said, bowing her head to act as if she were reflecting. "Bud Veitch, truly, was larger than life itself; an elder statesman who fought tirelessly for all the right things, all the right results, and all the right people. The cliche of *'owning a room'* gets thrown out there all the time, but let me tell ya, that man not only owned every room he walked into, he pulled everyone in that room to him. His charisma helped him establish political accomplishments the likes of which no one had ever seen before; policy that helped to preserve our freedoms, our liberty, and our firearms. He was a man who-"

All of a sudden, a shackled 6'6" man with long hair and a fiery red beard in an orange prison jumpsuit that read "INMATE" on the back made it through the entryway of the sanctuary, accompanied by two guards on each side of him. The balding, unkempt hair on his head flowed down to his shoulders like greasy flames, while the top of his scalp started to show through the thinning top. To Jill, he looked as if Leif Erickson had time-traveled to the present day to participate in the grunge movement. Vicky's paling complexion became even more severe as he entered the room. She looked over at Peter, who was perked up like a dog who heard the word "walk" uttered.

"Welp, I made it!" he announced, his arms extended forward only to be put back down by the guard on his left. "Big Dale is in the house!"

"Dale?!" Grant exclaimed in utter confusion.

"Dale!" Grace shouted, smiling as she booked it with her walker as fast as she could to see her son. "My sweet Dale! You've come home!"

"Christ almighty," Roy muttered as he shook his head.

Grant followed closely behind her to make sure she didn't fall over, as the two were now face-to-face with Dale Veitch for the first time since his sentencing three years ago. At that time, the 43-year-old music journeyman and his band,

"Walking Pneumonia" had spent the better part of two decades trying for their big break. Grace adored Dale for his free spirit, love of animals, and being the blithesome boy she could never forget. He and his four-man band traveled coast-to-coast in an old Volkswagen van in an attempt to find their footing in the music undergrounds of various cities and towns, constantly revamping their style in order to pinpoint their niche.

One of the towns was Waco, Texas, where they took up residence at Mount Carmel and joined the Branch Davidians in the summer of '92. Though they initially welcomed the band into their cult, tempers quickly began to run hot after they got high and ate most of the food rations stored for the impending apocalypse. After just three weeks at Mount Carmel, infamous cult leader David Koresh kicked them out of the compound after leaving for a recruitment trip and coming back to a kegger where the bassist and drummer were caught hooking up with two of Koresh's wives. Koresh punished the women by making them apologize to the entire congregation and cancel their subscription to the Sears catalog.

The band's raucous behavior wasn't the only reason they failed to find sustained success. Unfortunately, they just weren't very good. What they lacked in musical talent was nothing compared to what they lacked in lyricism. Dale convinced his bandmates that the criticism of their lyrics meant that they were counterculture–something he insisted all the great bands experienced before making it big. The reality, however, was that every song was just a nursery rhyme altered with overtones of destruction. An excerpt of one of their songs includes shouting lyrics and is accompanied by the backing of heavy guitars and drums:

Mary had a little lamb,

Little lamb,

Little lamb!

Mary had a little lamb, and the lamb of God

Is out-for-blood!

Blood! Blood! Out for blood!

Out for blood! Out for blood!

The lamb of God is out for blood

His wool will put you in the mud!

(guitar solo with dispensed fog machine)

After returning home to Minnesota, to their own surprise, Walking Ammonia found that their most reliable venues were birthday parties for kids with metalhead parents and arcade restaurants–so long as they toned down the lyrics and supplied the 20-something manager with weed. The amount of money they received proved unreliable for housing or new equipment, but just enough for gas and fast food. The crown jewel of those venues was the Chuck E. Cheese in Bloomington.

One day, a Chuck E. Cheese gig got canceled halfway through after a child threw up in the ball pit. The manager made the band stop playing and evacuated the facility, citing that it was Chuck E. Cheese's company policy to thoroughly clean the contaminated area and prohibit guests from using the equipment. That was all well and good until he refused to pay the band compensation for playing. A heated argument broke out between Dale and the manager, which ended in futility. While the other bandmates were ready to cut their losses, Dale took matters into his own hands.

He stormed back into Chuck E. Cheese's, head-butted the manager, and took money directly out of the register before running back to the van and speeding away. The other bandmates panicked as an enraged Dale sped down the highway, only making it a few miles before the van was pulled over. All in all, he ended up receiving an assault charge, a robbery charge, and a possession charge. He ended up falling on the sword with the pot in the van after realizing the position he had put his bandmates in. The judge ruled that Dale would spend 10 years in the penitentiary, sending the eldest son of the embattled Bud Veitch behind bars.

"I brought a hot dish, Ma," Dale said as he looked over to the stoic guard on his right, who was holding a dented pan covered with tin foil. "We had some stuff left over from a baby shower that we threw this Crazy Eyes Eddie guy on my cell block. He's not out for another six years, but I guess his conjugal visit went well."

"Oh, I'm so glad that you're making friends, sweetie! Your new buddy sounds lovely," Grace stated as she gave him a big hug.

"No touching," the guard on the right barked.

"It's fine, Steve. I think we can let this one slide," the other guard rebuked.

"Oh, and you brought your camp counselors with you!" she said, coming face-to-face with Steve. "Thanks so much for taking care of my sweet Dale."

Grant made a shrugging motion behind her to signal to the guard to just play along with it. Catching on to her senility, he obliged.

"Um, you're welcome..." he replied, "Can I set this down somewhere?"

"I can take that," Jill offered as she walked over and took the pan from the guard to place it in the kitchen with the other two hot dishes.

"Dale, we had no idea you were able to come," Grant said in a lower tone that his mother couldn't pick up on.

"Yeah, man, I'm sorry for dropping in unannounced on ya. Once I heard the news, I knew I had to pay my respects to Pops. A few strings had to be pulled with the warden, but there ain't no way I was going to let this situation go all 'Cats in The Cradle' on me," Dale said, as some snot from the cold started collecting into his facial hair.

"That's admirable, I suppose," Grant replied as he walked backward down the aisle to make introductions. "You remember Vicky's parents, Roy and Rose, I assume."

The three men walked forward in synchronized steps as the chains rattled in front of Dale's body. The towering man looked down at the dainty couple like an asteroid over an archipelago. He smiled down like a happy giant as Rose grimaced and Roy remained sneering. Returning from the dining area, Jill stood in the back corner of the sanctuary and watched as if the whole interaction was a soap opera.

"How goes it, Turners? It's good to see you again," he cooed.

"You as well," Rose stammered, nervously avoiding eye contact as she tightened her clutch on her purse.

"They let you out for this, huh?" Roy said, with his arms folded. "Back in my day, real prisoners worked the railroads all day without complaining. But I can see this country continues to transform into a nanny state."

Dale continued to smile down at him, unphased by the remarks. He gripped his hands together in front of him like a monk.

"There's nothing wrong with a little compassion, Mr. Turner," he replied.

"Ha! Compassion, he says," Roy rebutted. "I'm not going to take lessons on civility from a yardbird. If your daily routine includes not dropping the soap, you have no ground to lecture me on compassion."

"Not dropping the soap?" Rose asked innocently.

"Butt sex, Rose. It's like a Roman bathhouse in those prison showers. You can't turn on the facet without opening yourself up to sodomy," he interjected, shaking his head. "I bet a big fella like you gets his fill too."

Vicky looked on, sweat dripping down her back, as she watched her dad berate her brother-in-law. She looked over to Peter, who was scribbling away in the corner on his notepad, undoubtedly highlighting this in his piece. Normally, her dad's antics would annoy her to no end. The more attention that was redirected away from the casket, however, was what she needed. Dale's smile fell. Like a yoga instructor, he took a dramatic deep breath as everyone awaited his reply.

"There's nothing wrong with that either, Mr. Turner," he deflected. "Live and let live, as I always say. You seem to be really curious about it, though, given your extensive knowledge of the subject. Maybe you should give it a try sometime."

Rose's eyes widened like a frightened owl. Roy scrunched up his face in disgust, his blood pressure rising to near conniption levels. He muttered a mesh of incoherent profanities under his breath as his wife squeezed his arm. Dale's smile returned to him as he and the snickering guards took a couple of steps forward toward the casket.

"Jim, can you lift the cover for me?" Dale asked, awaiting the face of his father.

As the guard reached for the top half lid of the casket, Vicky leaped up and covered it with her hands. Holding it tightly shut, she whipped her head toward Dale, facing him for the first time in years.

"It's a closed casket, Dale," she quipped sternly.

"Vicky, it's good to see my favorite sister-in-law," Dale said, smiling down at her. "I promise I won't take long. I just want to say my piece to him one last time."

Strengthening her stance as if she were blocking an entrance, she stared him down and crossed her arms. She caught Peter out of the corner of her eye, reminding her to stay calm.

"Dale...I don't think it's appropriate for you to just drop by unannounced and assume you can just do whatever you want," she said calmly but firmly. "We want a closed casket, and that means it remains closed."

Dale tilted his head and looked at her as if he were talking to a pedantic retail customer. Even the guards looked befuddled at her demands.

"Vicky... he's my dad," Dale pleaded, inching his face closer to hers. "I just want to say goodbye to my dad."

"Well, you can say goodbye to him in a shut casket. I don't see what the difference is. He's gone either way," she argued.

Her heart started to race as all eyes were on her, feeling as if, at any moment, the casket would open and be revealed to all. Jill wondered why Vicky was so insistent on a closed casket. If it really was to shield her mother-in-law, couldn't they just distract her and let Dale say his goodbyes? Peter continued to write on his notepad as he watched everything unfold.

"Fine," Dale relented, "I don't need the casket open."

"Good," she said with a sigh, "feel free to—"

"—but I still get to sing my song," he interputed, standing firm like a confident Norse warrior.

"Your...your song?" she asked, not knowing if she opened herself up to something worse.

"Yes. *My song*," he announced, "I wrote a song in remembrance of my dad. I put my heart and soul into it, and I'm not budging until I get to share it with him."

"Dale, he can't even hear it. He's dead," she replied, feeling the turmoil bubble in her stomach.

"Song or open casket. You pick," he said.

She looked at the guards, hoping that they would interject and forcibly remove him from the front of the altar. The guards, however, stood silent. Oddly enough, it seemed as though they were completely aligned with Dale on this request. If they were going to bring a prisoner out through a storm, he ought to be able to have his wishes honored. Vicky bit her bottom lip in anger and exhaled like an angry dragon.

"Fine," she huffed, stepping aside, "sing your song then, Dale."

Dale took in a deep breath and closed his eyes in preparation for his piece.

"Steve, can you give me a beat? Have it go like 'bum...ba dum...ba dum dum...ba dum' and repeat," Daleinstructed, looking down to the man to his right.

"What?" Steve asked.

"Come on, Steve. The man's dad just died," Jim replied.

"Well, why don't you do it then?" Steve relented.

"I'm deaf tone," Jim said, pointing to his ear.

"It's tone deaf, Jim," Steve said, shaking his head.

"Cripes. This is why he asked you to do it. You clearly know what you're talking about," Jim replied.

"Unbelievable," Steve said, still shaking his head.

After a heavy sigh, he caved in, starting up softly with the vocal beat.

"Bum...ba dum...ba dum dum...ba dum...bum...ba dum...ba dum dum...ba dum"

Dale closed his eyes again and began bobbing his head to the beat while Steve reluctantly maintained it. In his mind's eye, he was on MTV Unplugged performing a B-side gem with a profound backstory. With his best Kurt Cobain singing voice, he began to sing.

Daddy Buddy sat on his wall...

Daddy Buddy had a great fall...

We all tried to put him back together...

But none of us could predict the weather!

Feeling left out, Jim began to snap on the beat. The raw emotion made its way up Dale's throat as he began to belt out the chorus.

Horses and kingsmen! Ooooooooooooooh

Horses and kingsmen! Ooooooooooooooh

Horses and kingsmen! Ooooooooooooooh

Horses and kingsmen! When will we meet again?

Dale bowed his head at the conclusion of his performance. After five seconds, Steve realized he was finished singing and stopped his vocal beat. Jim had a tear in his eye.

"Are you looking at my arm right now?" Jim asked Dale. "Goosebumps. I'm covered in goosebumps."

"Thanks, Jim," Dale buzzed, tears dripping down his face, "I really needed to hear that."

"Bring it in, big guy," Jim said as he embraced the inmate with a long, brotherly hug. Steve stood there with his arms crossed and rolled his eyes.

Vicky looked around the room to see the reactions to this unforeseen spectacle. Her parent's scowls turned into looks of concern; Grant looked more embarrassed than she'd ever seen him; Grace sat with a wide smile, ready to applaud the performance; and Peter's mouth hung open as if he were covering a once-in-a-lifetime historical event. She knew now that the article would be tainted with excerpts on family dysfunction. Her only hope was to lobby him for mercy later on to save face. It was a cherry of hopelessness on top of a catastrophe sundae.

"Oof," Grant uttered in an attempt to break the tension in the room. "I am feeling pretty hungry. Shall we head over to the next room and get started on lunch?"

"I think that's a great idea, Grant," Vicky immediately interjected, "let's all head over to the dining room, everyone!" The congregation of misfits waited and looked at each other, hesitant to be the first to move, until Grace powered forward with her walker, unphased by anything that had just occurred. The rest followed behind her single file into the dining room entrance that Jill held open. Each casserole's aluminum foil was removed, revealing the tuna noodle hotdish, tater tot hotdish, and what looked to be a mixture of hamburger, broccoli stumps, Kraft singles, rice, and unknown prison spices. As paper plates were dished out, each group elected to sit at separate fold-out tables and avoid conversing with each other. The scene was a modern-day painting of Nighthawks coming to life.

Jill still didn't know what to make of Vicky's threat. She assumed a similar declaration had already been made to Grant, but why? Why was she so adamant about keeping the casket closed? Maybe she didn't want the reporter to photograph the body, she thought. But even if that were the case, what kind of non-tabloid reporter would take pictures at a funeral without asking? No matter what, she felt uneasy about being bullied out of the wishes of the next of kin. Especially coming from her former bully. She took a breath and remembered that the procession would start in a little over an hour, regardless.

"Miss...miss!" Grace squealed, waving Jill over. "I'm a little chilly. Is there any way we can turn up the heat?"

"I second that," Roy chimed in, "I feel like I'm a frozen dinner."

"Quit being so dramatic, Roy," Rose replied.

"It's not a problem at all. I'll get right on it," Jill obliged as she walked out of the room and into the main hallway to the thermostat.

As she walked up to the yellow-stained Honeywell thermostat, she remembered that she had recently put a locked cover over it. She suspected that Randall and Patrick kept adjusting it, one wanting it cool and one wanting it hotter, and the constant fluctuation was getting on her nerves. Realizing her pockets were empty, she walked into her office to see if the keys were lying anywhere on her desk, covered in loose papers and knick-knacks. The lanyard was nowhere in sight. She wondered if she left it in her car but remembered unlocking the front doors earlier. They had to be somewhere, she thought.

Retracing her steps, she found her way back into the sanctuary. She recalled her conversation with Anna and wondered if she had sat them down in one of the pews or something. After checking, the pews came up empty. Still no keys in sight. The realization hit her like a freight train. They were sitting inside the casket.

She remembered Vicky's threat as she looked over at her own arm. She couldn't just let her keys burn with someone's loved one. Cautiously, she looked at the closed dining room door, lifted the lid up, and pressed her opposite shoulder against it to keep it open. The keys greeted her like a shining treasure in a dark sea. Grabbing them, she quickly pulled out her hand and closed the casket. Suddenly, a chill ran down her spine.

She felt a wet, almost sticky sensation covering her hand but was too afraid to look down. Finally, she did. As the keys sat in her hand, a smear of blood coated the inside of her palm. A lump formed in her throat. Every instinct in her body told her not to open the lid back up, but for some reason, her brain ignored the signals completely. She lifted the lid, seeing a thin pool of blood lining the right side of the casket and staining Bud's jacket. The blood led to a silver duffle bag that was tucked beside the right side of Bud's legs. Jill pulled it toward herself and began slowly unzipping.

Much like a dinosaur watching a meteor barrel toward the planet, there's nothing that can prepare another human being for the unexpectedness of seeing a severed head. Absolutely nothing. Air sours in your throat. A frozen chill runs down every channel in your body. Time stands still.

Jill was now face-to-face with the head belonging to Vicky's staffer, accompanied by a hand and foot that were poking out as well. She could see the shock in the cold, dead eyes that stared back at her. It was as if she were staring into a photo of someone at their most terrifying moment. Shaking, she stepped back and closed the casket. As she did so, something hard and metallic poked her in the back with authority.

"Make a noise, and you're dead…" Vicky whispered in her ear. "Move toward the front door."

Nodding slowly, Jill walked down the aisle and into the hallway, the gun firmly entrenched at her back. The two women walked forward out of the front metal doors, the storm billowing out in front of them.

Chapter 14

Hound Dog

Vicky tightly gripped Jill's sweater, her sharp nails digging into her back as she pushed her forward into the snowfall outside, making their way alongside the eastern side of the building. The barrel of the revolver was pressed against her right kidney like a metal finger, leading her to her demise. Despite her own life being in jeopardy, Jill's mind raced with concern for what she might do to everyone in the viewing room. Most of all, she feared for Randall. Vicky was vindictive enough to hurt him and far from being above it in moments like this. Deep regret settled in, knowing her last words to him were so contentious. For that, she hated herself. She only hoped that maybe he had run away for good, somewhere safe.

"Get going! Faster!" Vicky instructed, jabbing the gun deeper into her side.

Heavy snow and wind permeated the evening sky and started to cover their hair and clothes like thousands of white flies on a pile of discarded fruit. As they kept walking forward, Jill's arm hovering above her head, they approached the backyard of the funeral home. The hanging lamps on the backside of the building shined twenty meters out into the white abyss of the backyard.

Jill noticed a gray rabbit struggling as it hopped through the snow bank as they got closer. For a moment, she felt as if she were that rabbit who, too, was stuck in the elements as it faced certain doom as helpless prey. The snow drifts brushed against the bottoms of their feet and ankles as they approached the dirt mound in the snowy yard. Still holding her arm above her head, she turned around to face the pliable, botoxed face of rage behind her. Vicky looked like a sinister cat, eyeing a small bird with pure antipathy.

"You know, it makes too much sense that awkward little Jill Grinager would end up working with the dead," Vicky said, slowly moving the gun back and forth. "I give all the praise in the world to the guidance counselor who looked at a lost cause like you and realized that the only working relationship a freak like you deserves is with someone without a pulse."

Jill shuddered in the cold air as an all-too-familiar pain formed a lump in her throat. She swallowed, pushing it further down into the pit of her stomach. Her lips clamped together as she tried to remain calm in her silence. Vicky took a step toward her, forcing her to backpedal slowly.

"But to think...that one day, that same freak would try to ruin everything I've worked for? Ruin my future? That's low, Jill...lower than the people you put in the ground," she explained, licking the side of her inflated lips. "Luckily, I won't have to deal with it."

"Vicky, look, I promise I won't say anything," Jill pleaded in a raised voice as the snow continued to pile on top of them. "I'm sure there's a perfectly good explanation why you hacked your assistant to pieces and stuffed him into a duffle bag...I can't think of one, but I'm sure there is...you could pass it off as an accident or something; just please, please, don't kill me too."

Vicky paused and exhaled as if she were truly contemplating Jill's words. As she took a few slow steps forward, her boots crunched against the fresh snow like an old door creaking. Now face-to-face, her eyes looked down at Jill's feet and slowly made their way up like an aging elevator in an old metropolitan building.

"An accident? Yeah...that makes sense," Vicky said, looking off to the side, deep in thought. "Maybe you're right...maybe we just ought to call them up and straighten this out and–"

Suddenly, Vicky struck the side of Jill's face with the revolver, knocking her to the ground. Her glasses flew off her face and into the snow as blood started gushing down the side of her right cheek. With a whip, Vicky hit the other side of Jill's face, cutting her cheek wide open. She flipped over on her back and flailed her arm as Vicky hovered over her.

"Oops," she sneered, holding Jill down as if she were a tied-up animal struggling for its freedom. "Looks like I had another accident, Jill. We better let them know about that one, too."

Jill groaned in agonizing pain as snowflakes fell onto the tender gash on each side of her face. Each passing moment was greeted with a more excruciating sensation that pulsated throughout her head and neck.

"Hard to fight back when you're a human slot machine, huh?" she hissed as she held down Jill's arm with her own. "Do you know who I am, Jill? I'm the shooting star of American politics, Vicky Veitch. Do you think I got here by acting like a dainty little princess? Do you think I haven't done whatever I needed to do to make this climb? Do you really think I don't thrive off of being tested day in and day out in scenarios that would make a weakling like you crumble to the ground? People love me. And as long as I'm around, they will always fall in line to support me."

She slammed Jill's head backward, jolting it against the dirt mound. Jill saw a flash of light on impact, her vision becoming even more distorted as she looked up at the vicious eyes above.

"Oh, I bet this brings back old memories…stumpy little Jill trying to fight back with all of her might with her lonely little arm," she shouted with a laugh.

Jill's head was teetering on unconsciousness like a wobbly gymnast trying to stay on a balance beam. The taste of her own blood filled her mouth as she gasped for air. She helplessly pushed her arm upward and squirmed like a fish out of water, making no progress of any sort to free herself. Tears rolled down her face, burning inside the gashes, as she realized that she was hopelessly trapped. Images of the one-armed Barbie encapsulated in the storm drain flashed through her mind.

"Jill, Jill, Jill," Vicky said with another laugh, "There's no need to cry now! I'm sorry it has to end this way for you—truly, I am. And I'm sorry that people are going to think you left this world by your own hand. It really is tragic, given all that you've already had to overcome. But I'm going to be something big, Jill. A million times bigger than everyone in this no-name town put together, and I can't have you ruin that. A name that you hear every time you turn on the television or read when you open a newspaper. We're talking about *real* power here. It's everything, Jill. *Everything.*"

Still sitting on her sternum, Vicky let go of the arm. She sat up and started to point the gun back at Jill, who was still struggling for her life on the ground. She spat out some blood that was pooling in the side of her mouth onto the snow beside her. After letting out another groan, Jill rolled sideways and tried pulling herself up with her now-free hand, but to no avail. She flopped back onto her back and looked up at Vicky, whose barrel was pointed down at Jill's chest.

"I guess this is goodbye," Vicky mocked with a slight smile.

"What good is it..." Jill managed to belt out out as she gripped a clump of snow in her hand.

"What good is what?" Vicky asked.

Jill felt more blood run down the sides of her jaw as she lifted her shoulders up just enough to be a quarter of the way upright as she leaned her head against the mound.

"What good is all that power when your soul is a black hole?" she stammered, still breathing heavily from the blows. "When everyone you're supposed to love and care about is afraid of you...when you have to be heinous and hateful in your job...what good is it?"

Vicky dropped the gun to her side, tilted her head back, and began to laugh. Snow fell on her nose and cheeks, which she wiped away with her sleeve. Her hair extensions bobbed with a gust of angry wind. She looked down at Jill with a jeering snicker and smile.

"Oh Jill," she replied in a sinister tone, "do you really think I'm in this line of work to be some sort of humble, helping servant? That I want to build bridges, mend fences, lend a hand, or any of that spoon-fed Schoolhouse Rock bullshit? I knew you had it tough, but I didn't take you for a damn fool."

Vicky moved out of her power stance and began to pace back and forth. She used her gun in a gesticulating motion with her other hand as she talked.

"The name of the game is power. You get it, and you do whatever you can to hold onto it. It's your ticket to anywhere you want to go. A funnel for every money-making opportunity you could ever want! The ultimate aphrodisiac..."

Even in her feeble state, Jill found enough energy to cringe at the thought of Vicky's power-inspired sexcapades.

"It's an automatic legacy, and there isn't anything in the whole world as important. No one remembers the monk in his monastery, but everyone remembers the names in the history books. Mine will be among them," she proclaimed, pointing her thumb to her chest.

During Vicky's tirade, Jill heard a faint, odd shrieking in the distance that went undetected by her captor. While she couldn't quite make out what it was, it sounded like it was coming from the west, out into the distance. Maybe it was someone yelling from the building, she thought. Perhaps it was just the wind. For all she knew, it could have been ringing in her ears from the blows to the head from the revolver. Trying to conceptualize it, she realized Vicky was still ranting and waving her gun in the air.

"Poor, poor, stumpy little Jill. You wouldn't last one day in the arena, would you? That's okay. Not many can." Vicky flashed her vein smile once more.

Jill collected herself from the distraction and returned to the conversation.

"That's true," Jill replied. "I'm no politician. I don't know where you've been or what you had to do to get there,

Vicky...but I do know one thing: anyone can do well for themselves...but it will never be enough to do well if you don't give a damn about doing good..."

Jill spat out a glob of blood and cocked her head to the side, unafraid of her captor.

"You've really earned your reputation, Vicky..." she rebutted, as her breath returned to her. "You can take your legacy and go back to Hell where you belong."

Vicky's facial muscles twitched in rage. Her smile drooped, and she began marching forward toward Jill, kicking her in the side of the face with her right leather boot. The wound on her face opened further like a bad blister, lingering in an indissoluble pain.

"I bet you feel so high and mighty with that little sanctimonious speech, don't you, freak?" she raged, digging her spur into Jill's left leg. "You aren't better than me! You'll never be better than me. You're just going to die here, alone, with nothing to show for it. No one will remember you but a handful of townies stuck in one place their entire lives. That's your legacy! Not mine!"

As she pointed the gun at the dazed Jill, an unmistakable bellowing noise came from the west. Both women sharply turned their heads to face it.

Neeeeeeeyuheeeeee!

With her blurred, distorted vision, Jill looked out into the distance at a shadowy white figure in the field, one hundred meters away. Perhaps she was hallucinating in her final seconds. She squinted to see what appeared to be a glowing white figure in the distance in the shape of a horse. She squinted again, attempting to make out what looked like a matching white figure riding atop the steed, holding something high in the air. It looks like Gandalf and Shadowfax, she thought.

The animal bellowed another cry, standing on its hind legs before coming back to the ground. Kicking its feet forward, it began to charge at them with a thunderous trot, like a bright light lost in the snow-filled air.

"Get back! You get back!" Vicky screamed into the howling wind.

The figure ignored her warning and began to pick up speed like a freight train, the Gandalf-like rider pointing his object out in front of him. Vicky stumbled as she fired her gun once at the figure with a deafening bang. Jill watched in her blurry line of sight as it got closer and closer to her captor amid the blinding snow. She made out the figure of the massive white stallion, whose thundering gallop ran past Vicky as the figure in white swung his weapon. Metal-on-metal clanked as the figure exclaimed a familiar-sounding "Woo hah!" The gun flew out of Vicky's hand and vanished into the snowy abyss. Vicky fell violently to the ground, now parallel with Jill, who still fought to hold onto her senses. The horse and figure disappeared momentarily until the resounding gallops slowly got louder. As Jill slipped into unconsciousness, the last image in her eyes was the horse, now standing tall on its hind legs. As the stallion stood tall with its front hooves in the air, Vicky realized that she recognized this particular horse.

"Shit," she yelled, just as it came crashing down.

Chapter 15

Suspicious Minds

In his 13 years as the Sheriff of Rockdale, Jack Jorgenson never participated in a homicide investigation. Other than breaking up the occasional bar fight, the only violent crime he had to deal with was five years ago, when a disgruntled man drove his car into the storefront of Delmer's Pharmacy when they wouldn't refill his generic Viagra prescription. The man laid on the horn as he rammed his car through the window and into the cold and flu section. Thankfully, no one was hurt, but the jokes about the man "doing hard time" wrote themselves. But as he waited outside the funeral home, bundled up with his LPD-branded coffee thermos in hand on an early, blustery winter morning, he couldn't help but feel the rush of excitement this first homicide case gave him in the face of these grim circumstances.

A black SUV with tinted windows approached the parking lot. On the side of the passenger door was the black and yellow seal of the Minnesota Bureau of Criminal Apprehension. The car parked, and out walked a slender black man wearing sunglasses with a mustache so thick it looked like it could break any razor that attempted to remove it. On the back of his navy blue jacket, it reads 'BCA' in large, bright yellow letters.

"Alright, Jack," he said aloud to himself, "it's showtime."

As he approached him, the agent took off his sunglasses and placed them in his dress shirt pocket. Tucked underneath his left arm was a red leather ledger that looked as if it were as official as any holy book he'd ever seen. He stood in front of the sheriff with stoic eyes, looking at her with more confidence than fifty Navy Seals. He pictured him as a handsome gladiator gazing upon the battlefield in front of him before he took down a lion with his bare hands. Jack's heart skipped a beat just thinking about it. He nervously took another swing from his thermos.

"Special Agent Ben Lucas, BCA," he said, extending his right hand out to him.

"Hi, I'm Jack," he said before returning from his dazed wonderment. "I mean, I'm Jack Jorgenson...no, sorry–I mean, Jack Jorgenson, Sheriff of Rockdale. Yep, that's it. Oof, sorry, I clearly need some more coffee this morning!" he said with an embarrassed laugh.

"That's quite alright," Ben replied, his eyes wandering toward the entrance of the funeral home as he began putting on his latex gloves.

The two stood there in silence, John smiling as he continued to stare at him like a 7-year-old seeing a movie character mascot at Disney World.

"Well...shall we get to it?" he asked, breaking the silence.

"Oh geez, my bad. Right this way!" he agreed, scrambling to open the door. "You can go ahead and wipe your feet on the mat, right over there, by the coat rack so we don't track in any of the snow and stuff."

They walked underneath the yellow crime scene tape that hung in front of the door. As they wiped their feet down, Ben pulled out two forensic foot coverings to go over his shoes. A timorous Jack started searching inside the coat closet area to see if there was anything he could use to do the same. He found two stocking hats on the top shelf in the lost and found box and began trying to fashion them around his boots. While he struggled, Ben approached him like a disappointed parent.

"Sheriff, I have extras if you need them," he offered, holding two blue pieces of cloth in his hand.

He smiled and nodded as he took them from his hands. Internally, he began cursing at himself for looking so unprepared. The two began slowly walking down the center aisle of the chapel. The special agent stopped abruptly, causing Jack to almost run into the back of him. He took out his ledger and quickly scribbled something down with precision. After a brief pause, the two walked over to the casket, where the forensic team was still taking pictures inside of it while placing yellow markers around it. Ben crouched and examined the inside of the casket, where one body lay prepared and the other dismembered in a duffle bag.

"Jacob," Ben turned to the photographer who had just finished up a shot, "what's the initial observation on the deceased?"

"We IDed the victim as one, Ethan Bile, a twenty-seven-year-old Caucasian male from Marietta, Georgia. He's a political operative for Representative Veitch. No signs of struggle, so the gunshot to the head almost certainly came first," the photographer replied.

"Interesting. And what about the discharging of the weapon?" Ben inquired as he scribbled some more notes into his ledger with an onlooking Jack, his thermos still in hand.

"Surprisingly, the gun we found in the vehicle was the one of the two that was fired. It's a bit of an antique; my guys IDed it as a German Commercial Luger 9mm Pistol dating back to the early 20th Century. The accounts from the family and reporter claim the gun was a collector's item said to belong to the Red Baron," he informed.

"Which is just so freaking cool, right?" Jack interjected like a distracted child.

The two men stopped and turned to look at Jack with blank expressions on their faces. His excitement was doused as if it were a campfire that just got drenched with water. They turned back to resume their work.

"While there were no prints on the trigger, we examined the inside and found that not only was it recently fired, but the sear was completely worn inside the gun. This likely caused the firing pin to release. Wear-and-tear with age is not a surprise, given the age of the firearm. When we arrived at the cabin last night, we initially thought that given the spacing and trajectory of the shot, it was a close-range execution, but given those conditions, I don't think we can rule out a misfire."

Ben scribbled some more notes down while turning the chin of the body to examine all sides of the head. Jack looked in intrigued wonderment as though he were reading him an exciting bedtime story.

"Do we know *why* she was carrying around an antique pistol in the first place? Especially when she already had another gun on her?" Ben asked as he stood back up.

"I can answer that, Special Agent," Jack interjected.

The two men looked back at him simultaneously with the same perplexed look on their faces. The special agent walked toward him and leaned his hand on top of the edge of the altar.

"Go on," Ben said, his voice deep and smooth like a tub of butter.

"Well, from what I gathered in the questioning of this Time Magazine reporter, they were doing some political profile piece about her and her recently deceased father-in-law. Now, I'm no Ike Eisenhower, but arranging a political puff piece on the day of a funeral makes as much sense as having a funeral on Ash Wednesday in the first place," he stated with a smile that was met with still faces. "Anywho, to each their own, I 'spose. But according to this reporter and his photo film, she used the Red Baron's pistol as a prop to pose with and show off. You know how people get when they want to show off a cool toy or collection to look impressive. I tell ya, my dad just bought this brand new Zenith TV, and he hasn't stopped talking about it since—"

"—Thank you, sheriff," Ben interjected, cutting him off. "That, uh, helps clear things up... Daniel, what's your read on the dismemberment?"

"Our gun theory corroborates that this was a hack job to dispose of evidence and the body, which was also apparent in the buried torso we found," he said, putting his hand in the casket toward the duffle bag and unzipping it. "Arms and head were a clean cut, but it's clear that there was a struggle getting through the femurs in one swing. The guy also has a medical discharge bracelet from the night before on his left arm that we traced back to the Hennepin Emergency Room."

The sheriff watched the two men examine the opened duffle bag as they hovered over the casket. Knowing from every nighttime crime drama he watched (typically in his underpants), the body examination is what separated the men from the boys in the world of criminal justice. He imagined it was like being a part of an exclusive club–you could only talk about this sort of thing with other fellow big-shot detectives. The general public just couldn't handle it. Alright, Jack, now is your chance to play with the big boys, he thought.

"I think I should also take a look at our records here as well. Ya know...for the sake of quality insurance and such," he said, incorrectly using the first term that popped into his mind as he took a few steps forward.

"That's quite alright, sheriff," Ben said, without turning around. "We're just making a note of the lesions and condition."

"No, no, I insist," he said, continuing to barge his way forward. "Accuracy is key for our reporting, so I better get in there."

Daniel and Ben looked at each other, saying much to each other with a single glance. After letting out a sigh, he relented.

"Alright...if you insist, sheriff," he replied.

Jack waddled up to Ben's left side, feeling a certain swagger of importance overcome him. He looked down to see a trail of dried blood by the body of Bud. This trail led to the open duffle bag, where a severed head lying on top of a pile of limbs stared him dead in the eye. The contents of Jack's stomach immediately started curdling.

"Good Lord!" he shouted before feeling his esophagus fill up.

Running back toward the front of the altar, he began vomiting loudly on the first pew. Daniel shook his head and muttered to himself as he watched the doubled-over egg-shaped man continue to regurgitate his breakfast at the crime scene. Ben sighed and walked slowly down to the sheriff, patting him on the back.

"Are you going to be alright there, Jack?" he asked.

"Mother of God!" he yelled, wiping his mouth with his sleeve, "What kind of Frankenstein shit did I just look at?!"

"It's going to be okay," Ben assured him, giving another pat on the back to the keeled-over man. "That's not the first time this has happened. Just catch your breath, and we'll get this cleaned up."

As the agent kindly came back from his vehicle with some towels, the two men cleaned up the front pew. Embarrassment caught up with Jack, who was now cursing himself internally for his own bodily reaction. He'd never have Ben's gravitas, he thought. He feared people would forever see him as a donut-loving Chief Wiggum type, too useless to be instrumental in any sort of big-time case. A podunk sheriff for a podunk town.

He watched as Ben began scratching his chin, pacing over to the front of the altar, his eyes looking up at the wooden cross behind it that went up to the ceiling. As he did so, he watched in wonder as he finished wiping the last bit of puke off the front seats. Even Daniel, watching from behind the casket, looked confused about what he was doing. Ben took the ledger out once more and took a minute to write more notes.

"Sheriff, come with me to the back," he said before walking past her and heading toward the front doors.

A slight bit of confidence returned to Jack as he paced behind the agent. Unfortunately, he tripped over the side of the pew, falling to his knees and dropping his thermos, which clanked on the floor multiple times.

"Doggonit," he stammered as he promptly picked himself up and grabbed his thermos.

Meanwhile, Special Agent Lucas was already out of the front door. He jogged for the first time in a decade to catch up. As he met up with him, he noticed that he was staring at the ground, examining it thoroughly. He stood beside him in silence, waiting for him to speak as his eyes followed the snowy tracks in front of him.

Jack followed, thinking to himself that Ben had the most upright posture of anyone he had ever met. It was as if he were a praying mantis, looking for prey and viewing its surroundings as it climbed up the branch of a bush. They made their way to the backyard and approached the second crime scene, where the yellow tape was tied around the backyard trees, forming a rhombus shape around an imprinted mound of snow and a revolver. He opened up his ledger and started to sketch as Jack waited for him in silence for another few minutes.

"Sheriff, what's the breakdown here?" he inquired, still sketching.

"You mean about this gun?" he asked, pointing at the revolver.

"No," he replied curtly, "I mean all of it. You made a key connection about this all being out of the ordinary— the funeral, the interview, Ash Wednesday, all of it— based on your interview with the Time reporter. I want you to do the same here by going through all you learned in your questioning."

Jack felt a rush of adrenaline and excitement pulsate through his body. It seemed as though the special agent was complimenting his analytical skills. Perhaps he wasn't some useless donut shop cop, he thought.

He quickly fantasized about the two of them as a detective duo in an HBO crime drama that was too intense for cable. Jack would be the encyclopedia of data, keen on observation, while Ben would serve as the suave inspector with stellar combat abilities. Their bond would be so strong that they would finish each other's catchphrases after hunting down the killer. Violent firefights would ensue at criminal compounds, where they would find themselves on the brink of death, only to pull off the impossible. After saving Ben from certain death, they'd become best friends, and he would start referring to Jack as his "brother from another mother" while giving him a cool secret handshake in front of the entire police force.

"—Sheriff?" Ben interrupted as Jack stood staring into space with a wide smile on his face.

"Oh! Right, sorry, I was just trying to collect everything I made a mental note of," he stated before clearing his throat.

He paced around the yellow tape bordering the revolver and imprint, pretending to deeply examine the scene before him.

Ben watched him walk back and forth, his hands folded in front of him, unsure of what he was doing.

"Well, as I said before, the Representative brought this gun to show off for this political piece. And I also want to reiterate that I'm no political Pat here, but if there's one thing I do know about political types, it's that they love their exposure when they can get it. The bigger, the better," he concluded, rubbing the back of his neck. "What doesn't make much sense to me is thinking someone like that straight up murdered someone, especially someone who worked for her— and by her husband's account— worshiped the ground she walks on. Unless there's something we don't know that happened between the two of them, murder doesn't seem like it would serve her all too well. Personally, I think the gun accidently discharged."

Rubbing his chin again, Ben began to nod slightly.

"I can see that," he murmured softly. "So the medical bracelet found on his wrist is interesting. Do we know what they were up to the day before or why he went?"

A warm feeling of acknowledgment poured over Jack, who became more animated with his hands.

"Oof...let me tell ya, that's a can of worms right there. So we still have to wait for the court order to approve getting the medical records as confirmation, but you're never going to believe this," he added, getting in a crouched position as if he were telling the story around a campfire: "My cousin Dan is a fire chief down in the cities. He calls me up yesterday morning and talks my ear off for over an hour to tell me he got called in the other night to the ER to help this scrawny guy with a bowl cut. The guy–who I presume to be our victim–was in possession of this bag that's filled with...I guess you would call them made-in-China marital aids," he said, starting to blush.

"Made in China marital aids?" Ben quizzed with one eyebrow raised.

"Oh, ya know, they're like toys for someone who spends a little too much time scrubbin' their carrot. Anywho, we found the bag in the vehicle, and the receipts trace back to Colton Lorenzo, who also works for the Representative. Now, this Colton guy kept just a bunch of stuff in there, Ben. Just a bunch of stuff," he explained, shaking his head. "I mean, for Pete's sake, it looked like someone had disassembled a vacuum cleaner. And all of the items came in packages that had Mandarin writing on them," he pointed out before taking a deep breath and watching it float into the cold morning sky. "And well, this Ethan fella tries one of them out. He's a younger guy, so I don't know if he's stupid, lonely, bored, or if it's a sex thing between them-but long story short, he gets his ding dong stuck in the contraption and ends up having to go to the ER to get it off."

"I see," he said, "and this Colton, where is he now?"

"We can't find him," he replied, hanging his head. "We know from the husband that the guy flew in on Sunday and then checked out of his room at the Nites Inn Tuesday morning. Which is also odd because, according to the husband, he was supposed to be at the service but never showed up. He said it's not out of character for him to flake off, though...quite the ornery guy by the sounds of it. Still, something doesn't feel right about it. You think we oughta do a missing persons report?"

"Don't bother," he replied as he jotted down more notes in his ledger.

"Don't bother? With all due respect, Ben, we can't find him anywhere. What if he's in danger or worse? I just think in circumstances like this, we should make sure everyone is accounted for, don't ya think?"

He looked across the field to see a rabbit hopping across the snow bank. With each hop, the bunny plunged further into the snow as it tried to reach the shallow, barren cornfield twenty meters away. He knelt down and examined the revolver next to the yellow 'E' place marker. The charcoal body of the Smith & Wesson felt cold through his surgical gloves. He set it back down and stood back up.

"I've seen guys like this before," he replied, looking directly into Jack's eyes. "Sex toys from Asia, flakey, ornery, doesn't communicate. The man's a pervert, Jack. The kind of guy who would travel to the ends of this planet just to get his rocks off. I bet he hitched a ride to the airport and bought himself a one-way ticket to Bangkok. He's probably shacking up in some laundromat basement as we speak."

"Good grief," he exclaimed, putting his hands to her lips as unflattering images shuffled through his head. "I had no idea."

"Be glad that you didn't. Guys like that burn themselves out eventually, and it always turns out ugly," he replied as they began to walk just east of the hole.

Ben stopped and knelt down again, closely examining the deep-hooved footprints below. He drew a few of them in the ledger, leading them up to a circle labeled 'scene.' Jack looked over his shoulder in wonderment, as if he were watching a master chef at work up close at a Hibachi restaurant. Every little detail he wrote down felt like he was unfolding the mystery piece by piece. He prepared himself for a dramatic reveal where Ben would proclaim the case solved, much to the guilty party's chagrin. Still kneeling, he turned his head to the side and looked up at him with his deep brown eyes.

"Horse tracks at a crime scene, huh?" he noted, still staring at the tracks. "That's something you don't see every day."

"Yeah, no, definitely not," Jack replied. "The horse belongs to her father, and she apparently abducted it despite his wishes. They found the poor thing shivering by the post office."

"Why did she want the horse so badly?" he asked.

"Same reason she wanted the Baron's gun. She likes to be seen as a real cowgirl in the eyes of the voters, but to tell ya the truth, a lot of people around here know it's just a big act," he said with a shrug.

Ben paced around once more. He crouched to carefully examine the imprint mark of a body that looked like a one-winged snow angel.

"What's the account from the mortician?" he asked.

Jack exhaled as the incident played out again in his head.

"Well, she took a couple of strikes to the face with that gun when the Representative had her pinned down. She's still out of it, but the doctors say she'll pull through. Luckily for her, the fire alarm went off during the blizzard, which got everyone trying to locate her," he went on, turning his back to him and looking at the site. "Mrs. Veitch, on the other hand, took quite a horseshoe-sized doozy to the head."

"Bad luck for sure," he replied, standing back up and shaking his head. "Any update on her status?"

"Oh, not so good, Ben," he said with an uncomfortable grimace. "The doc said she's in a pretty deep coma. At best, I'd say she's going to get a lot of coloring books for Christmas from now on," Jack noted, shaking his head with his hands in his pockets.

"Jesus," he said as he took off his latex gloves. "Who the hell found them during a damn blizzard anyway?"

"That's the part we couldn't quite figure out. They were both found inside the backdoor after the fire alarm went off, but no one inside the funeral home even knew anything was going down to begin with. The only theory I have is that the mortician knew they'd both die out there, so she put on her old altruism cap and decided to save her assailant's life," he explained with a shrug.

"Does anyone else have access to the back door?" Ben asked with an eyebrow raised.

"Just the assistant director but he went home sick earlier in the day. She's also got this nephew who's a little different that lives with her, but we found him at home as well," he replied.

"What do you mean 'a little different'?" he asked inquisitively.

"Well, he's a really nice kid and all, Ben, but he likes to dress up as Elvis," he replied.

"Elvis? Like the singer Elvis?" he asked, dumbfounded.

"Yeah, it's just kind of his thing, I 'spose. I mean, I seen him around town dressed as other music folks, too. He walked up behind me at the bank one time dressed as Gene Simmons once and scared the daylights outta me. But yeah, Elvis is the one that people around here know him for."

"Is he...all there?" Ben asked, pointing to his head.

"Gosh, I don't think anyone truly knows. I guess we're all so used to having Elvis walk around our town that we just don't care if he is or not, to tell ya the truth," he said nonchalantly. "The kid's at the hospital right now and hasn't left her bedside. I don't know about you, but if I came out of a coma, I think seeing Elvis would make me think I'm still asleep," he concluded with a laugh.

The special agent stood with his arms folded, shaking his head. He was starting to wonder if he had been transported to some bizarre reality in the form of a small Minnesota town. The two started walking back toward the back of the church.

"I don't know if headlines could ever do this situation justice," he said, rubbing his face stressfully. "Did you get anything else out of the family and staff?"

"Not really. No one inside witnessed anything or even heard a gunshot. They were preoccupied eating hot dishes while her convict brother-in-law was singing REO Speedwagon a capella–apparently, he's got a set of pipes on him, according to one of the guards. I also questioned the assistant director, but not only did he go home sick for the day, but he ended up crying hysterically through the entire line of questioning. Poor guy...the innocent heart just can't handle something sinister like this," he continued, shaking his head. "What gets my goat, though, is that no one even pushed back when I asked if she was capable of something like this. Not even her own folks."

A cool breeze tickled Jack's nose and began fogging up the right side of his glasses. He took them off with the bottom of his dress shirt underneath his coat.

"That's certainly a telling statement," Ben observed as he sat down on the back steps of the church.

He pulled out a pack of Camel cigarettes from his jacket, looked up, and motioned the pack toward Jack as an offering.

"Oh, no, thank you!" he said politely before plopping down next to him. "I don't smoke. I'd be happy to sit with ya, though!"

As the two of them sat there, Ben lit up his cigarette and toyed with it in his fingers as he took a drag. He was lost in thought as he stared out into the snowy distance. Jack stared at him like an idol, wondering what connections he was making in his head. He took a breath, set his ledger by his side, and took another drag.

"So..." Jack suspired, eagerly awaiting for him to say something profound.

"So what?" he asked, tipping a fragment of ash off the end of his smoke.

"What do you think? Ya know, what's your assessment of everything here?" he inquired as he unsuccessfully tried to fold one leg over the other in anticipation.

He took another slow inhale from his cigarette and watched the smoke slowly dance out of his mouth and into the cold air above. Ben turned to look at Jack's face, which had an excited smile that made him feel like he was talking to his own son.

"I'm curious as to what you think, Sheriff," he said with a slight smile.

"What do I think?" he replied with uncertainty.

"I promise I'm not messing with you. You've been breaking everything down with great detail; you've been the lead on everything so far. Tell me what you think," he said, turning his body toward his own.

Jack paused fearfully as the uncertainty of whether or not he was about to embarrass himself crept in. He wasn't an expert. He didn't have a ledger or anything to go off of other than his own thoughts and hours of TV marathons. This world was foreign to him, and he felt as if he was about to be exposed as the donut shop imposter he feared he was deep down. Staying quiet wasn't an option, though, he thought. That was as bad as saying the wrong thing.

"Ya know, Ben, I gotta be honest," he began as he looked down at the concrete step in front of him. "I really don't know. Cripes, I'm sure you've already uncovered this whole thing like Sherlock Holmes himself, but to me, this just seems like one big calamity," he said, taking off his glasses and rubbing them on his shirt one more time. "Not to be personal or anything, but I sometimes think people like Vicky Veitch get too caught up in their own vanity to know whether or not what they're doing is right... someone who got herself so lost in those weeds that she turned a bad accident into something much worse. One minute, she's boosting her career, and then BAM! She accidentally ends up turning ol' bowl cut into a hollow jack-o-lantern," he shouted as he pointed an imaginary gun out in front of his body. "And then hopes to desecrate her husband's father's tomb in order to burn the evidence."

Ben took another long drag as he watched Jack, deep in thought, staring out into the distance.

"Ya know...it used to be that even if you didn't like 'em, you could at least feel alright about these political types. It felt like they were still trying to do a good job. I don't know; maybe some of them are still like that. But it seems like some will tell ya that they're sent by God himself. Then they go and act like this, and God sends a horse to kick 'em in the face...and well, it's a darn shame it has to be that way, if you ask me."

They sat in silence for a moment before Jack turned and put his two fingers up to his mouth, gesturing for a cigarette. Ben pulled the pack out of his pocket and handed one to him. He lit it for him as he cupped his hand around the end of it. After taking a deep, dramatic inhale, he started coughing.

"You alright?" he asked, patting Jack on the back.

"Yeah," he wheezed in a voice with little breath in it, coughing some more. "I'm good.'

Ben leaned on his fist as his fingers gently stroked his chin. He looked to the spot where the rabbit had been to see it was gone. Maybe it made its way through; he hoped so anyway.

"For what it's worth, I think you're right," he said.

Still stifling a cough, he turned to look at him with astonishment in his eyes. He felt as if he was in the middle of an episodic ending of his crime drama fantasy.

"You do?" he asked in complete shock.

"I do," he replied, "vanity ran amuck," he said, taking one last drag from his cigarette before ashing it on the concrete. "Sometimes, that's all it takes to act crazy. Even in a town that has its own Elvis."

"I guess so," he agreed, holding his cigarette away from his body to avoid taking another inhale.

While Main Street stood still, Jack could still hear the chatter from the townsfolk who were gathered outside the crime scene at the front of the funeral home. The two sat in silence momentarily as the cool breeze brushed through their ears. Jack, uncomfortable with silence, chimed back in.

"Boy, this weather has been something else, huh?

Prior to writing *The Wake of the Hound Dogs*, A.D. Matson worked as a political speechwriter, giving him a close-up of the bizarre side of America and the humor in all of it. Matson grew up in Sioux Falls, South Dakota, a place which inspired much of the material in his debut novel. He currently resides in Stillwater, Minnesota.

9 7 9 8 2 1 8 5 5 9 5 8 8